A Sam & Friend's Mystery

Book Two

Lake Monster Mix-Up

MARY LABATT • JO RIOUX

KIDS CAN PRESS

This is a work of fiction and any resemblance of characters to persons living or dead is purely coincidental.

Kids Can Press acknowledges the financial support of the Government of Ontario, through the Ontario Media Development Corporation's Ontario Book Initiative; the Ontario Arts Council; the Canada Council for the Arts; and the Government of Canada, through the BPIDP, for our publishing activity.

Published in Canada by
Kids Can Press Ltd.
29 Birch Avenue
Toronto, ON M4V 1E2

Published in the U.S. by
Kids Can Press Ltd.
2250 Military Road
Tonawanda, NY 14150

www.kidscanpress.com

Based on the book *The Secret of Sagawa Lake* by Mary Labatt.

Edited by Karen Li
Designed by Kathleen Gray
Printed and bound in China

The hardcover edition of this book is smyth sewn casebound.
The paperback edition of this book is limp sewn with a drawn-on cover.

CM 09 0 9 8 7 6 5 4 3 2 1
CM PA 09 0 9 8 7 6 5 4 3 2 1

Library and Archives Canada Cataloguing in Publication

Labatt, Mary, [date]
Lake monster mix-up / written by Mary Labatt ;
illustrated by Jo-Anne Rioux.

(A Sam & friends mystery)
Interest age level: For ages 7–10.
ISBN 978-1-55337-822-8 (bound). ISBN 978-1-55337-302-5 (pbk.)

I. Rioux, Jo-Anne II. Title. III. Series: Labatt, Mary, [date] . Sam & friends mystery.

PS8573.A135L35 2009 jC813'.54 C2008-907085-2

Kids Can Press is a Corus™ Entertainment company

To my family — M.L.

To my entire family, who is always there for me — J.R.

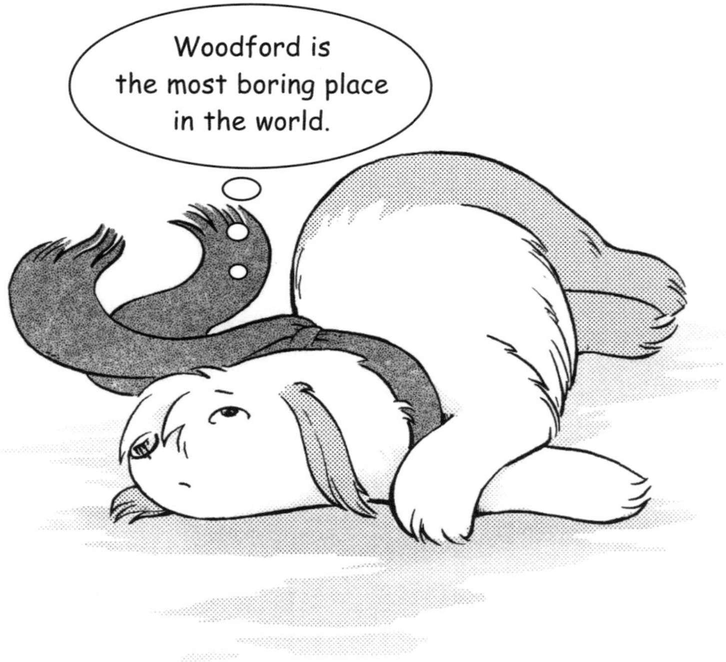
Woodford is the most boring place in the world.

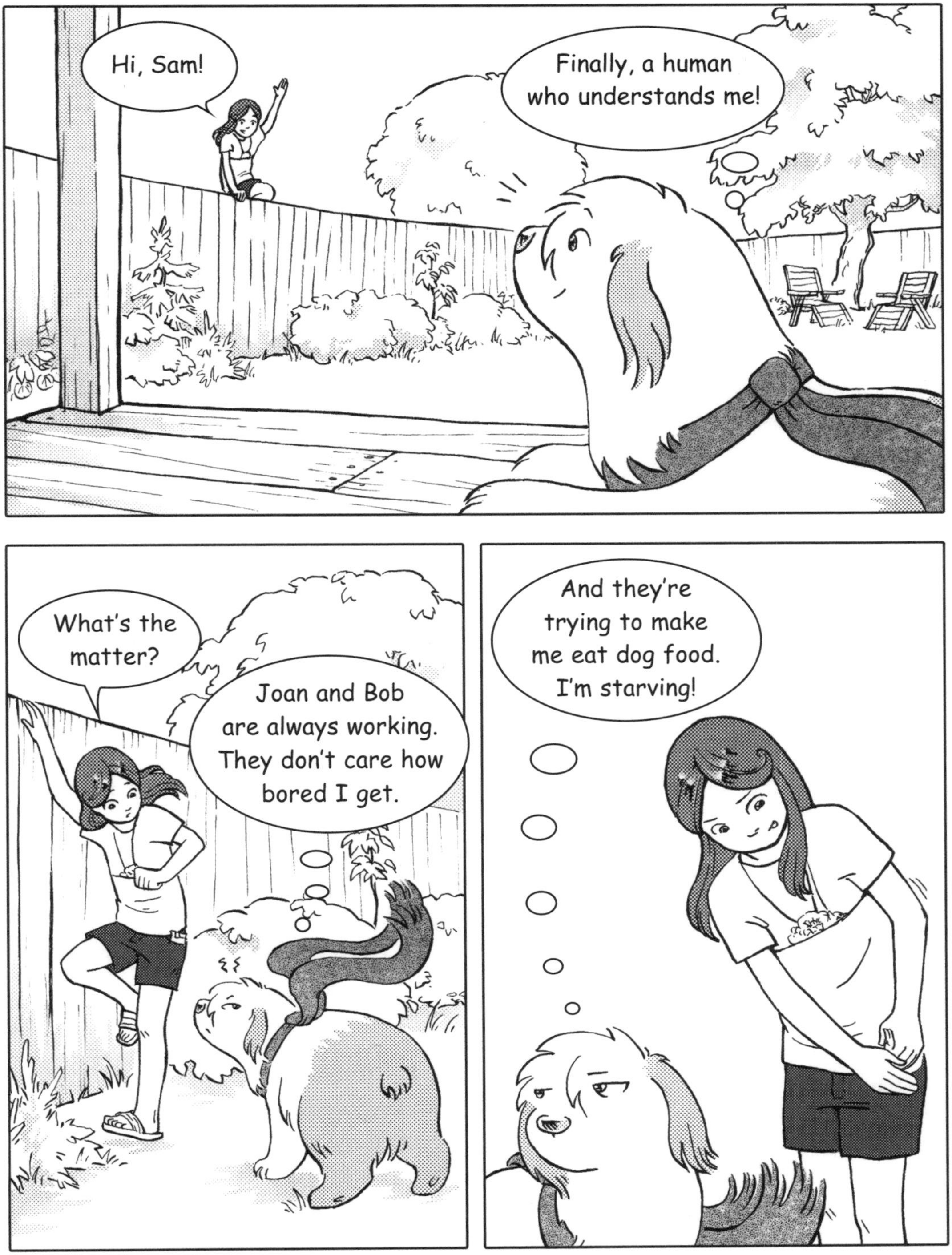
Hi, Sam!
Finally, a human who understands me!
What's the matter?
Joan and Bob are always working. They don't care how bored I get.
And they're trying to make me eat dog food. I'm starving!

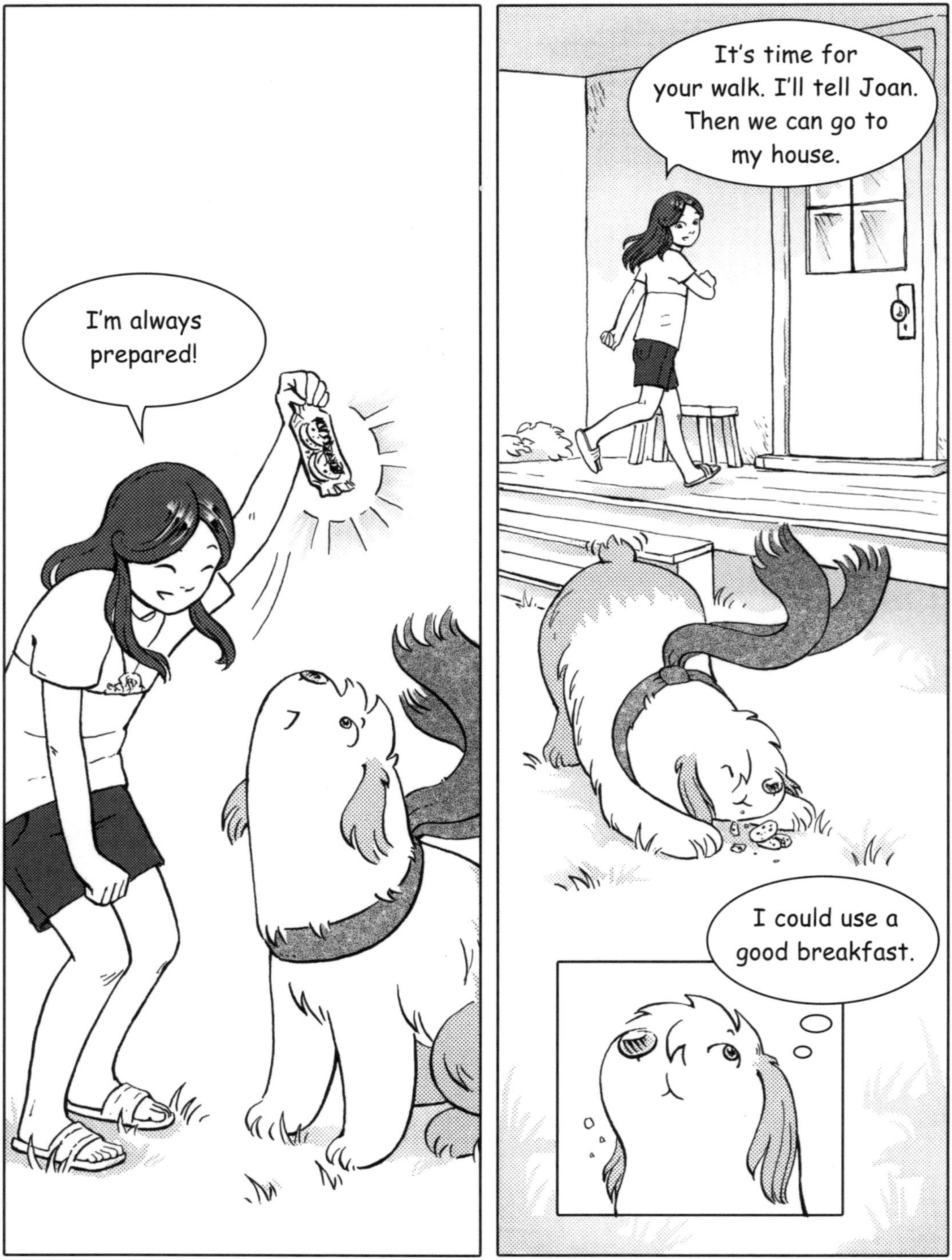
I'm always prepared!
It's time for your walk. I'll tell Joan. Then we can go to my house.
I could use a good breakfast.

Later that afternoon ...

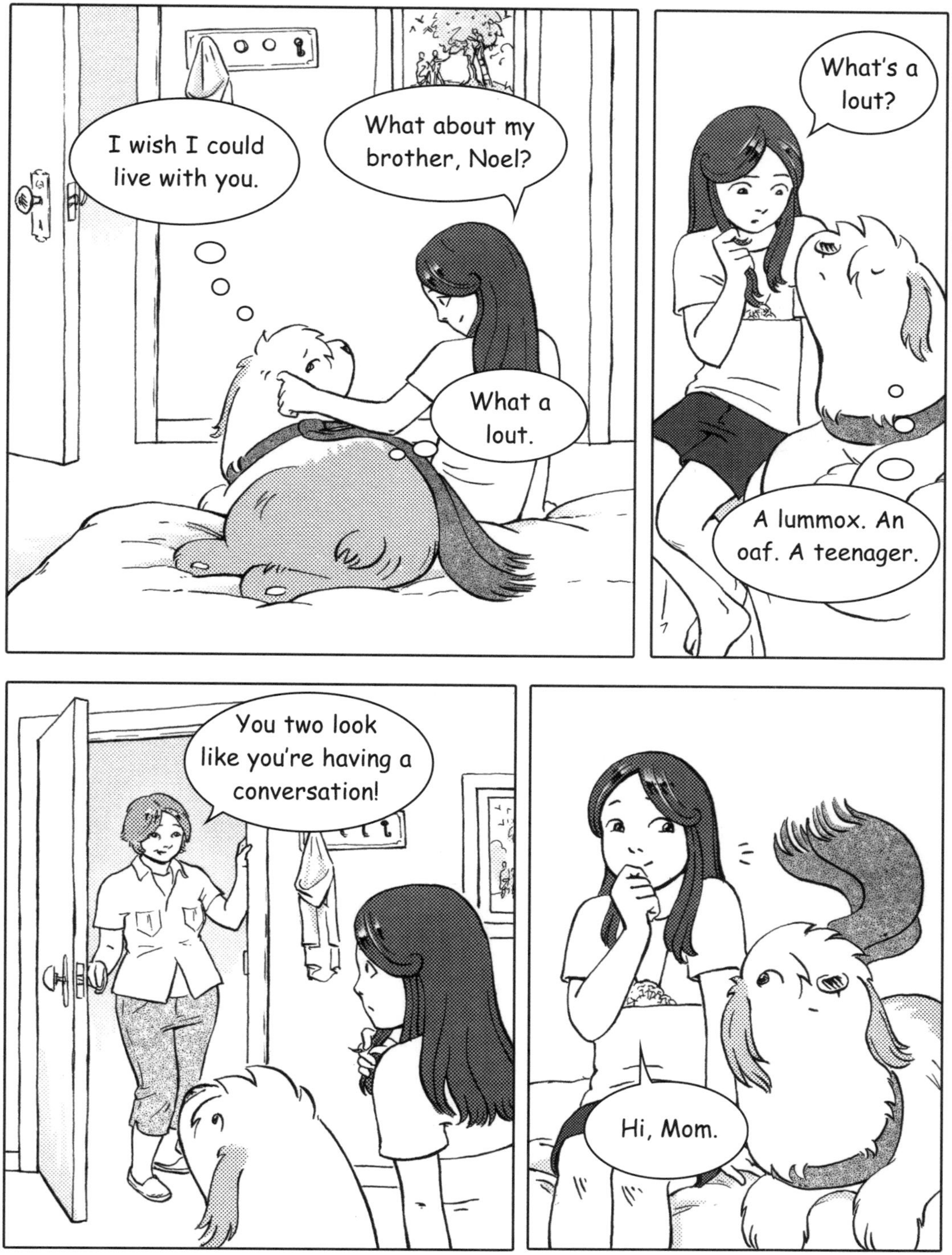
I wish I could live with you.
What about my brother, Noel?
What a lout.
What's a lout?
A lummox. An oaf. A teenager.
You two look like you're having a conversation!
Hi, Mom.

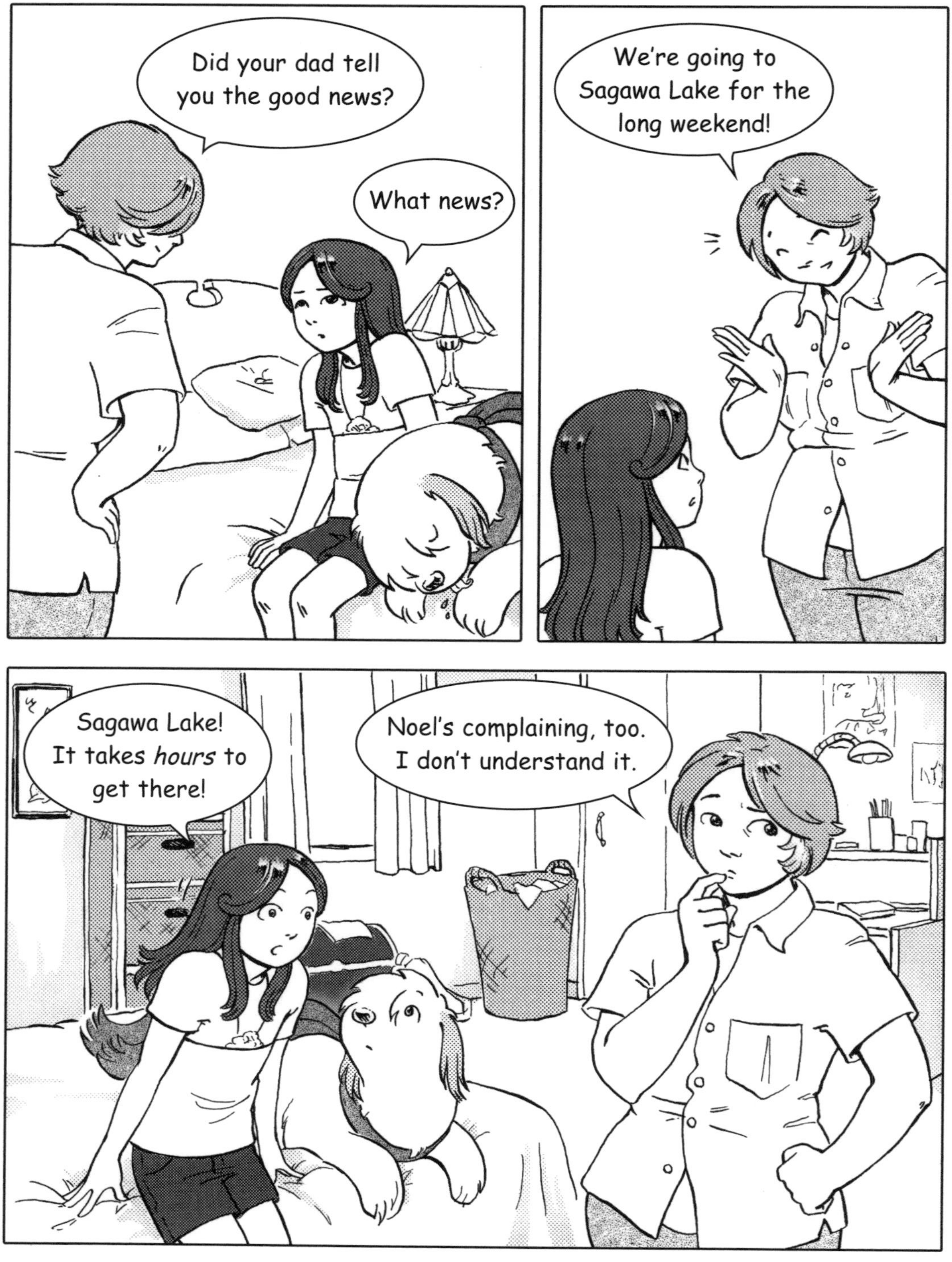
Did your dad tell you the good news?
What news?
We're going to Sagawa Lake for the long weekend!
Sagawa Lake! It takes *hours* to get there!
Noel's complaining, too. I don't understand it.

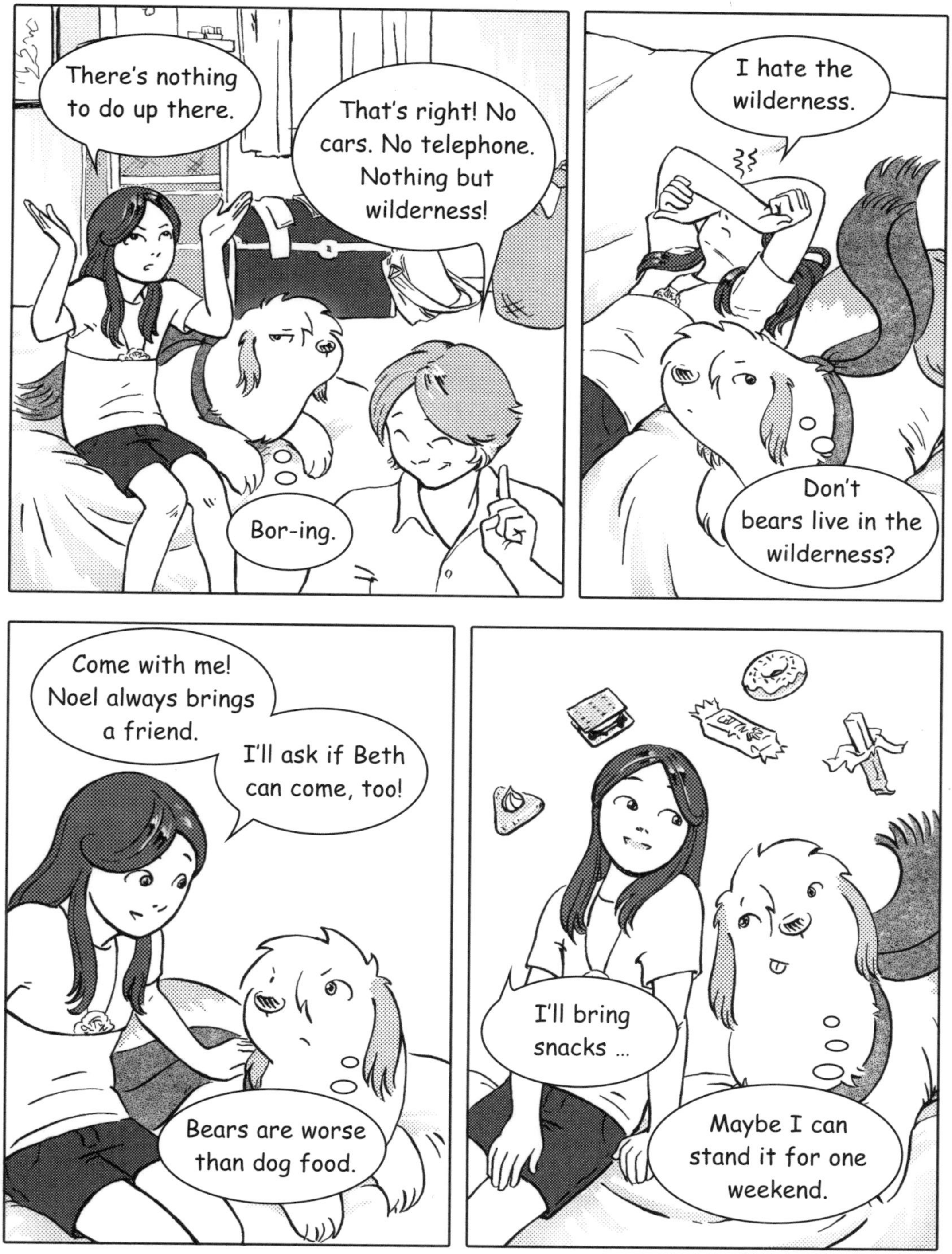
There's nothing to do up there.
That's right! No cars. No telephone. Nothing but wilderness!
Bor-ing.
I hate the wilderness.
Don't bears live in the wilderness?
Come with me! Noel always brings a friend.
I'll ask if Beth can come, too!
Bears are worse than dog food.
I'll bring snacks ...
Maybe I can stand it for one weekend.

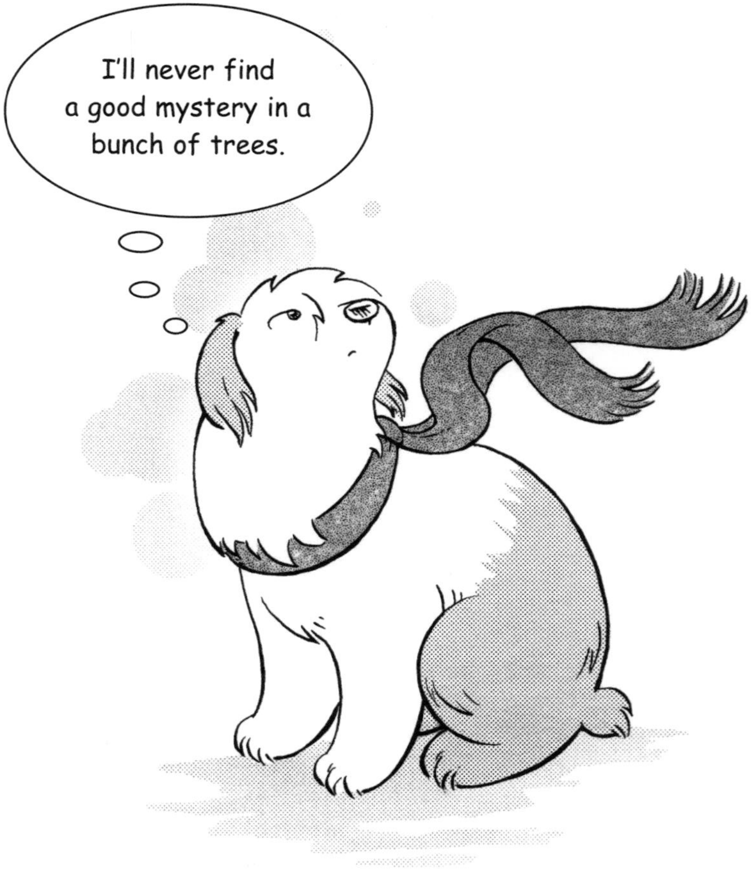
I'll never find a good mystery in a bunch of trees.

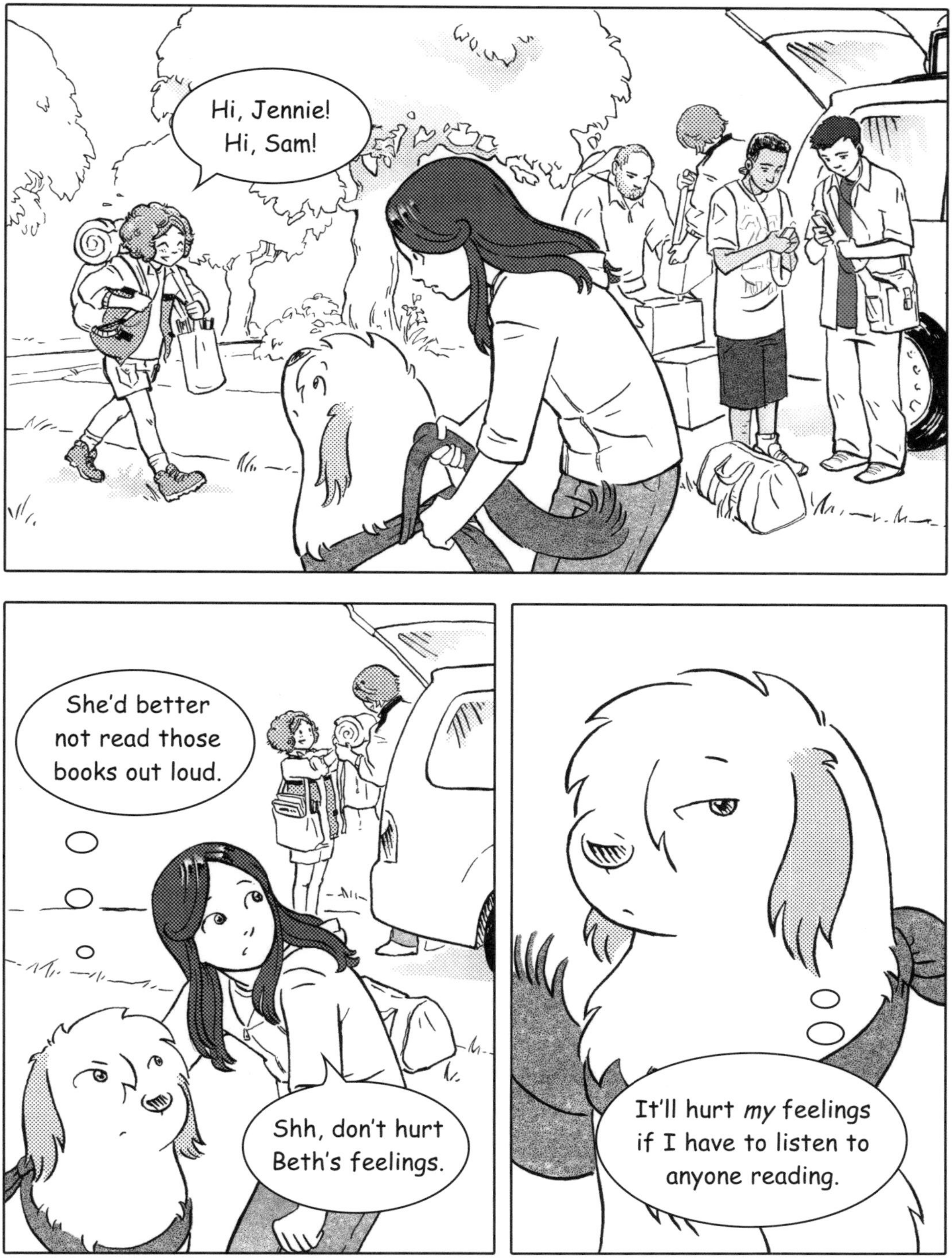
Hi, Jennie!
Hi, Sam!
She'd better not read those books out loud.
Shh, don't hurt Beth's feelings.
It'll hurt *my* feelings if I have to listen to anyone reading.

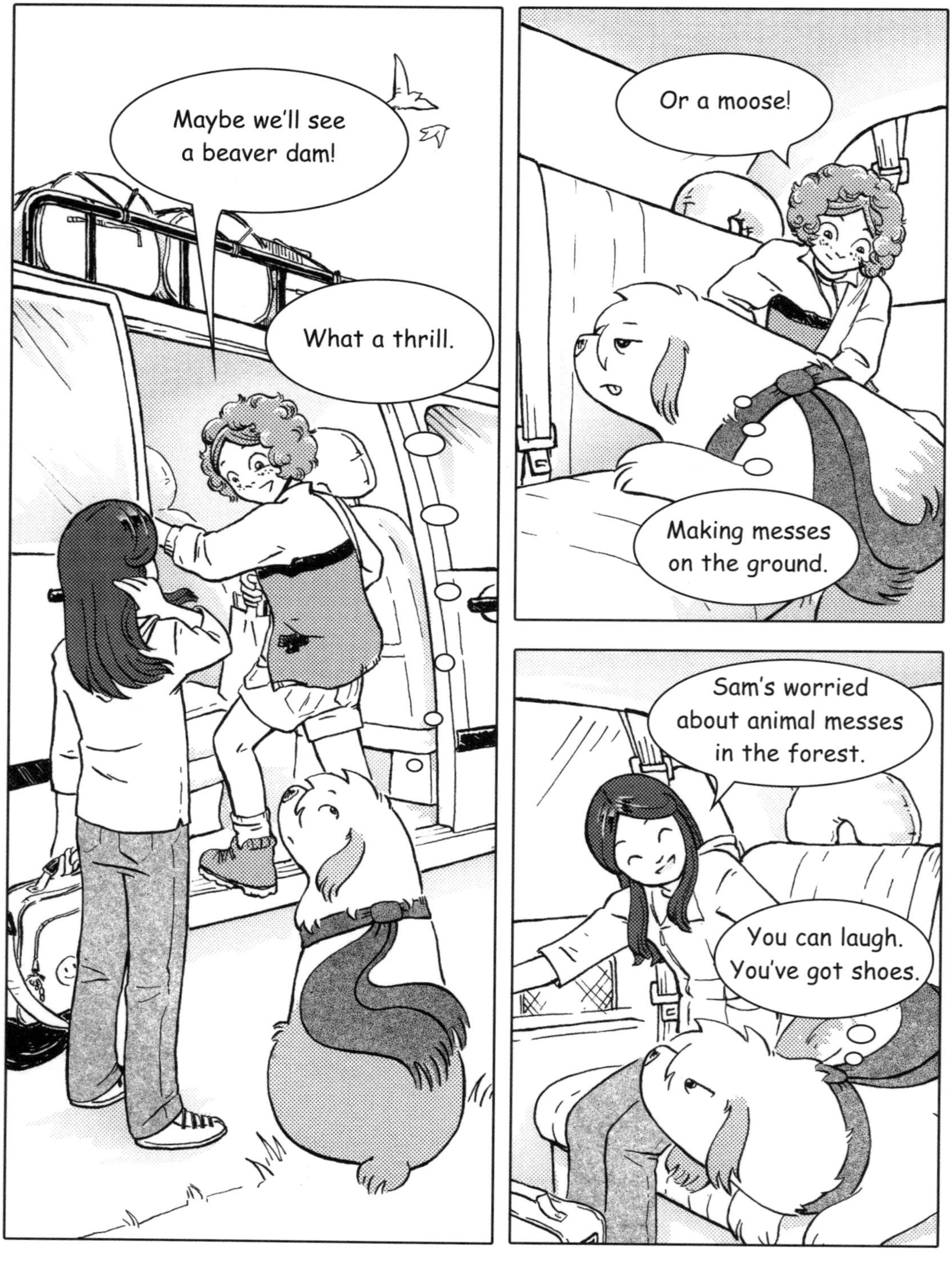
Maybe we'll see a beaver dam!
What a thrill.
Or a moose!
Making messes on the ground.
Sam's worried about animal messes in the forest.
You can laugh. You've got shoes.

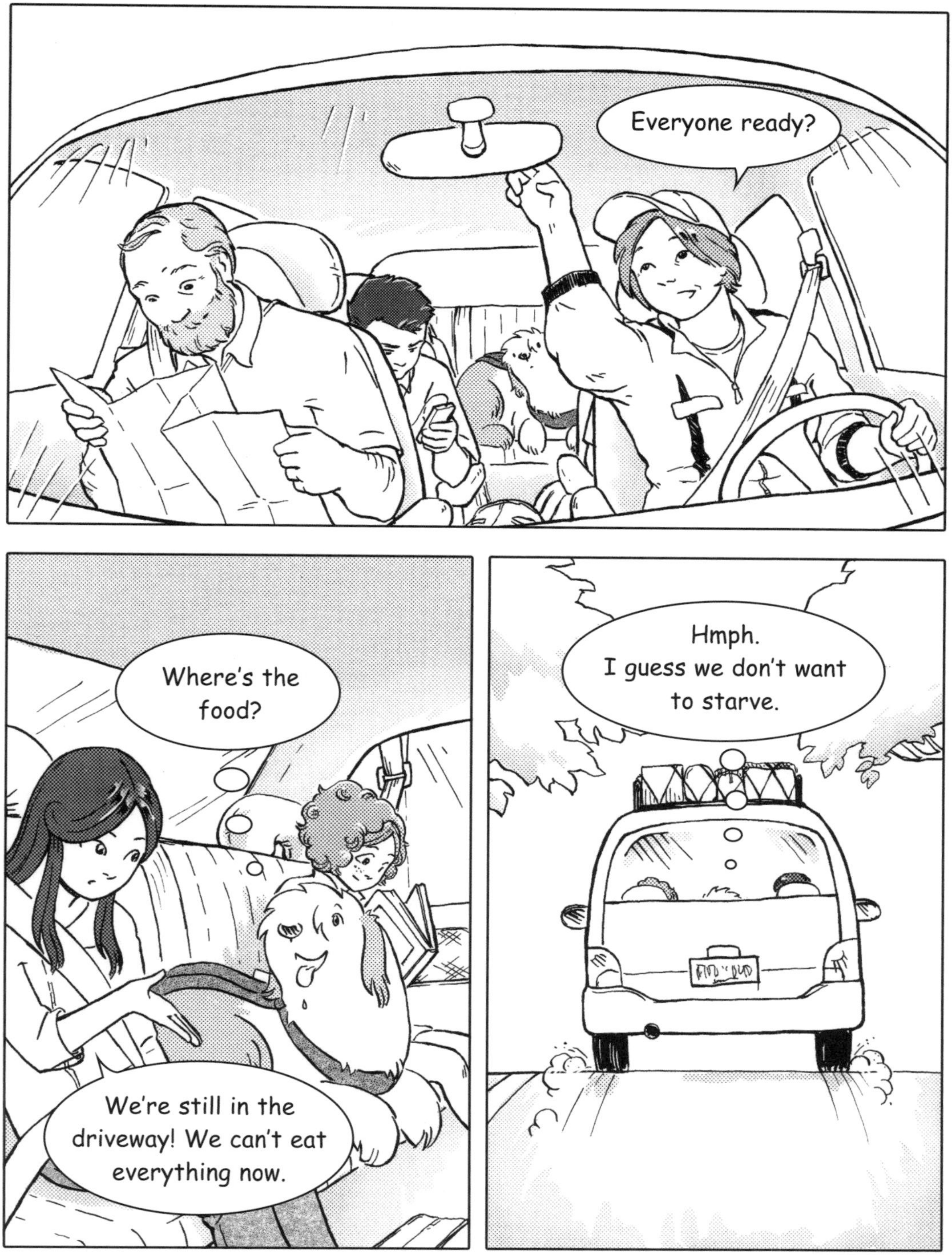
Everyone ready?
Where's the food?
We're still in the driveway! We can't eat everything now.
Hmph. I guess we don't want to starve.

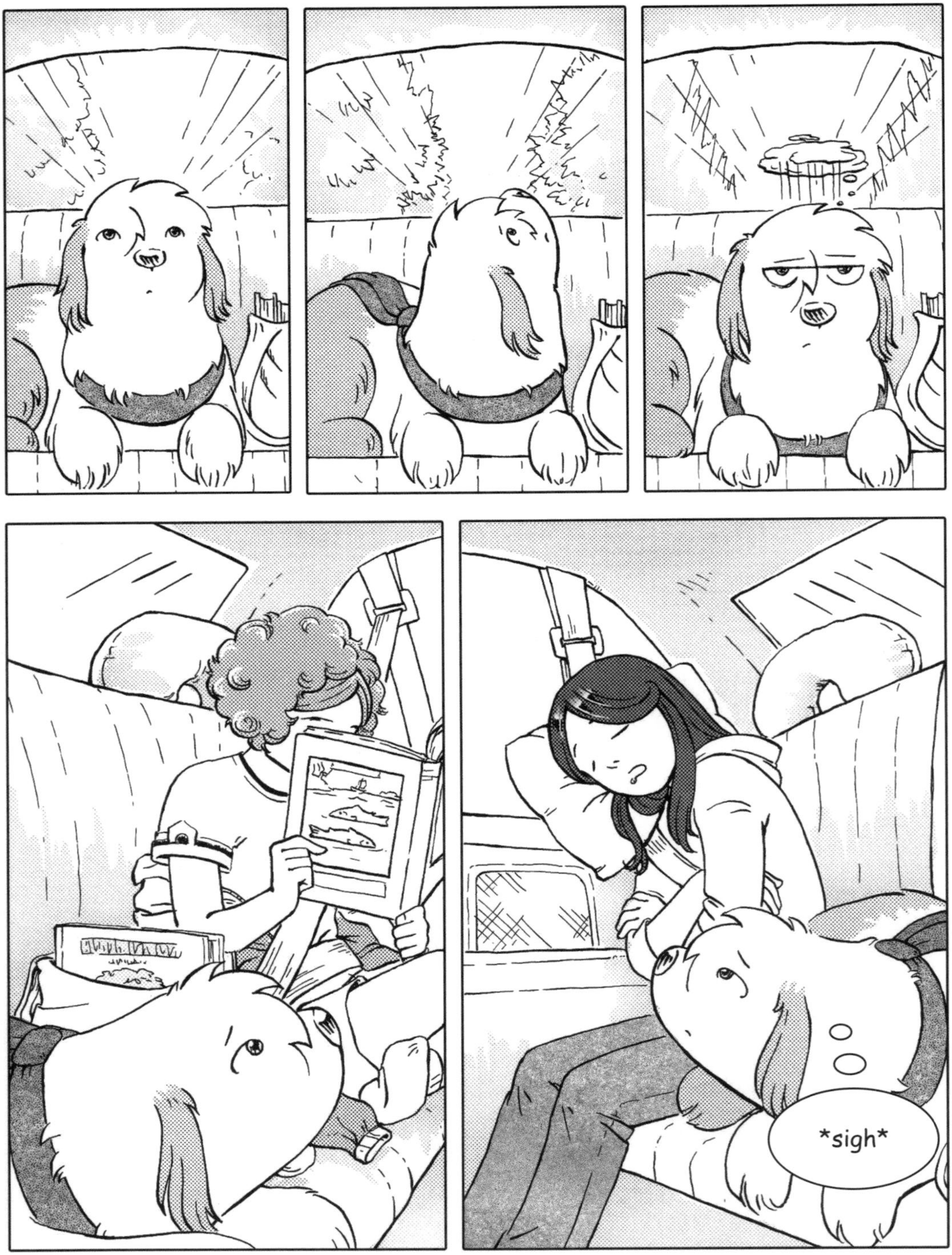
sigh

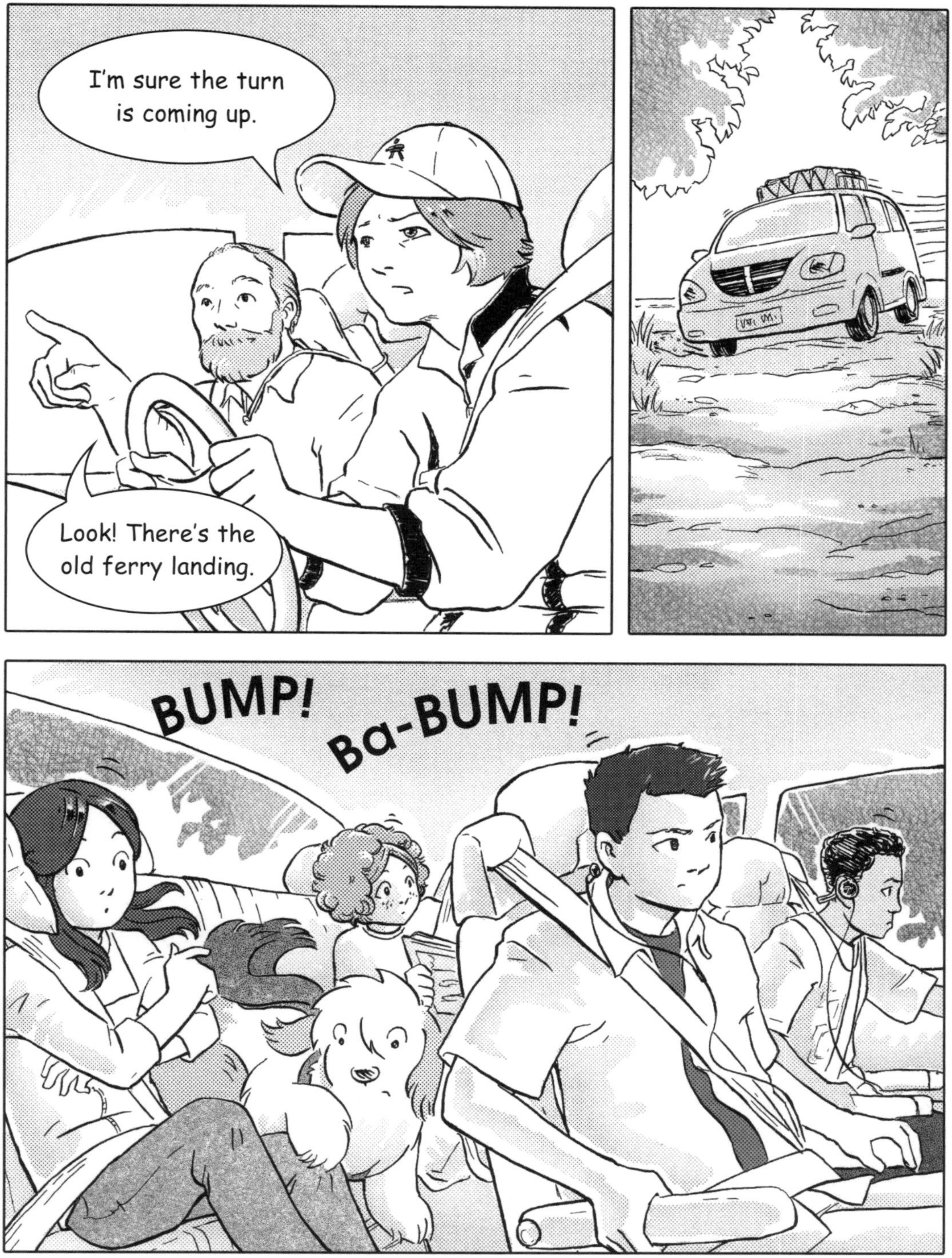
I'm sure the turn is coming up.
Look! There's the old ferry landing.
BUMP!
Ba-BUMP!

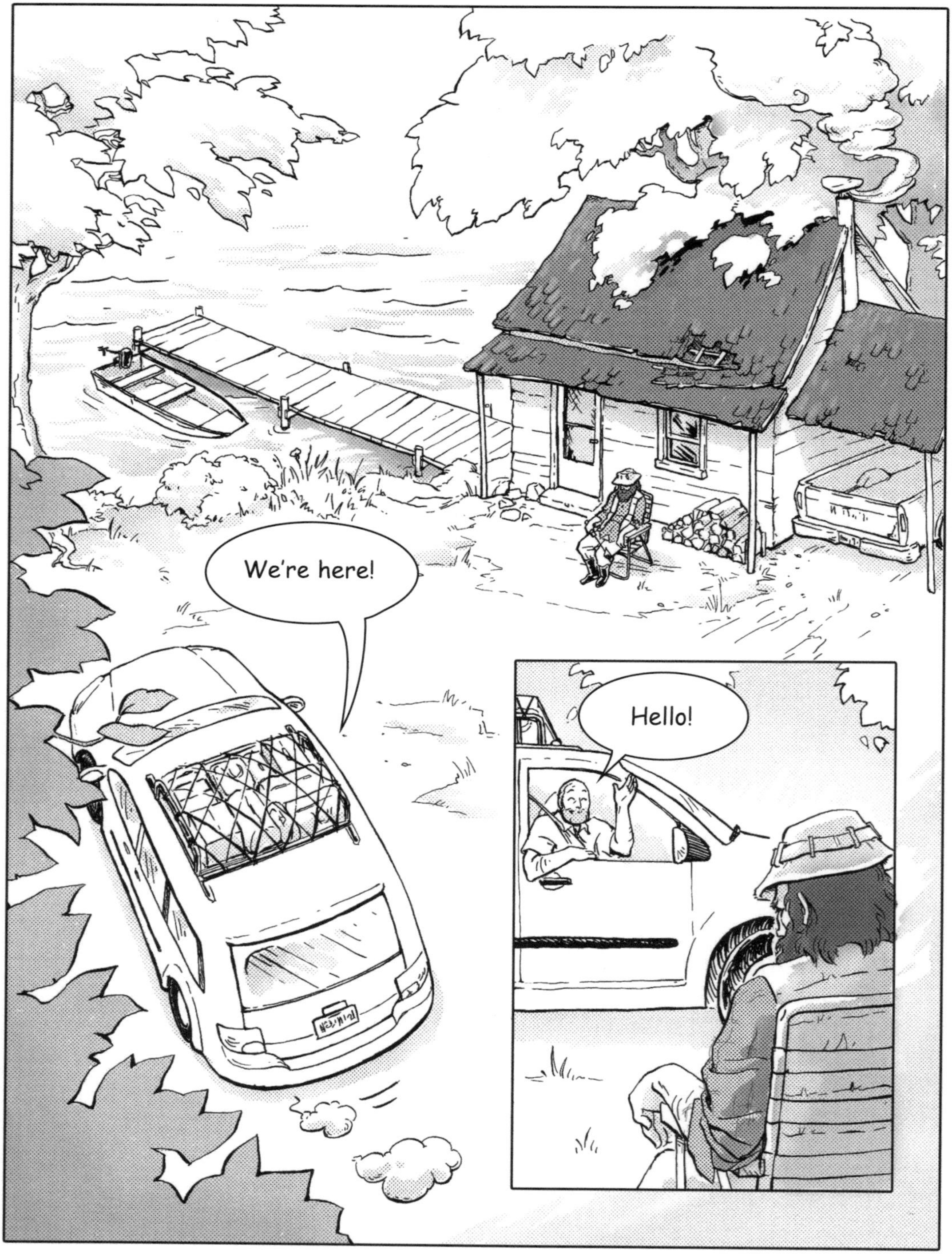
We're here!
Hello!

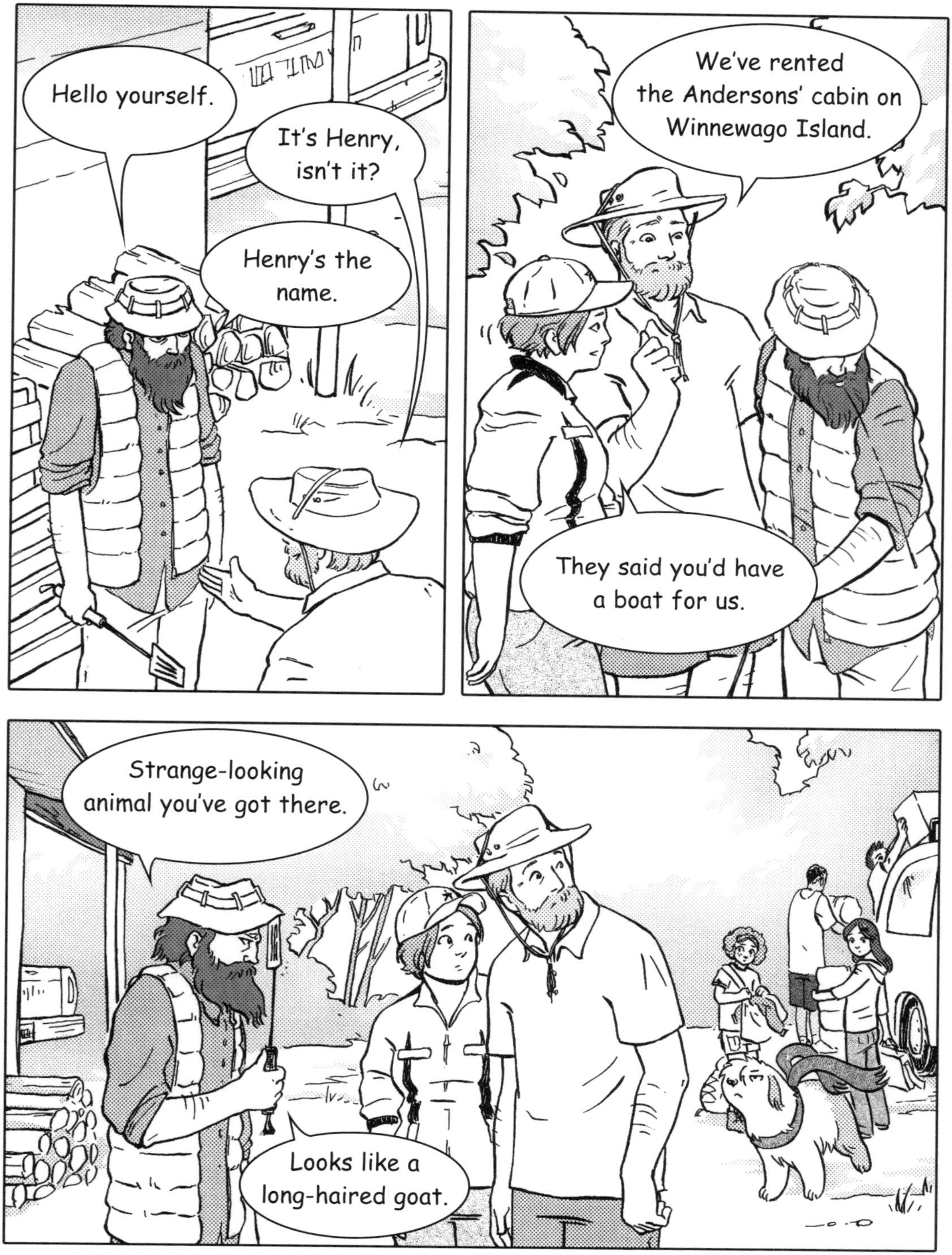
Hello yourself.
It's Henry, isn't it?
Henry's the name.
We've rented the Andersons' cabin on Winnewago Island.
They said you'd have a boat for us.
Strange-looking animal you've got there.
Looks like a long-haired goat.

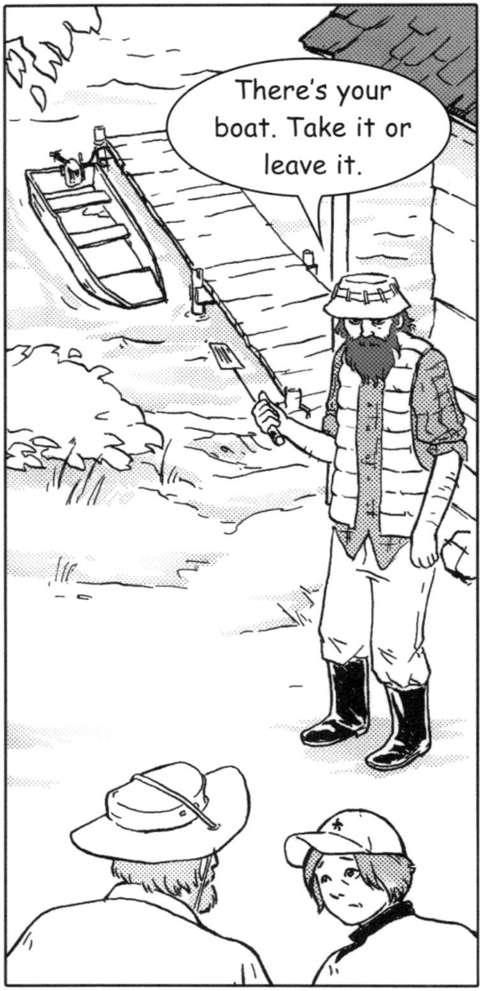
There's your boat. Take it or leave it.

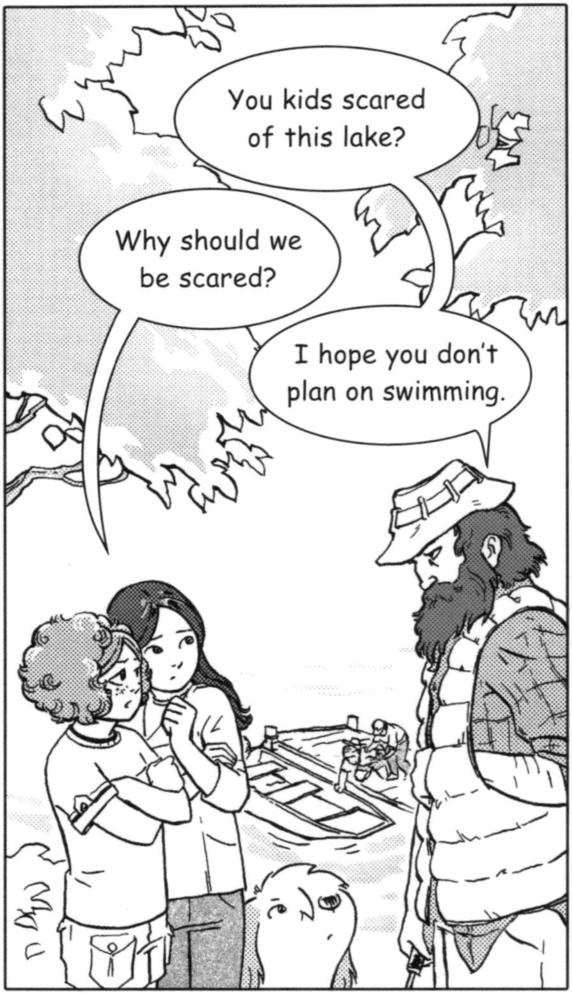
You kids scared of this lake?
Why should we be scared?
I hope you don't plan on swimming.

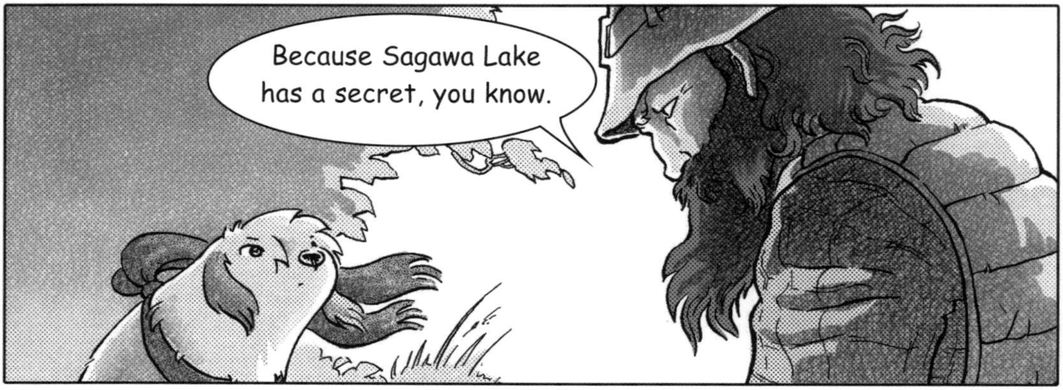
Because Sagawa Lake has a secret, you know.

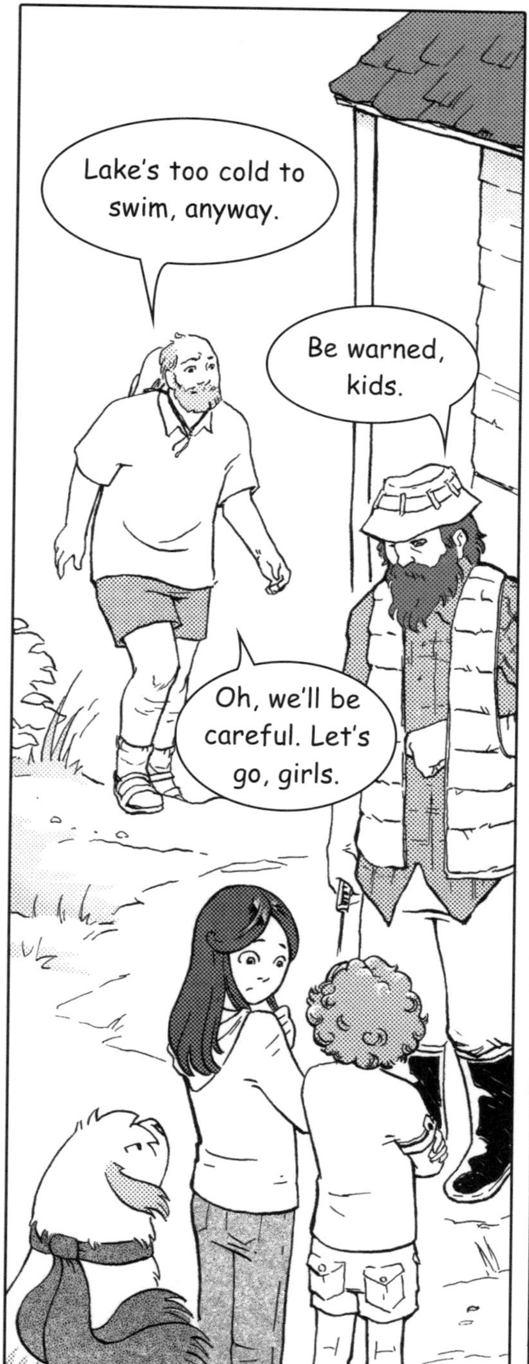
Lake's too cold to swim, anyway.
Be warned, kids.
Oh, we'll be careful. Let's go, girls.
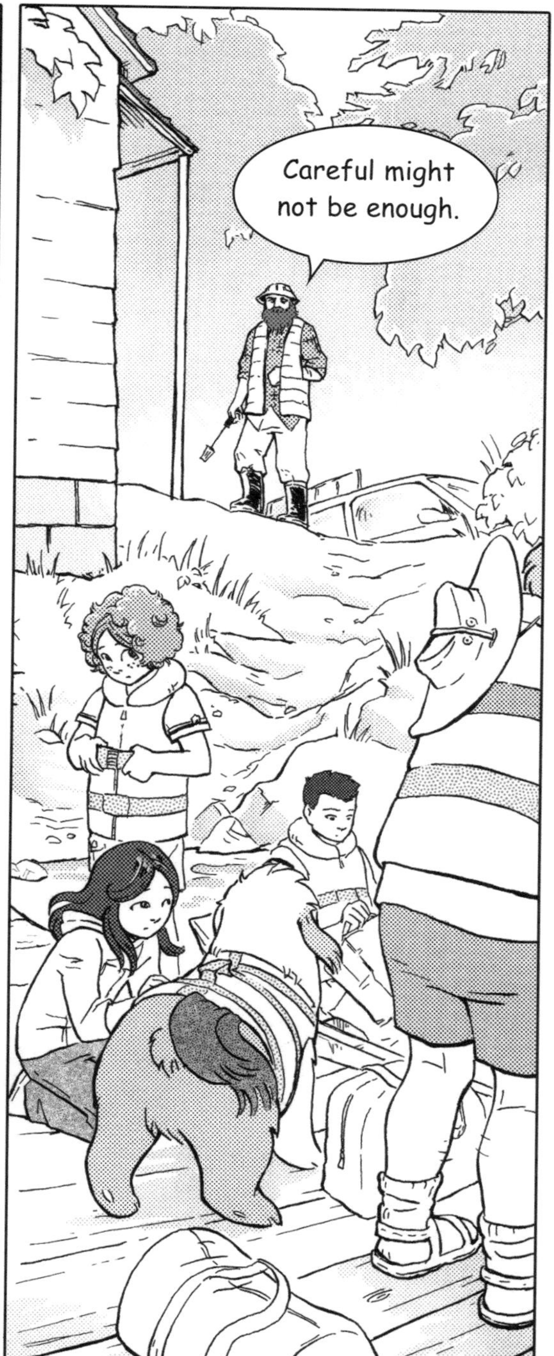
Careful might not be enough.

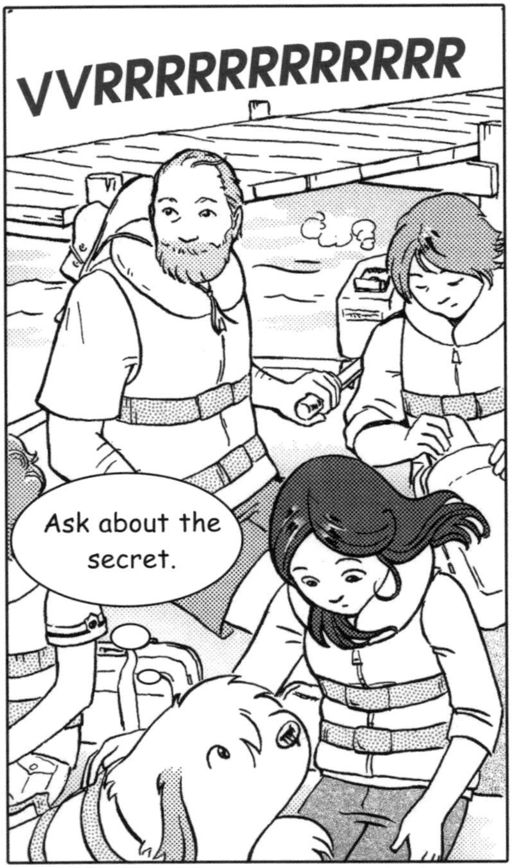
VVRRRRRRRRRRR
Ask about the secret.

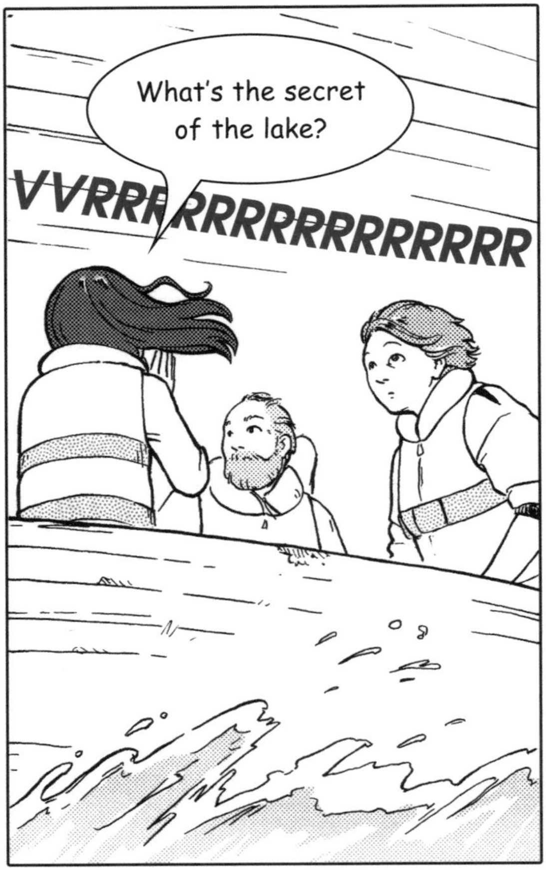
What's the secret of the lake?
VVRRRRRRRRRRRRRRRR

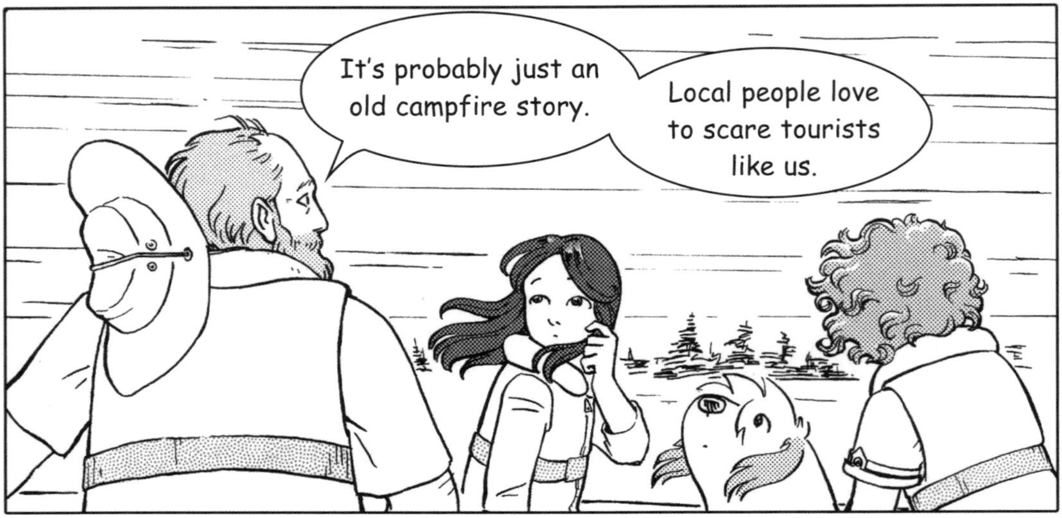
It's probably just an old campfire story.
Local people love to scare tourists like us.

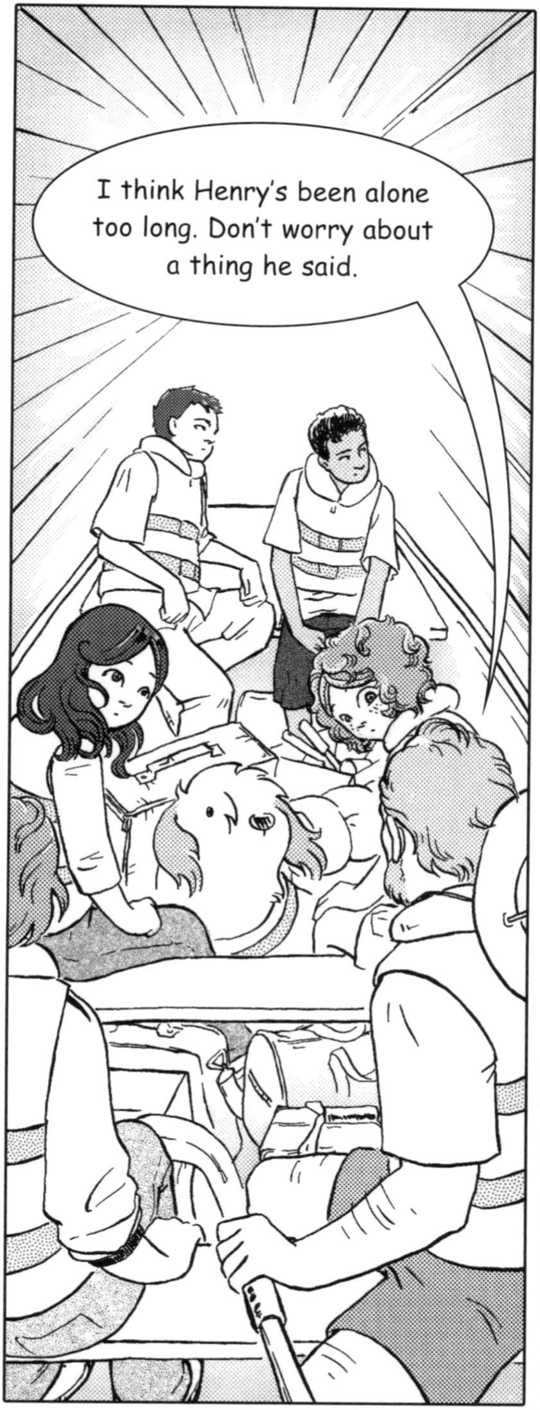
I think Henry's been alone too long. Don't worry about a thing he said.
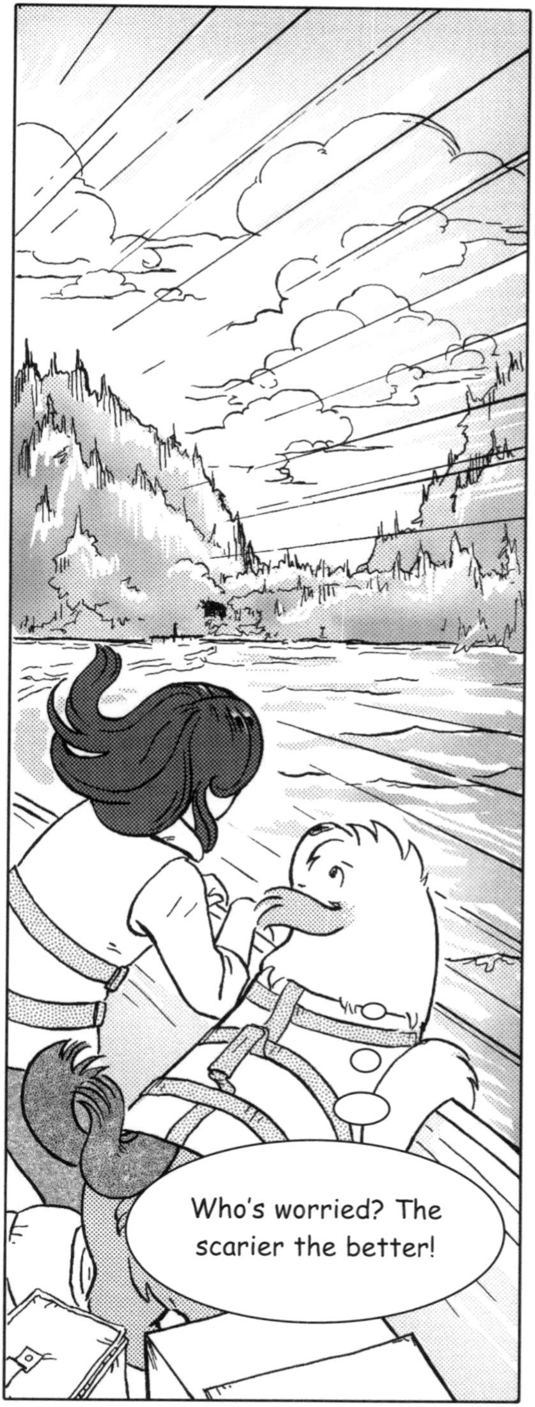
Who's worried? The scarier the better!

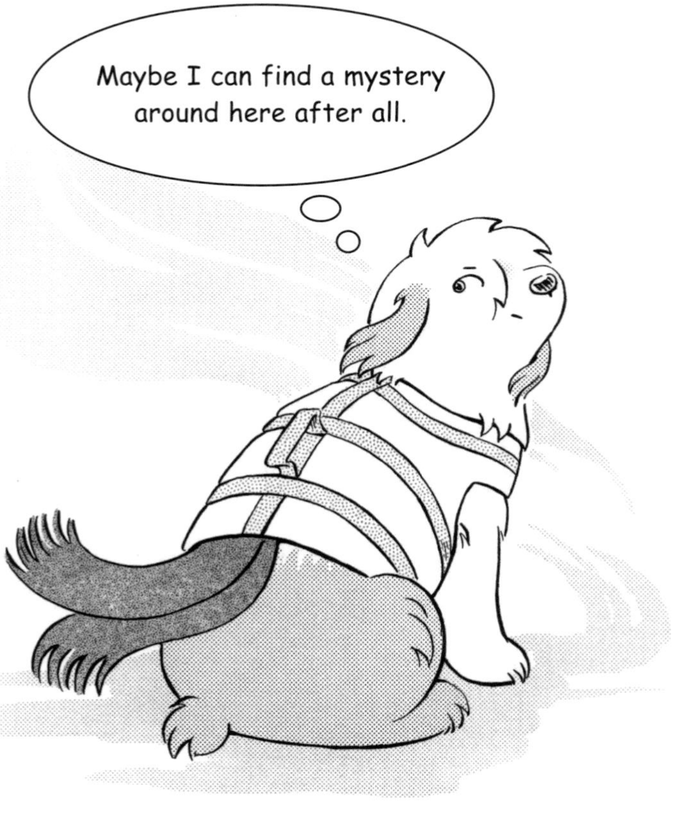
Maybe I can find a mystery around here after all.

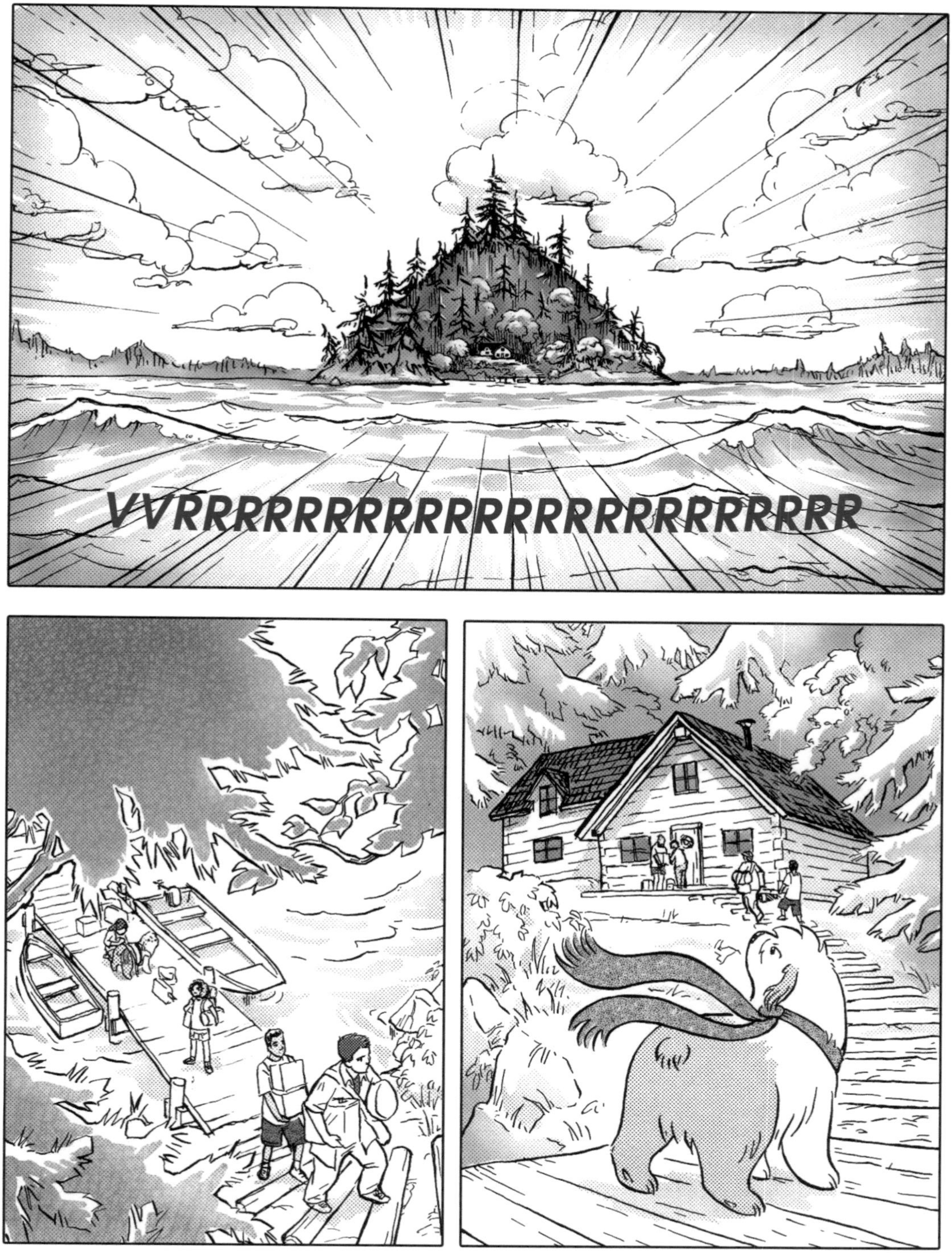
VVRRRRRRRRRRRRRRRRRRRRRRR

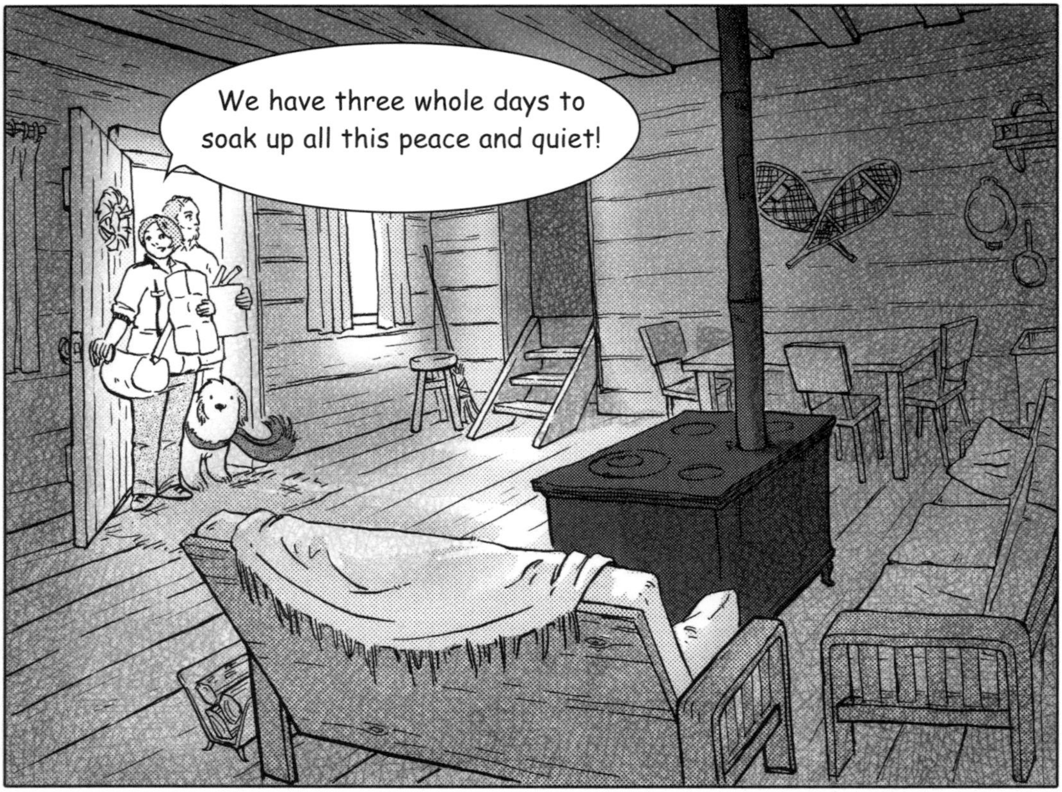
We have three whole days to soak up all this peace and quiet!

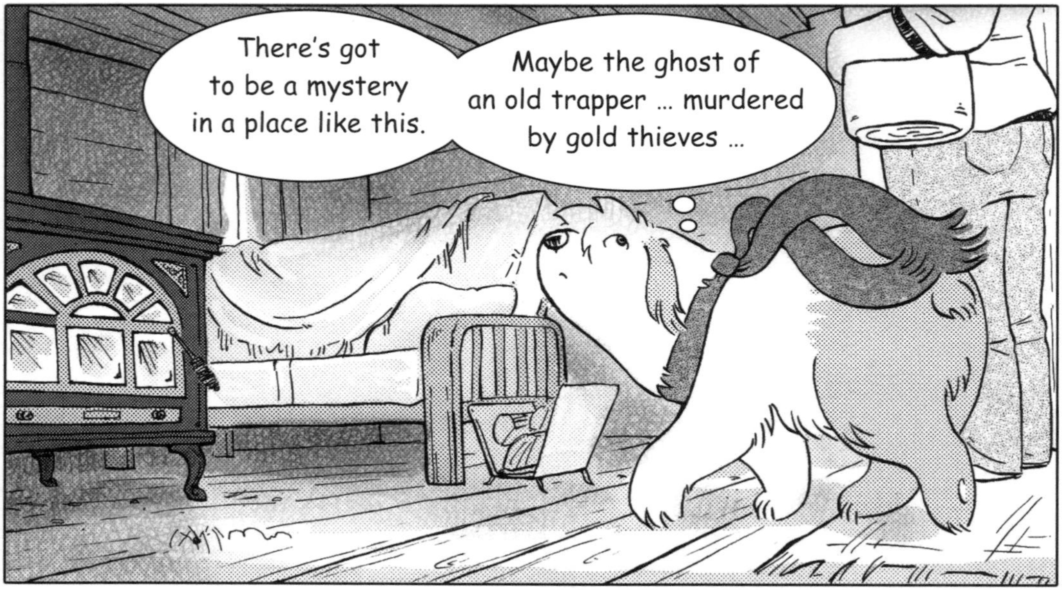
There's got to be a mystery in a place like this.
Maybe the ghost of an old trapper ... murdered by gold thieves ...

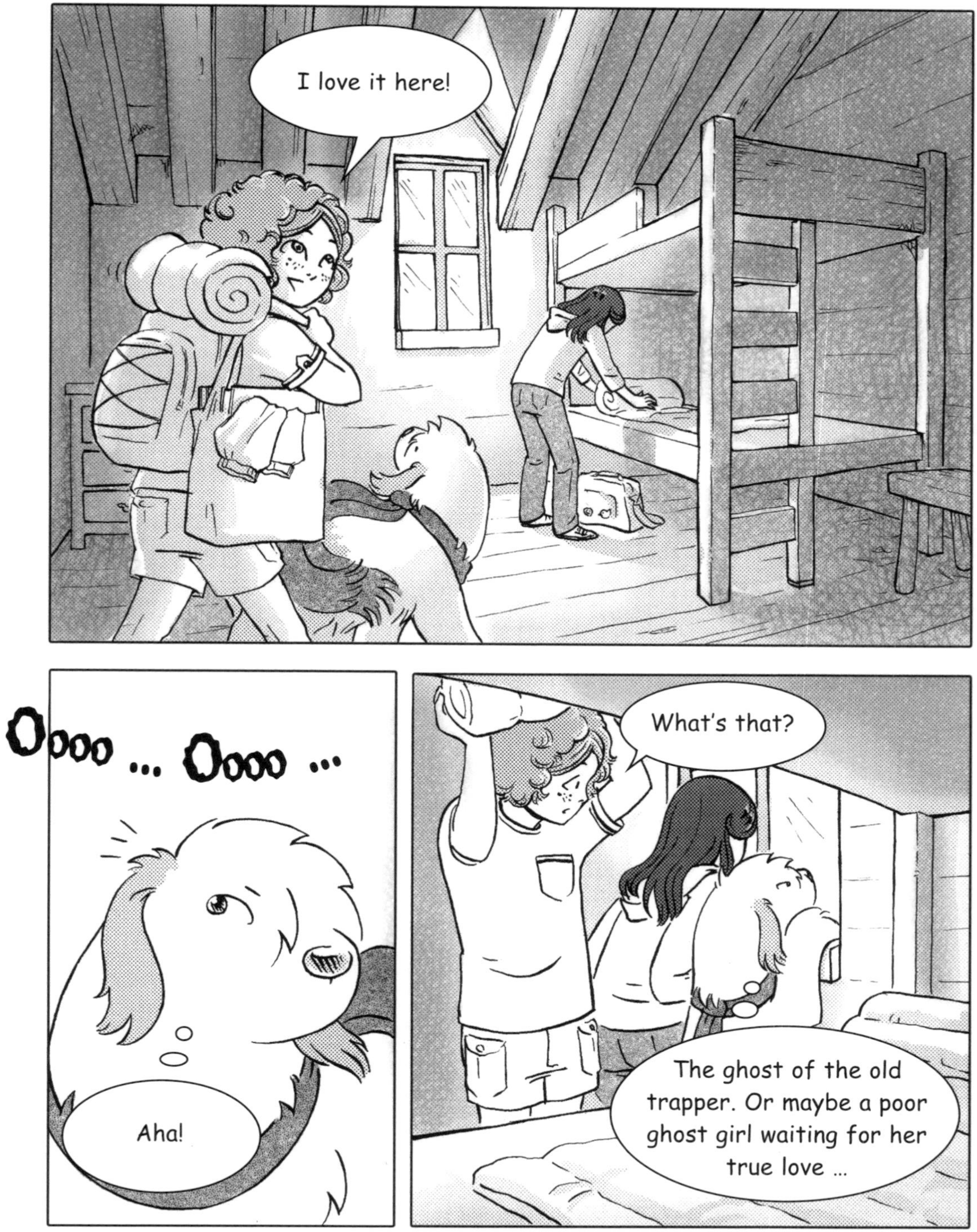

I love it here!
Oooo ... Oooo ...
Aha!
What's that?
The ghost of the old trapper. Or maybe a poor ghost girl waiting for her true love ...

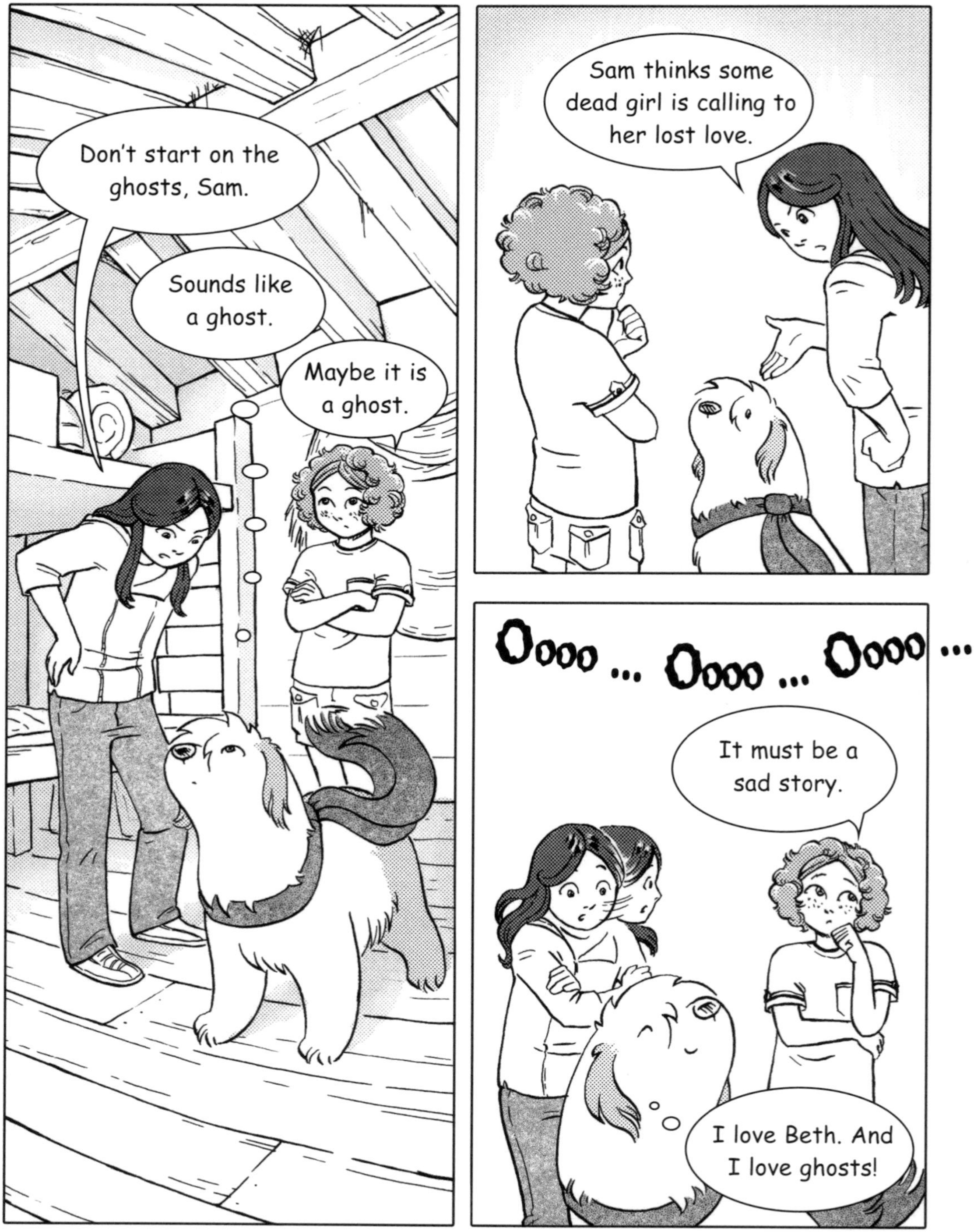
Don't start on the ghosts, Sam.
Sounds like a ghost.
Maybe it is a ghost.
Sam thinks some dead girl is calling to her lost love.
Oooo ... Oooo ... Oooo ...
It must be a sad story.
I love Beth. And I love ghosts!

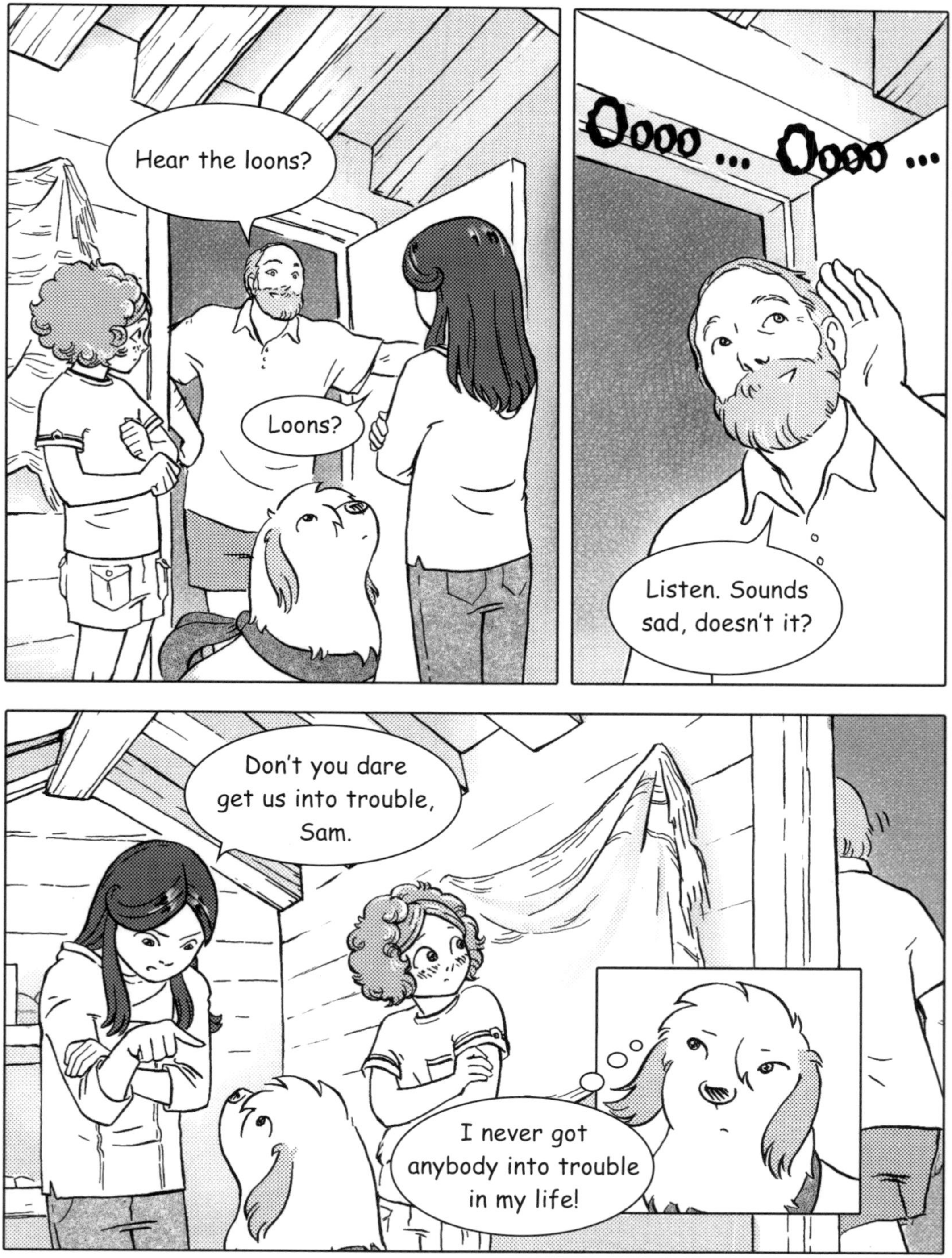
Hear the loons?
Loons?
Oooo ... Oooo ...
Listen. Sounds sad, doesn't it?
Don't you dare get us into trouble, Sam.
I never got anybody into trouble in my life!

Late that night ...

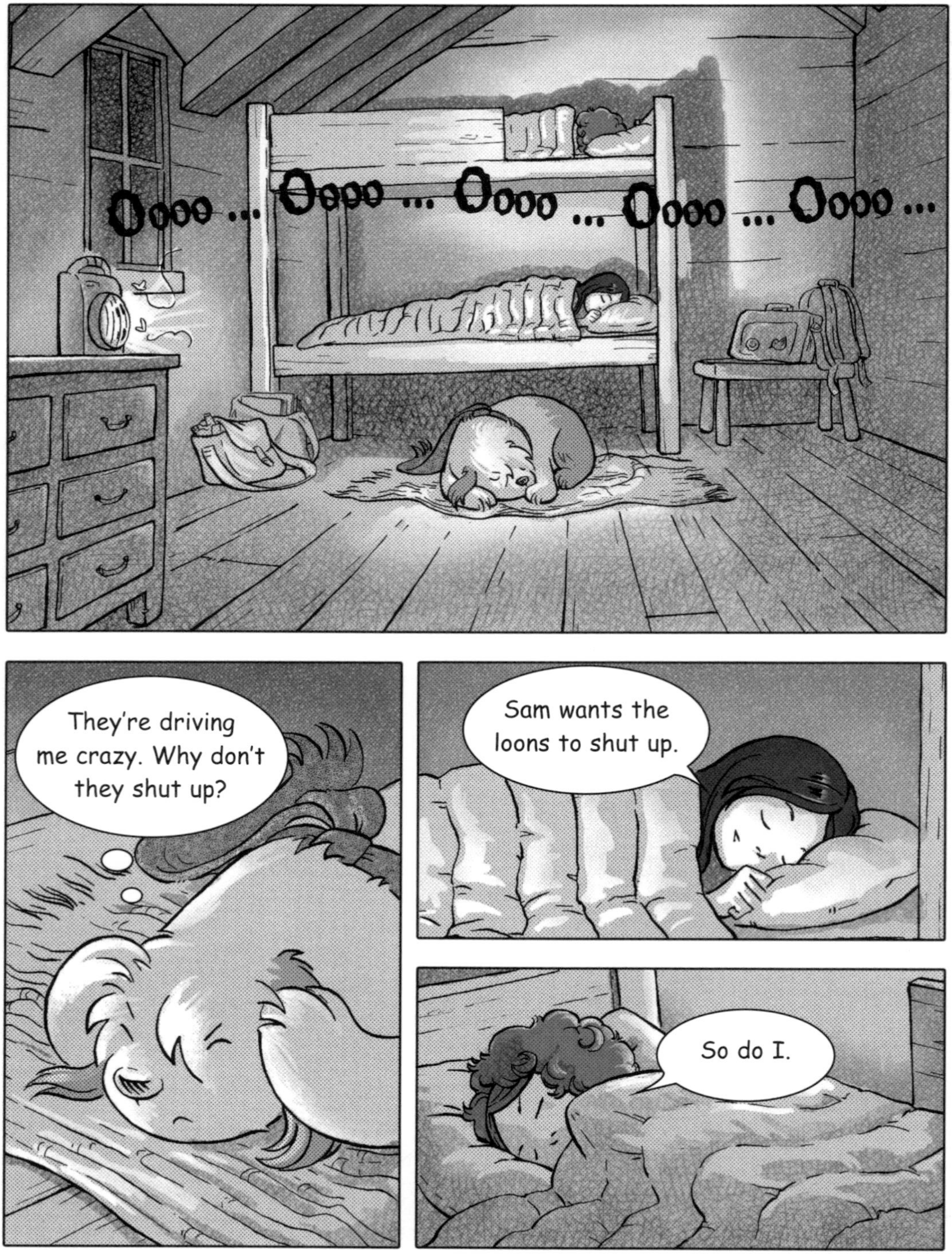

Oooo ... Oooo ... Oooo ... Oooo ... Oooo ...
They're driving me crazy. Why don't they shut up?
Sam wants the loons to shut up.
So do I.

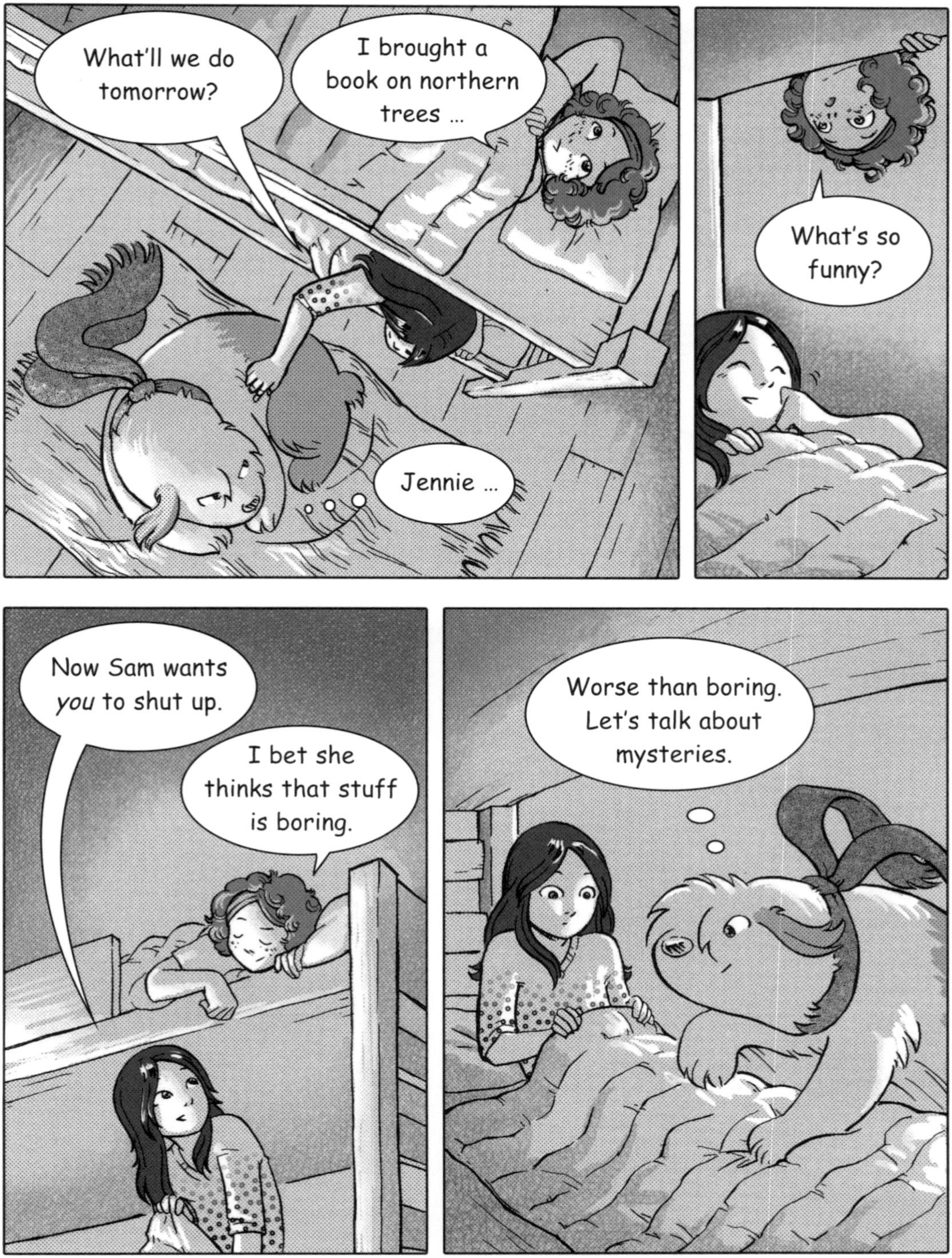
What'll we do tomorrow?
I brought a book on northern trees ...
Jennie ...
What's so funny?
Now Sam wants *you* to shut up.
I bet she thinks that stuff is boring.
Worse than boring. Let's talk about mysteries.

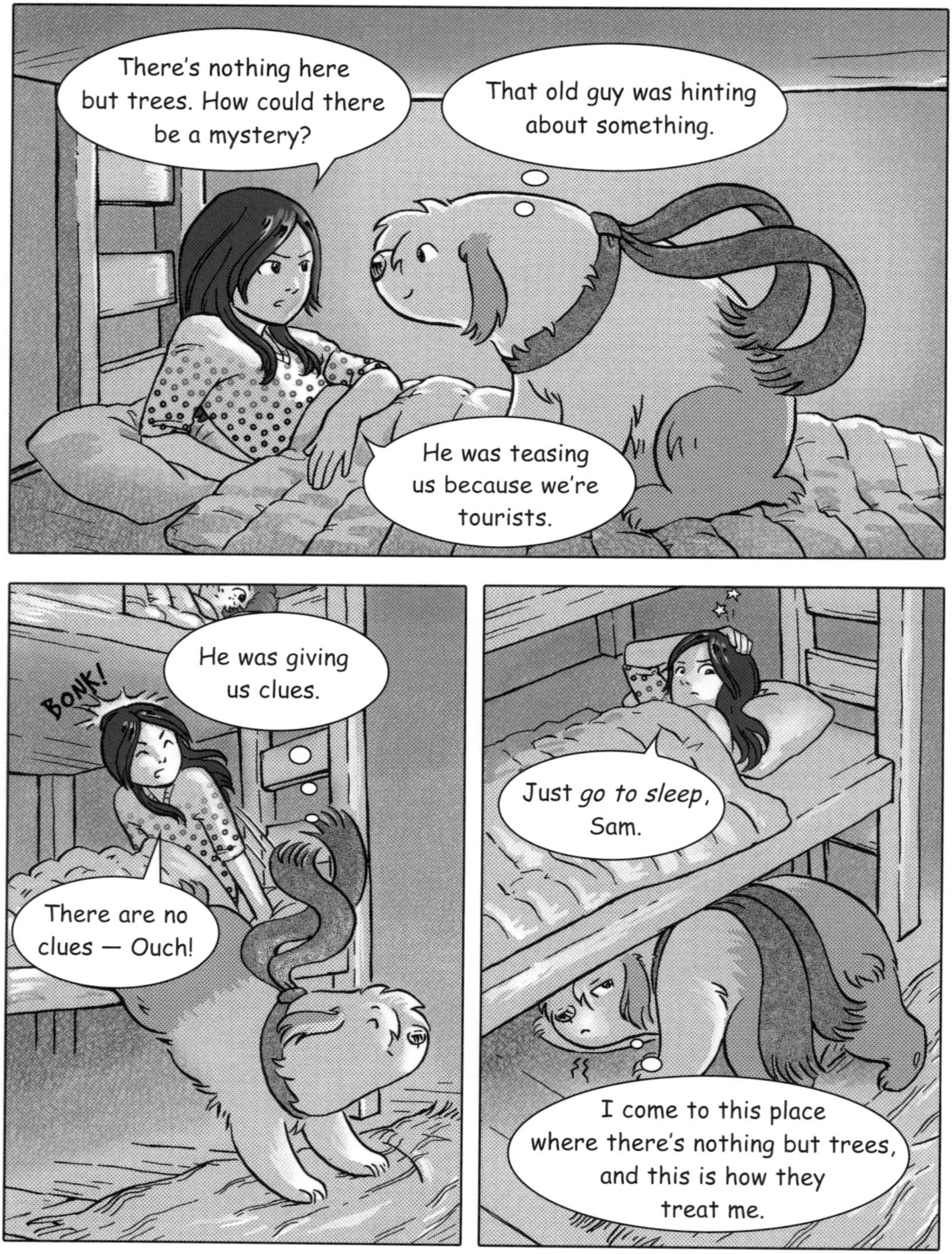
There's nothing here but trees. How could there be a mystery?
That old guy was hinting about something.
He was teasing us because we're tourists.
BONK!
He was giving us clues.
There are no clues — Ouch!
Just *go to sleep*, Sam.
I come to this place where there's nothing but trees, and this is how they treat me.

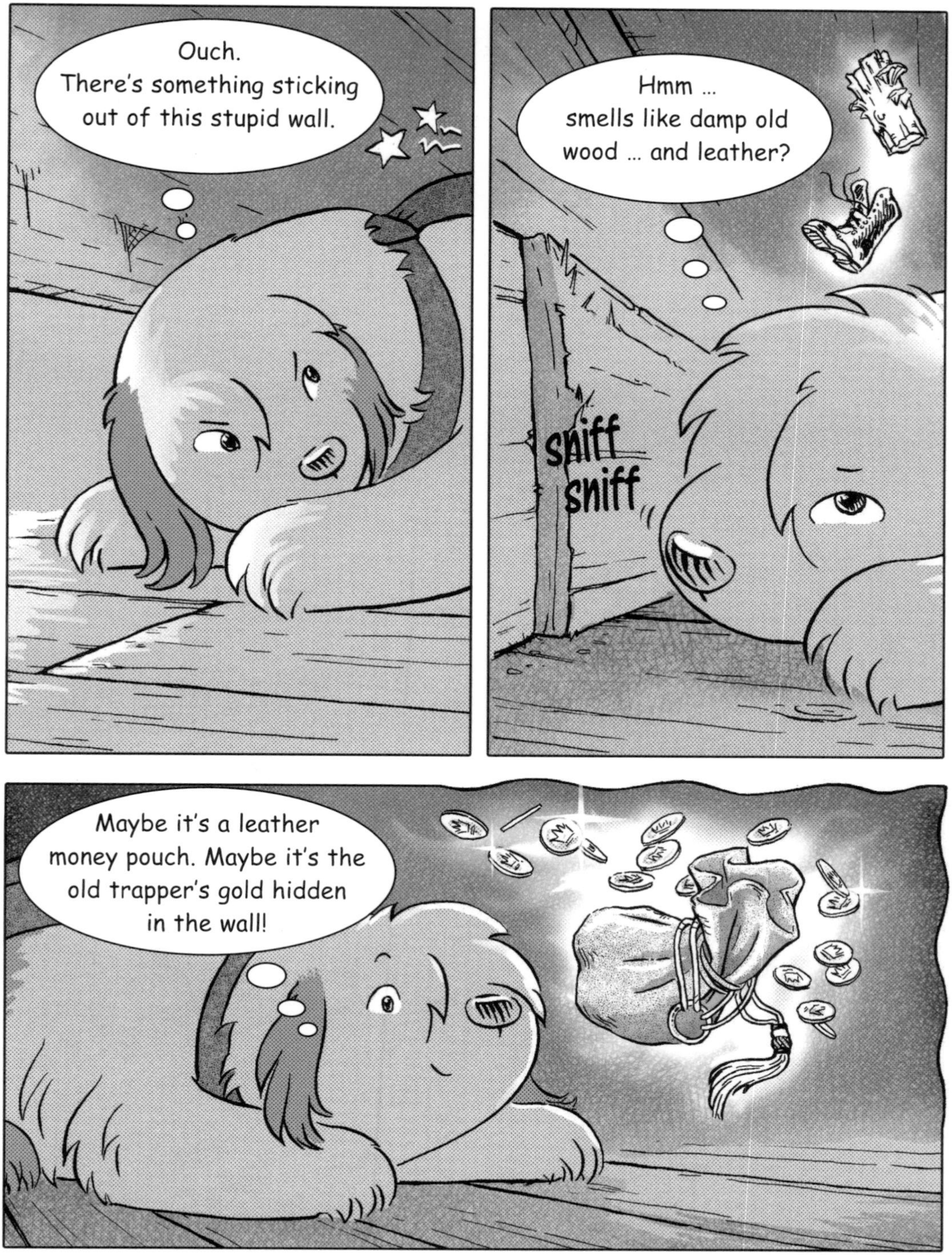
Ouch.
There's something sticking out of this stupid wall.
Hmm ... smells like damp old wood ... and leather?
sniff sniff
Maybe it's a leather money pouch. Maybe it's the old trapper's gold hidden in the wall!

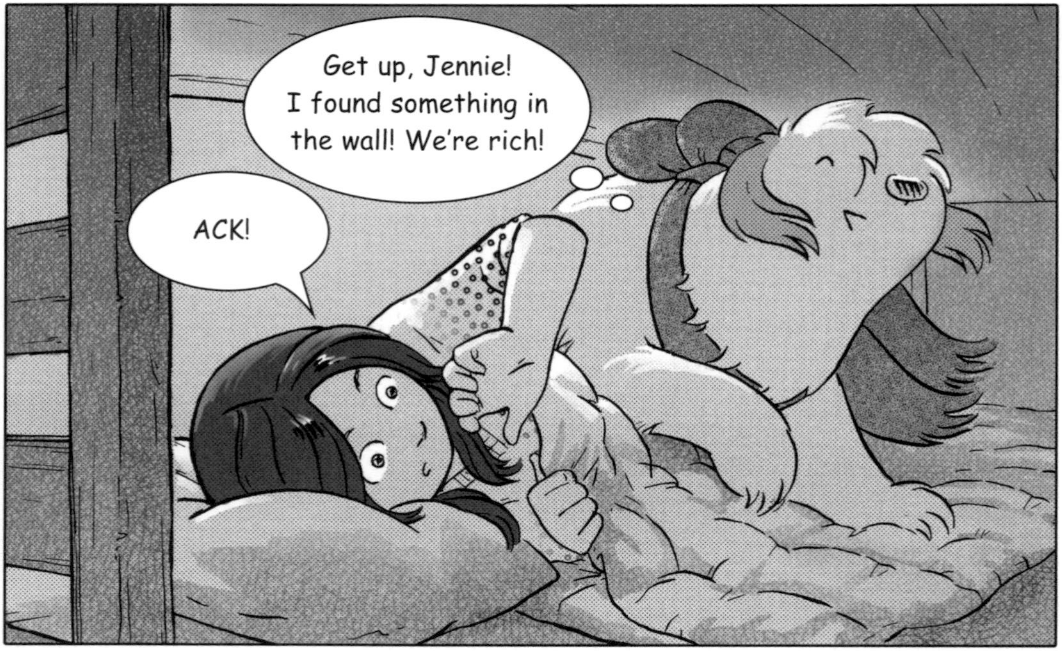
Get up, Jennie! I found something in the wall! We're rich!
ACK!

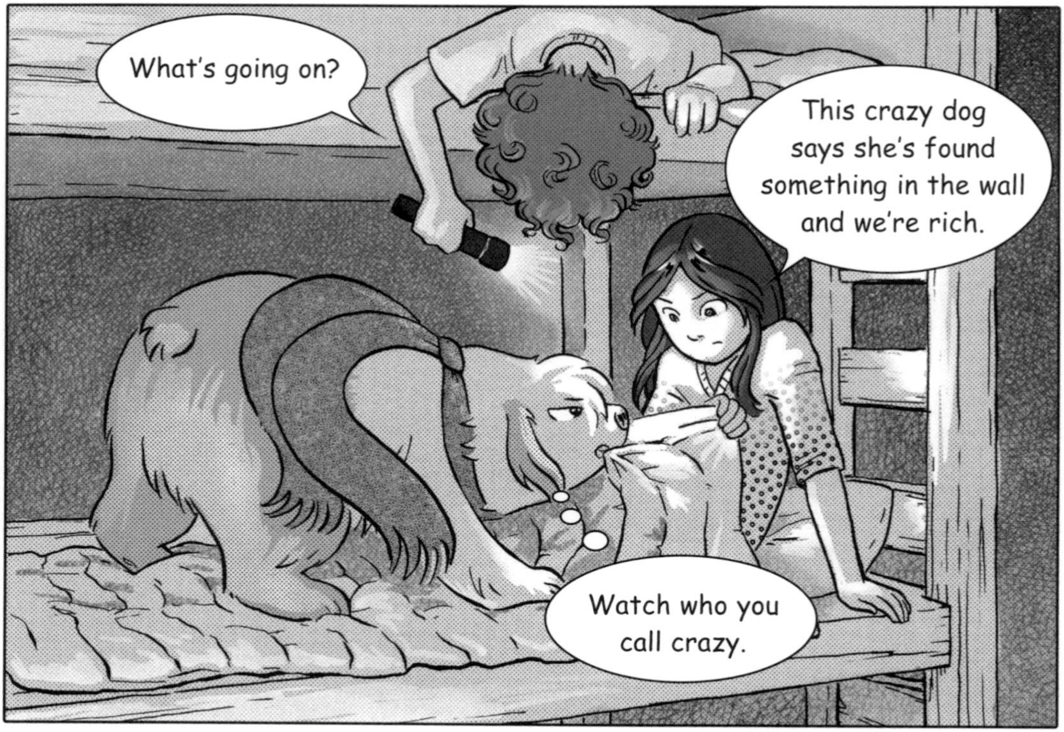
What's going on?
This crazy dog says she's found something in the wall and we're rich.
Watch who you call crazy.

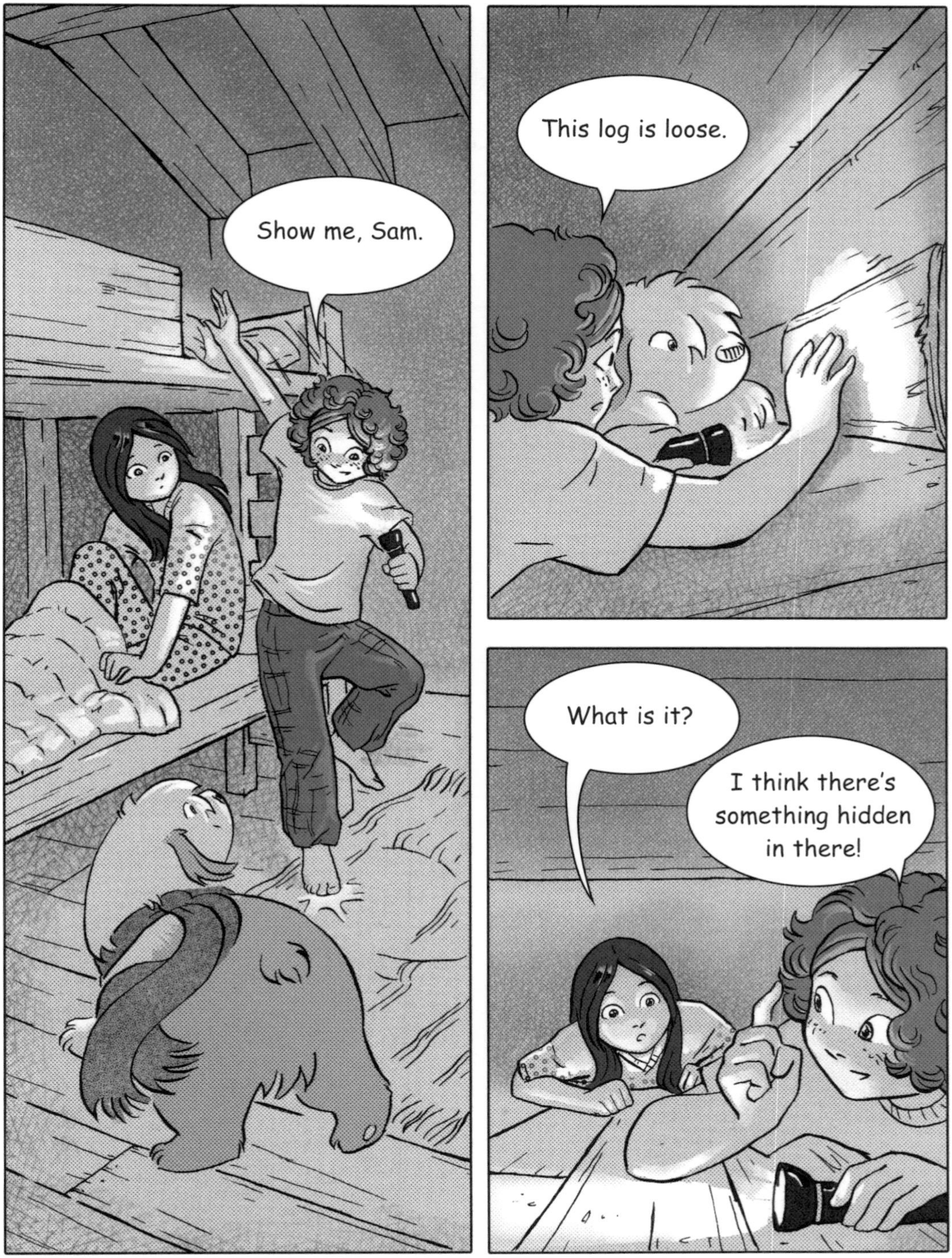
Show me, Sam.
This log is loose.
What is it?
I think there's something hidden in there!

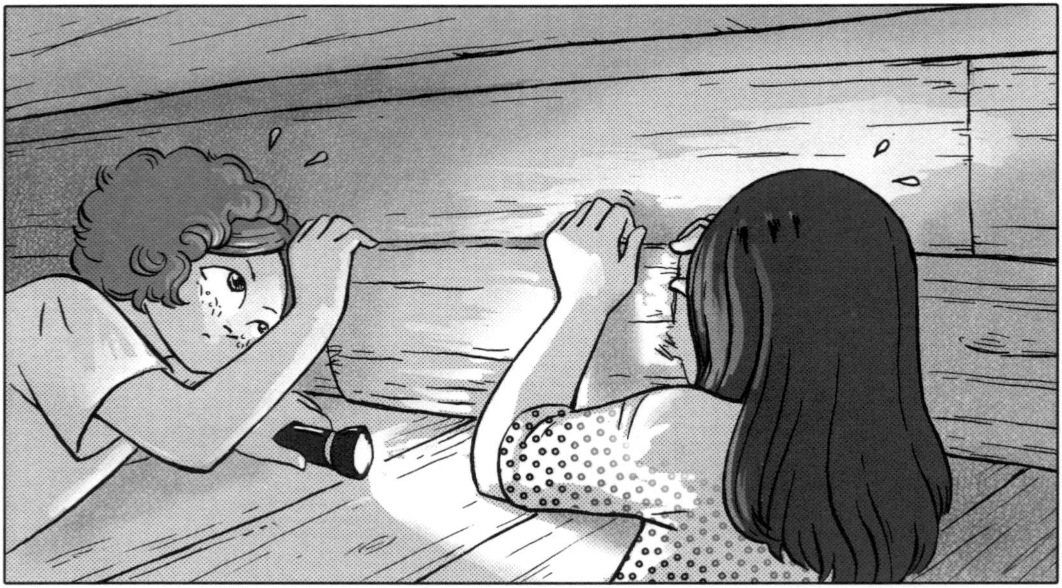

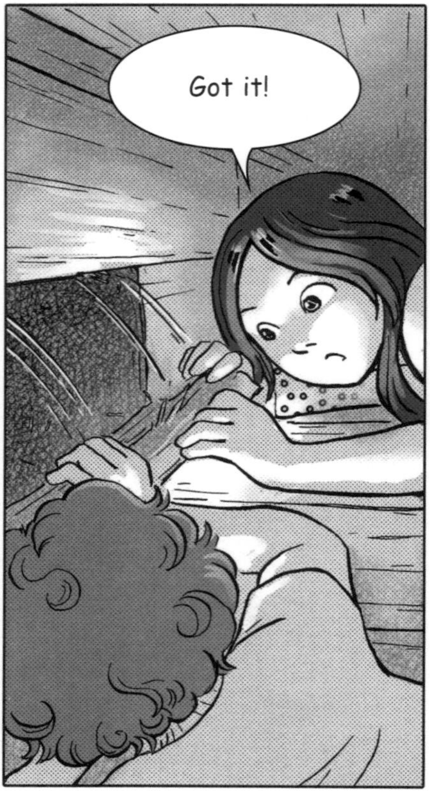
Got it!

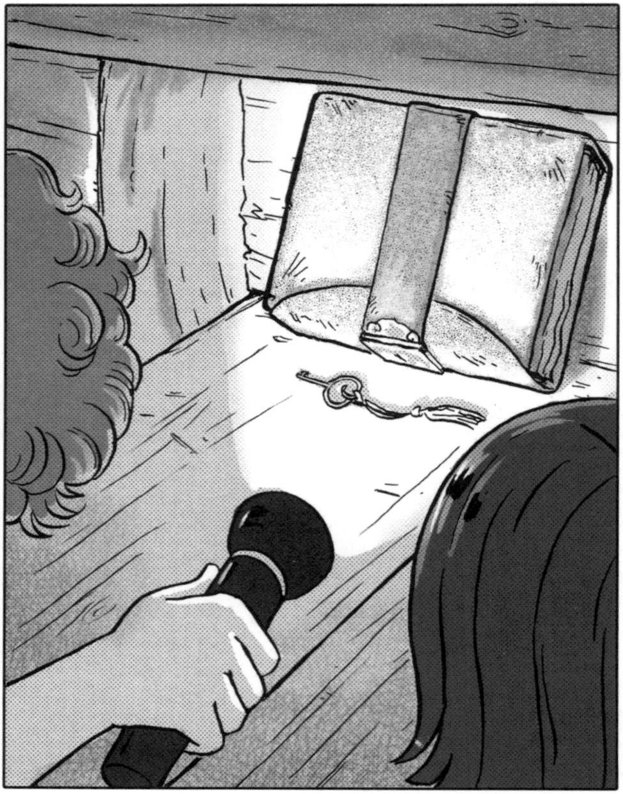

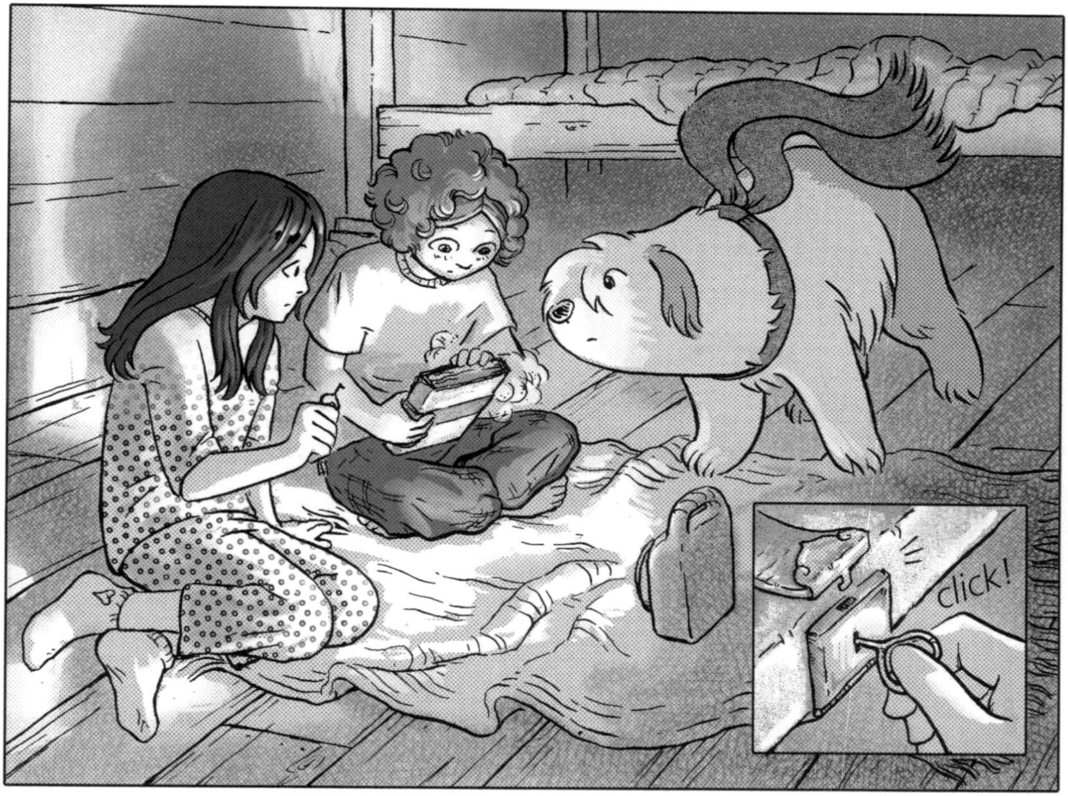
click!

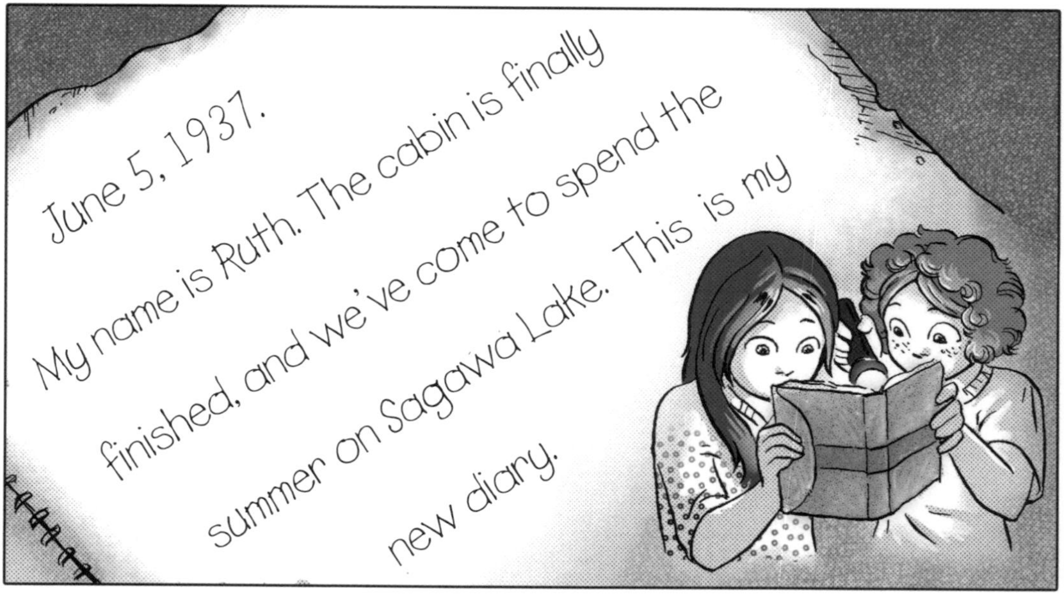
June 5, 1937.
My name is Ruth. The cabin is finally
finished, and we've come to spend the
summer on Sagawa Lake. This is my
new diary.

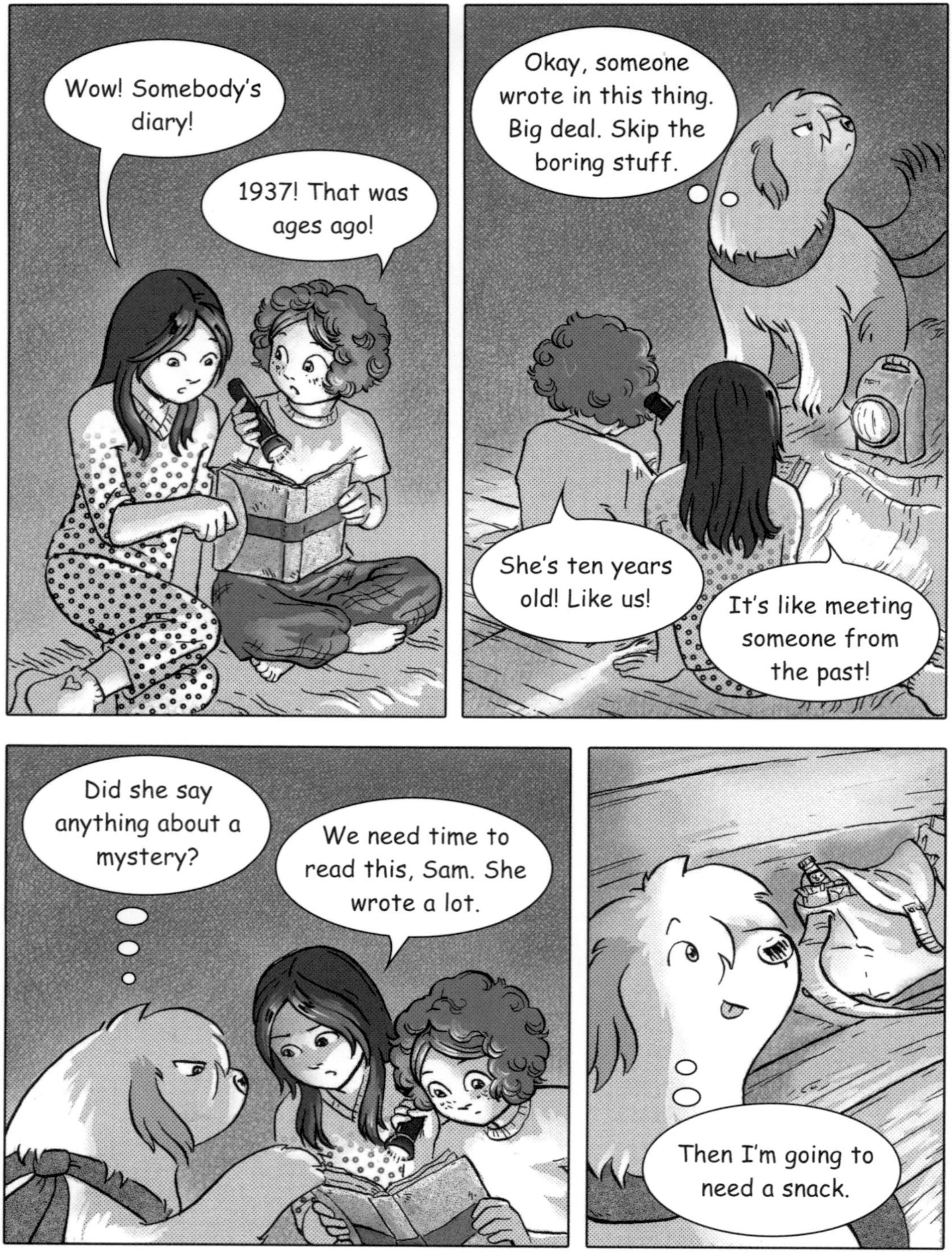
Wow! Somebody's diary!
1937! That was ages ago!
Okay, someone wrote in this thing. Big deal. Skip the boring stuff.
She's ten years old! Like us!
It's like meeting someone from the past!
Did she say anything about a mystery?
We need time to read this, Sam. She wrote a lot.
Then I'm going to need a snack.

Into the early morning ...

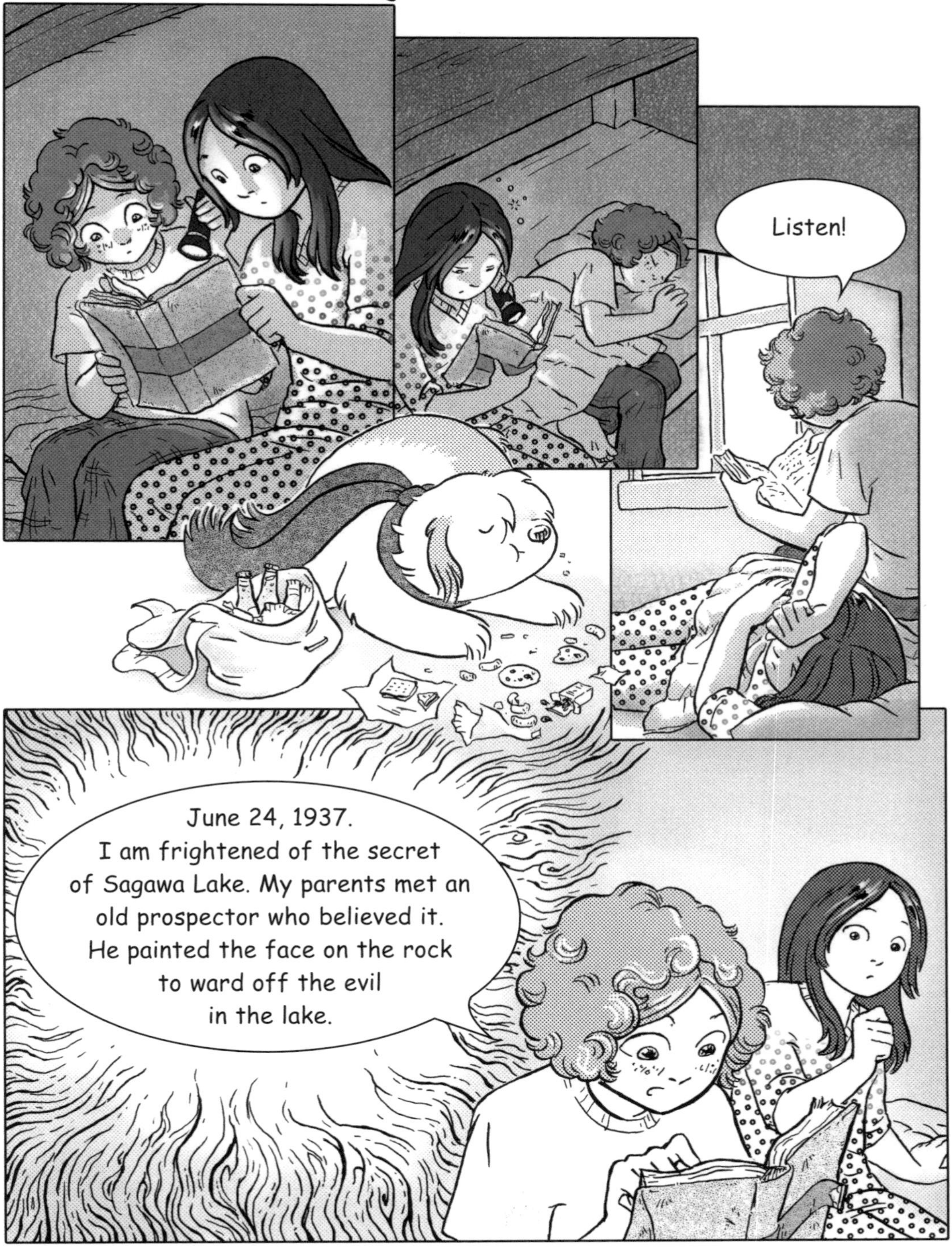
Listen!
June 24, 1937.
I am frightened of the secret of Sagawa Lake. My parents met an old prospector who believed it. He painted the face on the rock to ward off the evil in the lake.

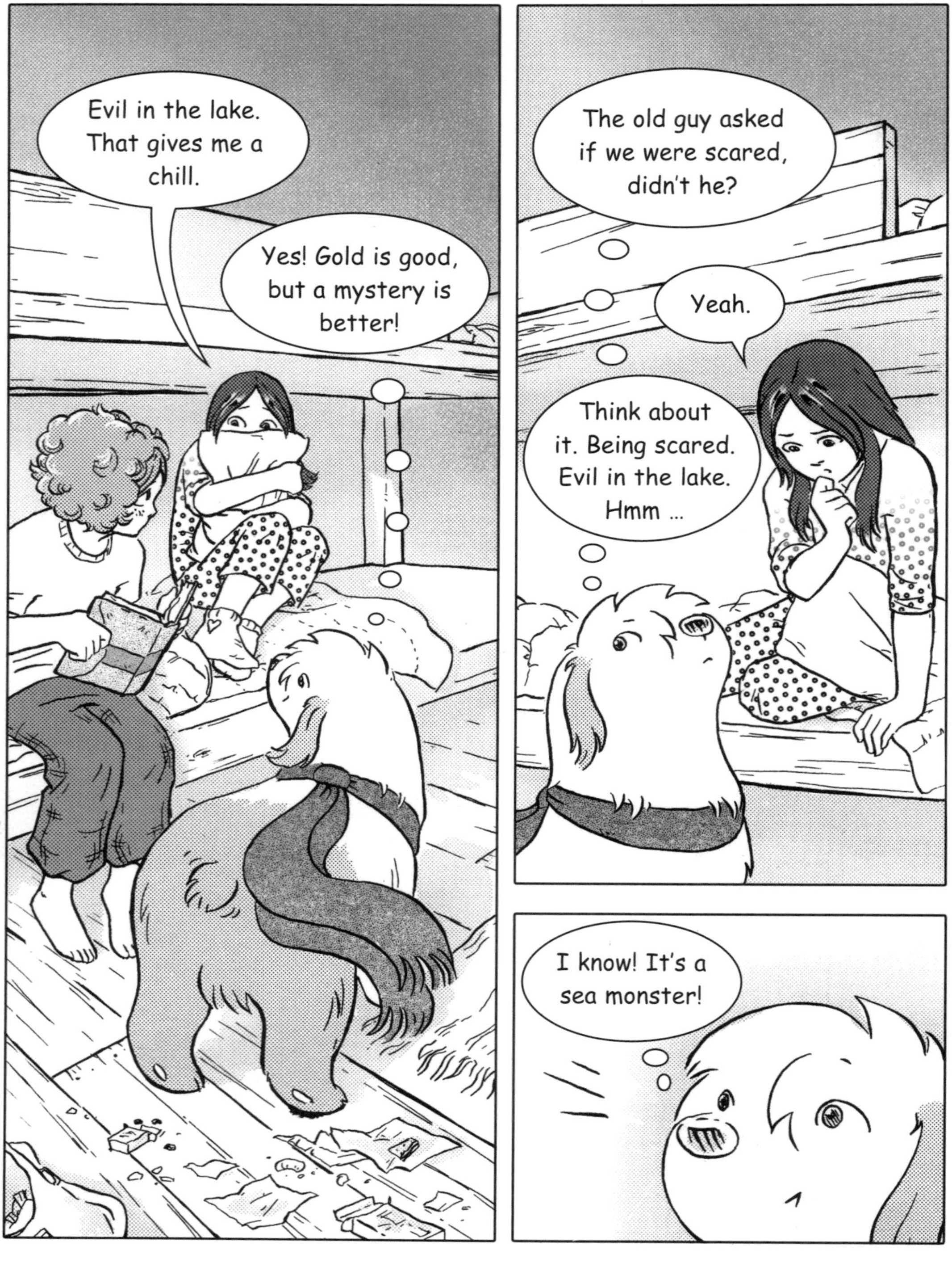
Evil in the lake. That gives me a chill.
Yes! Gold is good, but a mystery is better!
The old guy asked if we were scared, didn't he?
Yeah.
Think about it. Being scared. Evil in the lake. Hmm ...
I know! It's a sea monster!

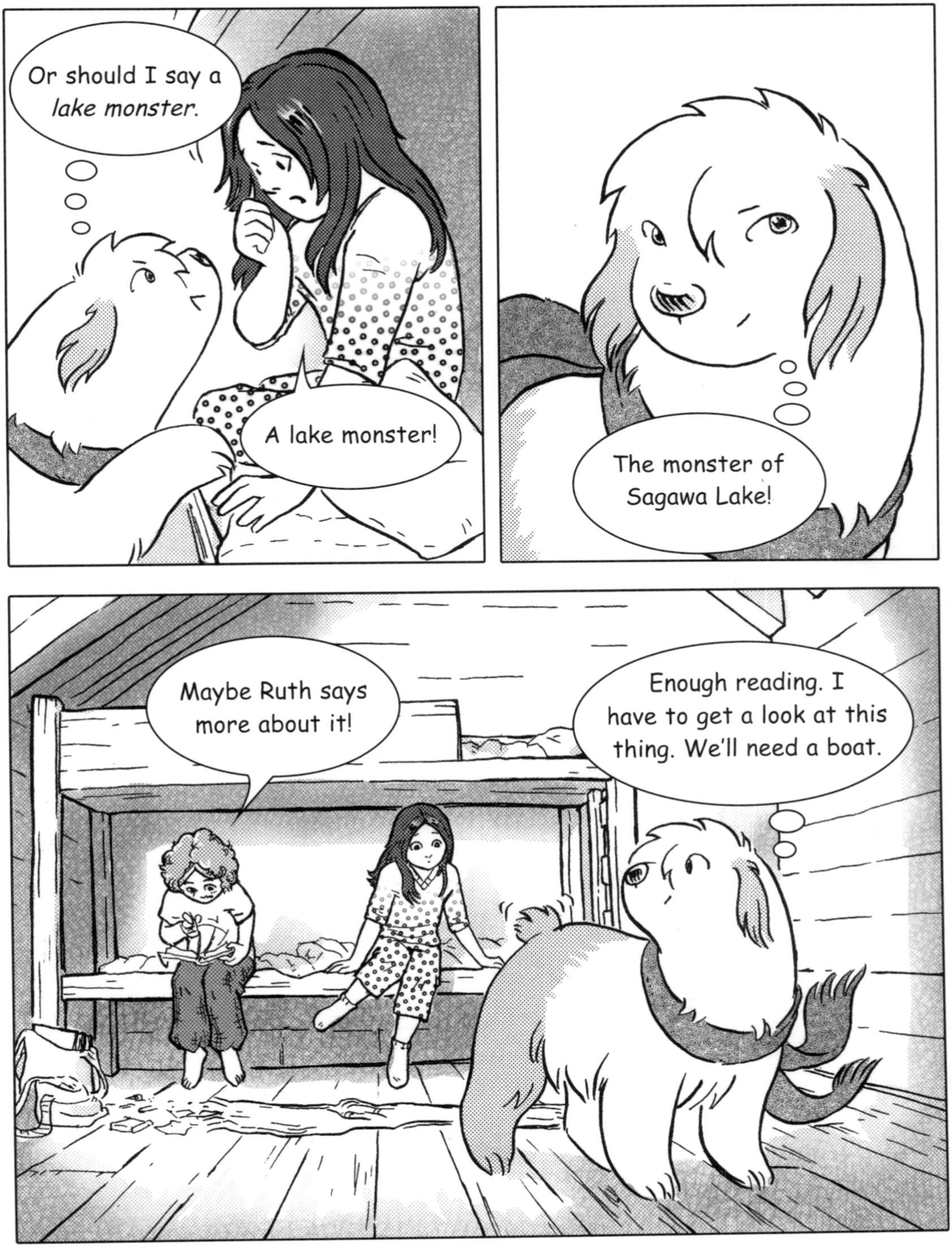
Or should I say a *lake monster*.
A lake monster!
The monster of Sagawa Lake!
Maybe Ruth says more about it!
Enough reading. I have to get a look at this thing. We'll need a boat.

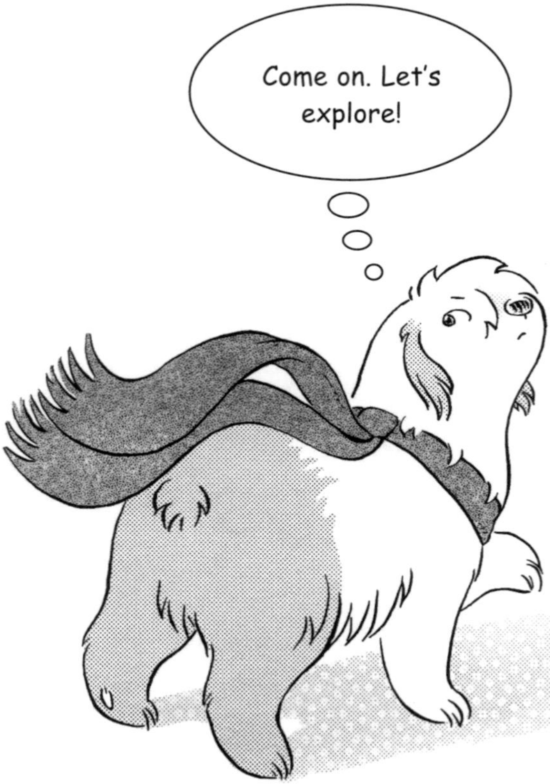
Come on. Let's explore!

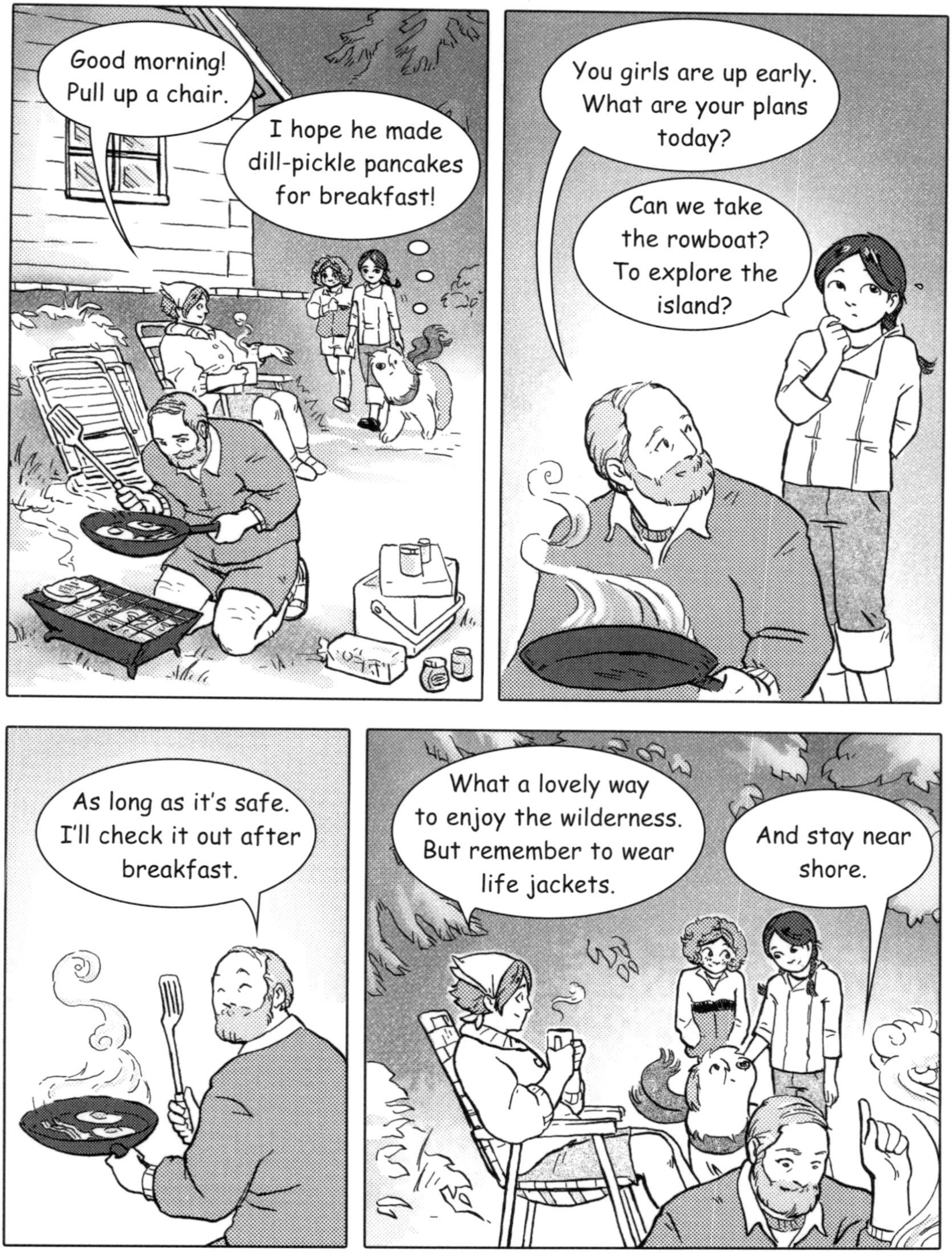
Good morning! Pull up a chair.
I hope he made dill-pickle pancakes for breakfast!
You girls are up early. What are your plans today?
Can we take the rowboat? To explore the island?
As long as it's safe. I'll check it out after breakfast.
What a lovely way to enjoy the wilderness. But remember to wear life jackets.
And stay near shore.

Soon ...

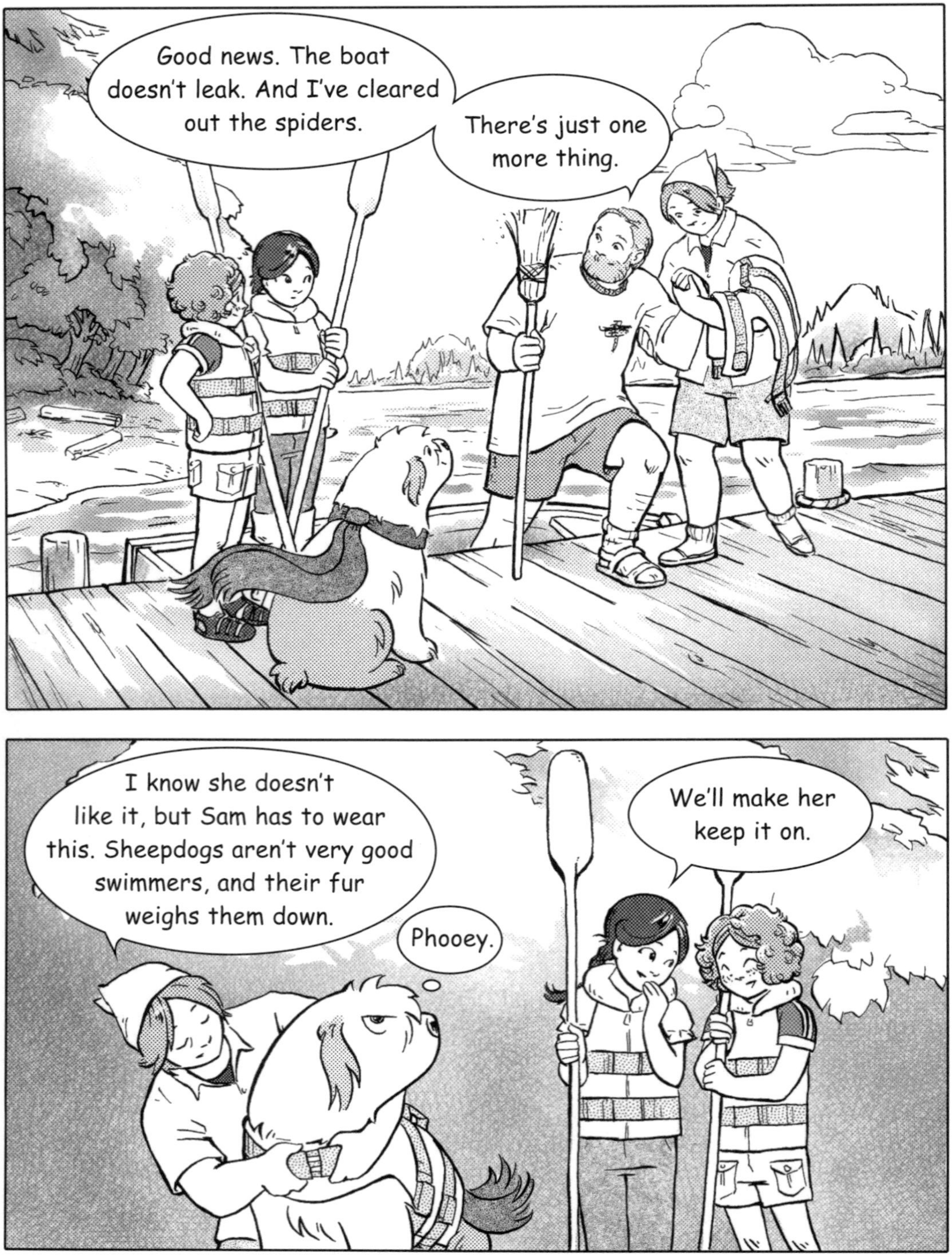
Good news. The boat doesn't leak. And I've cleared out the spiders.
There's just one more thing.
I know she doesn't like it, but Sam has to wear this. Sheepdogs aren't very good swimmers, and their fur weighs them down.
Phooey.
We'll make her keep it on.

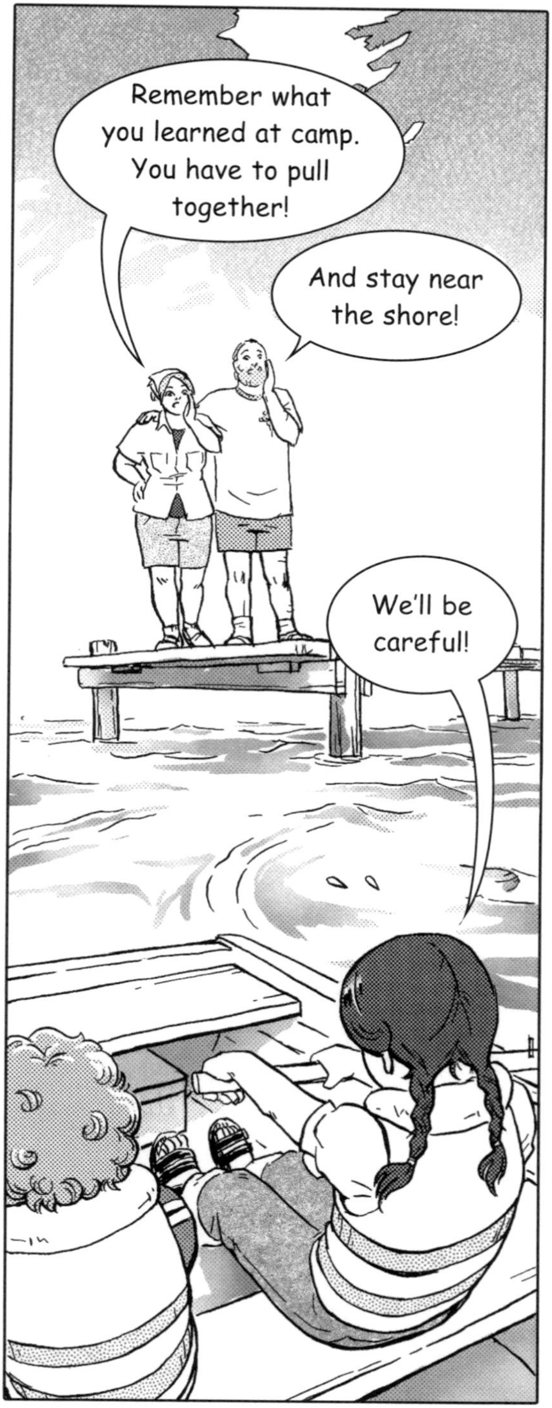
Remember what you learned at camp. You have to pull together!
And stay near the shore!
We'll be careful!

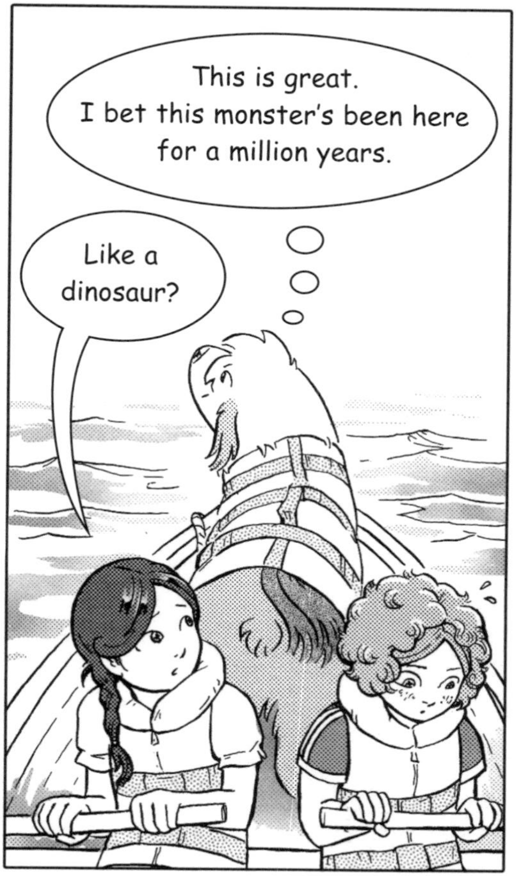
This is great. I bet this monster's been here for a million years.
Like a dinosaur?

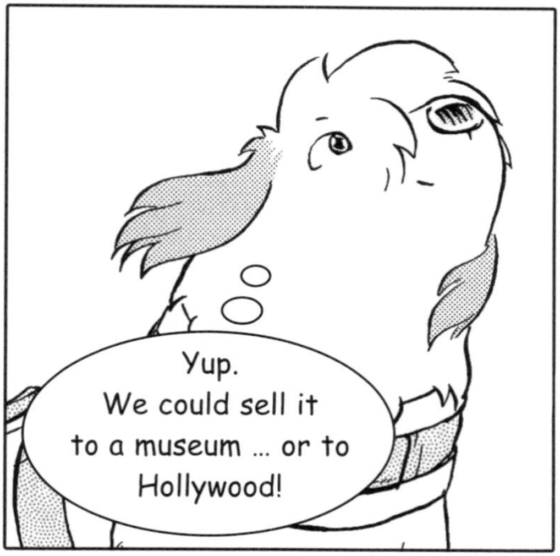
Yup. We could sell it to a museum ... or to Hollywood!

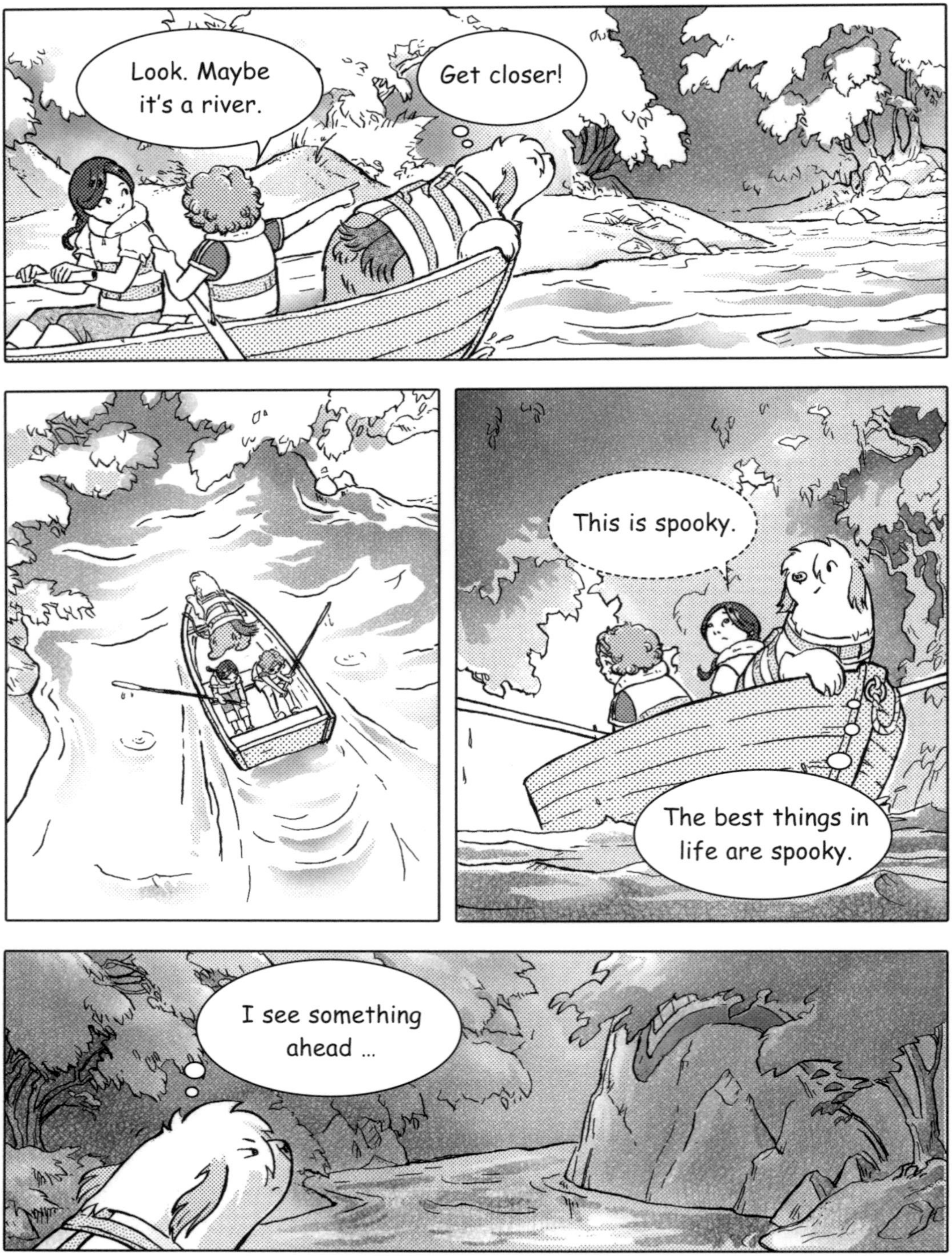
Look. Maybe it's a river.
Get closer!
This is spooky.
The best things in life are spooky.
I see something ahead ...

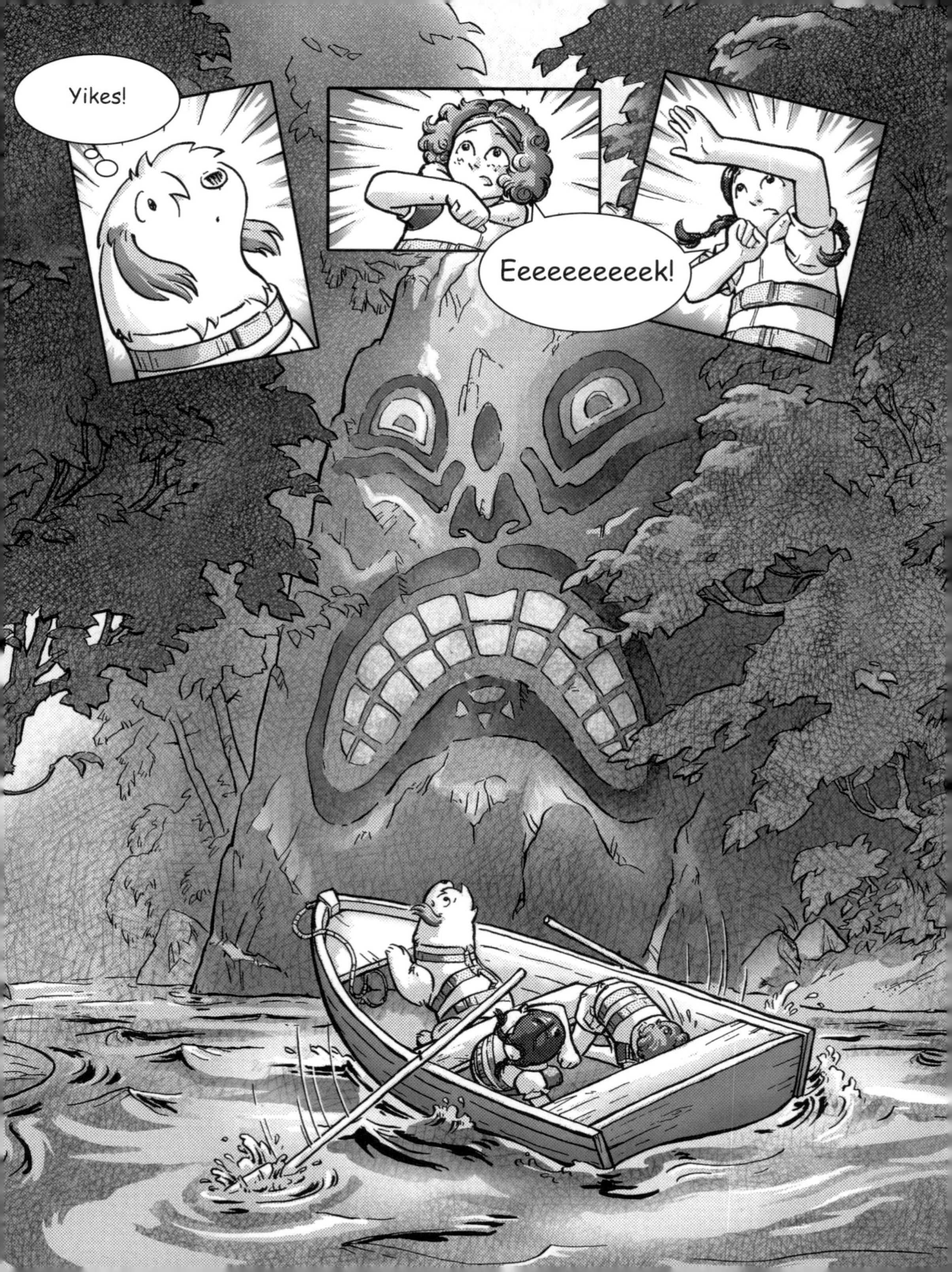
Yikes!
Eeeeeeeeeek!

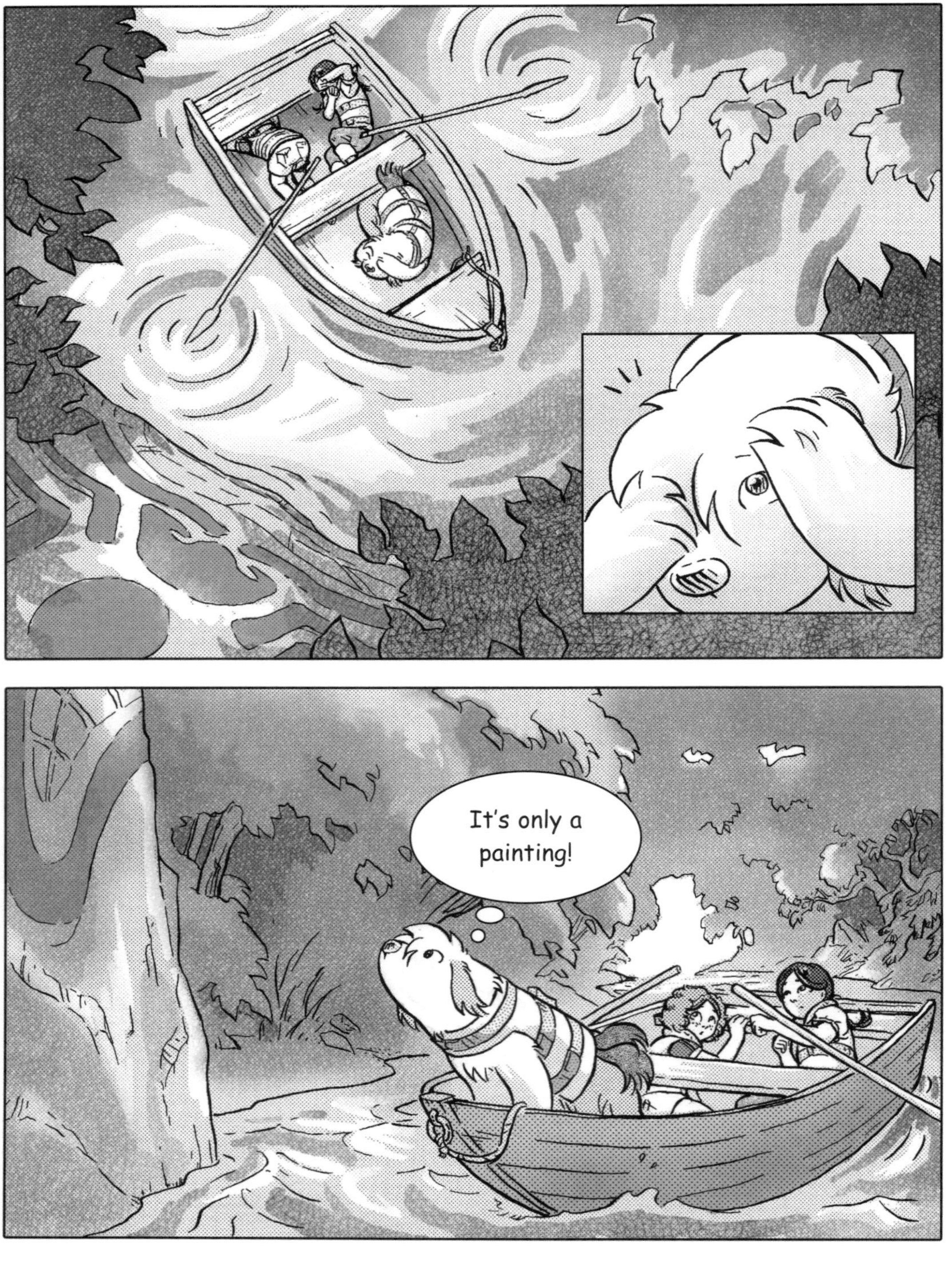
It's only a painting!

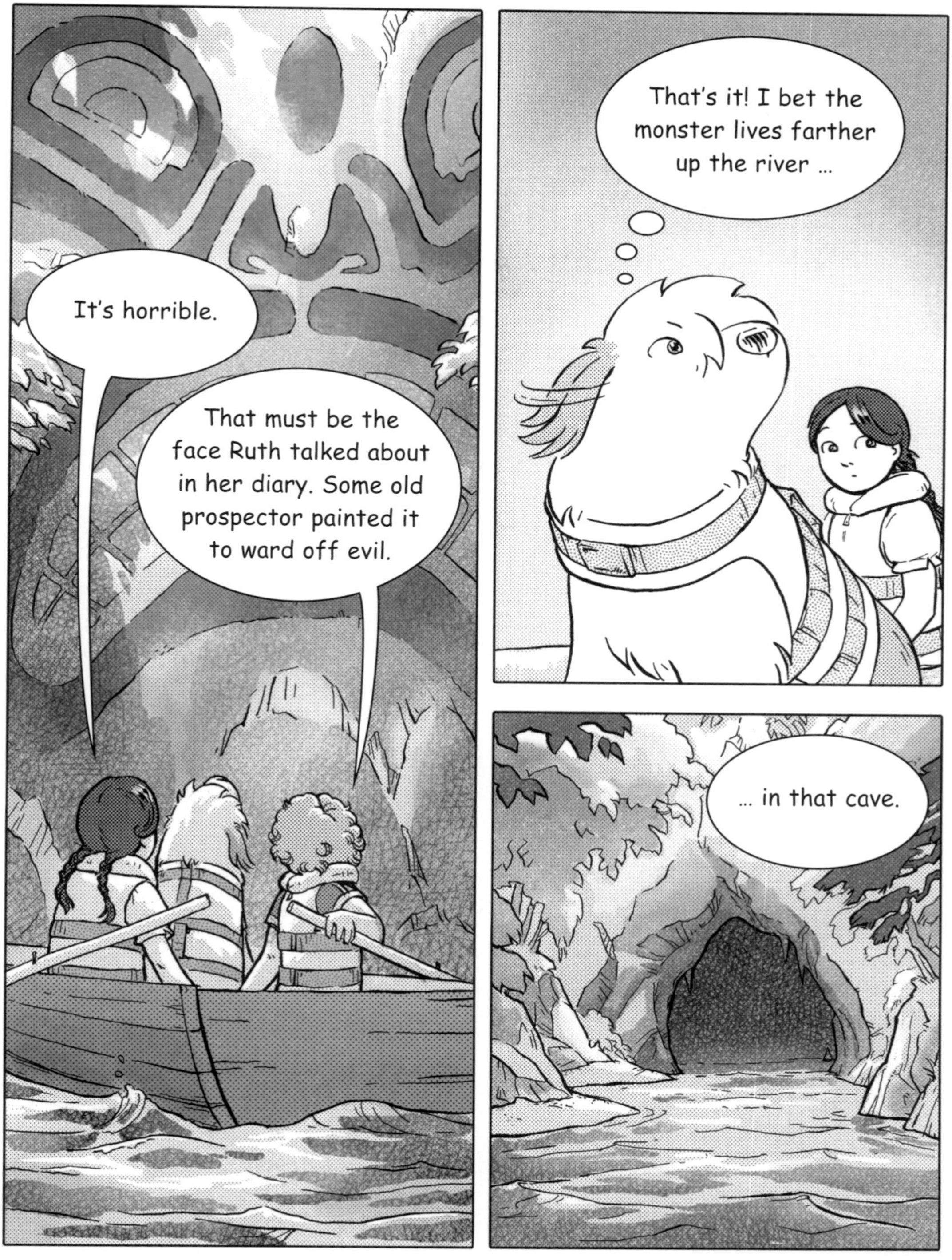
It's horrible.
That must be the face Ruth talked about in her diary. Some old prospector painted it to ward off evil.
That's it! I bet the monster lives farther up the river ...
... in that cave.

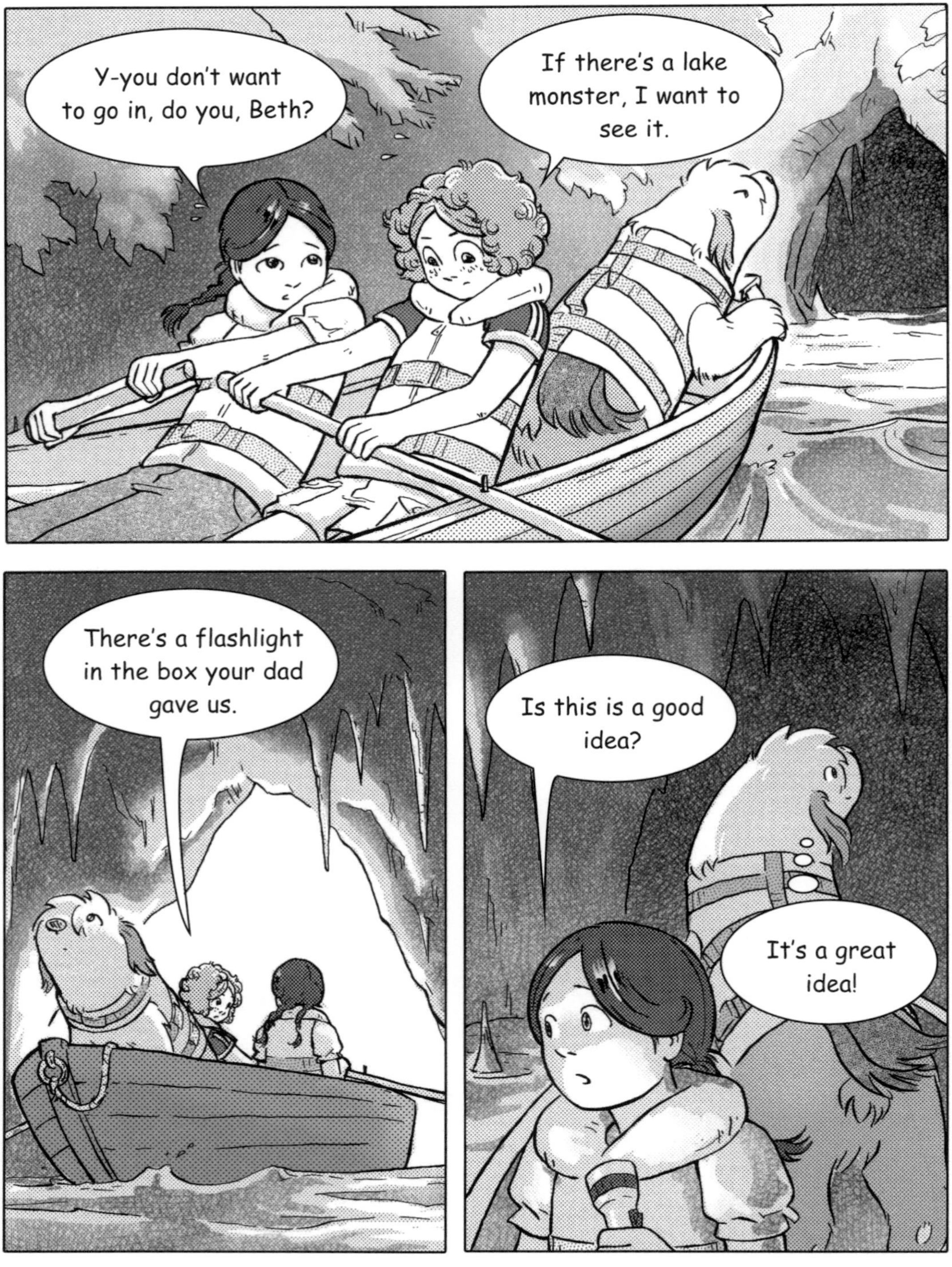
Y-you don't want to go in, do you, Beth?
If there's a lake monster, I want to see it.
There's a flashlight in the box your dad gave us.
Is this is a good idea?
It's a great idea!

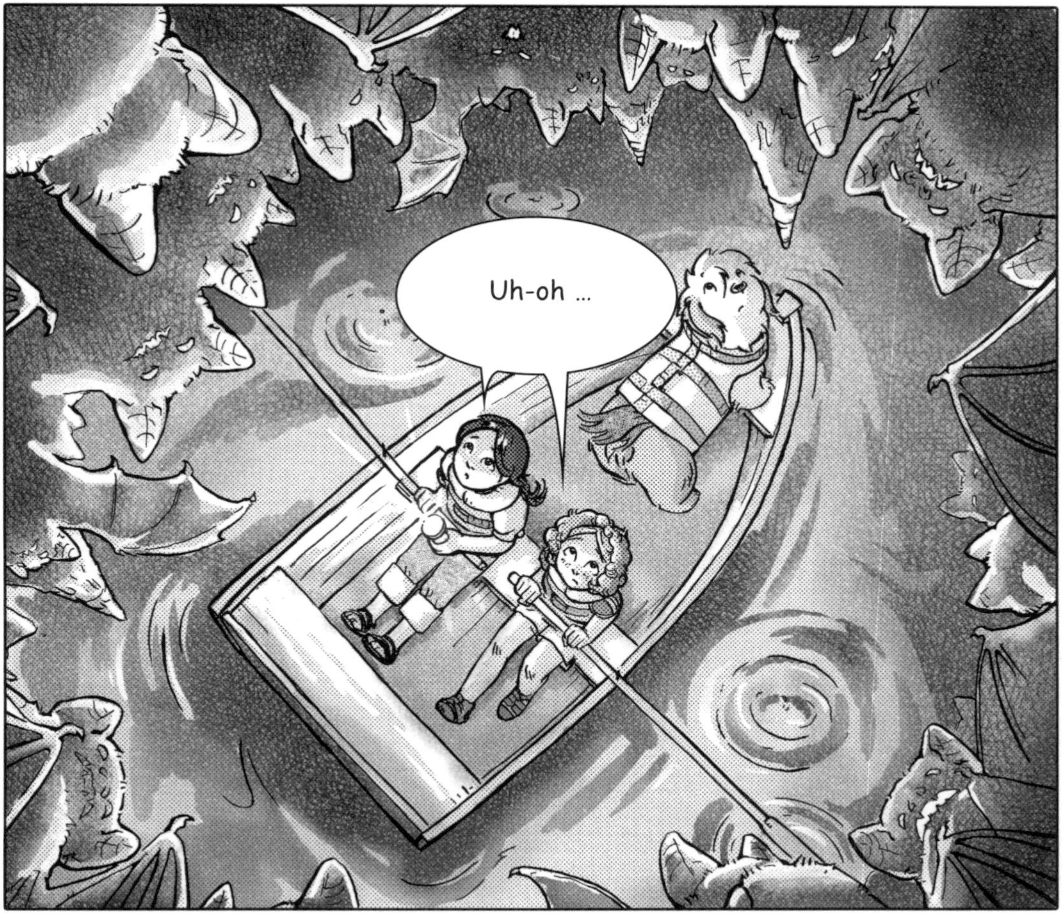
Uh-oh ...

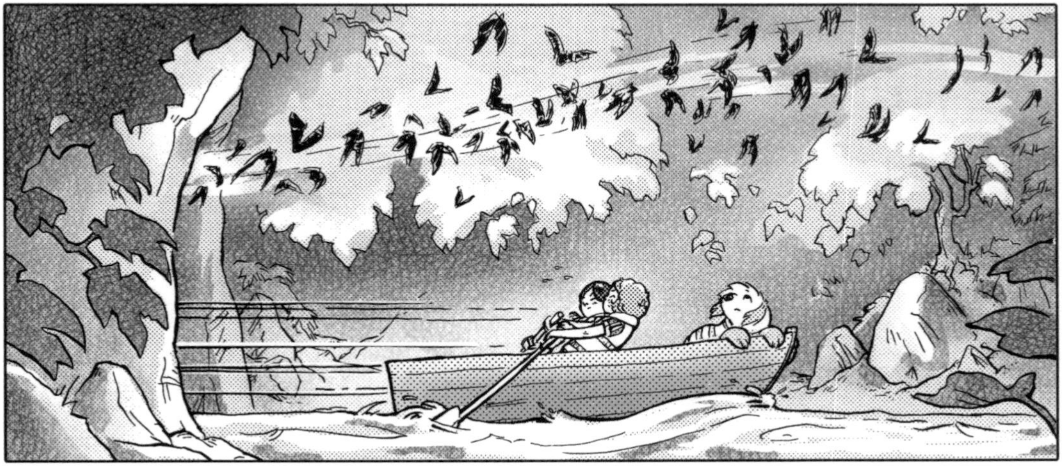

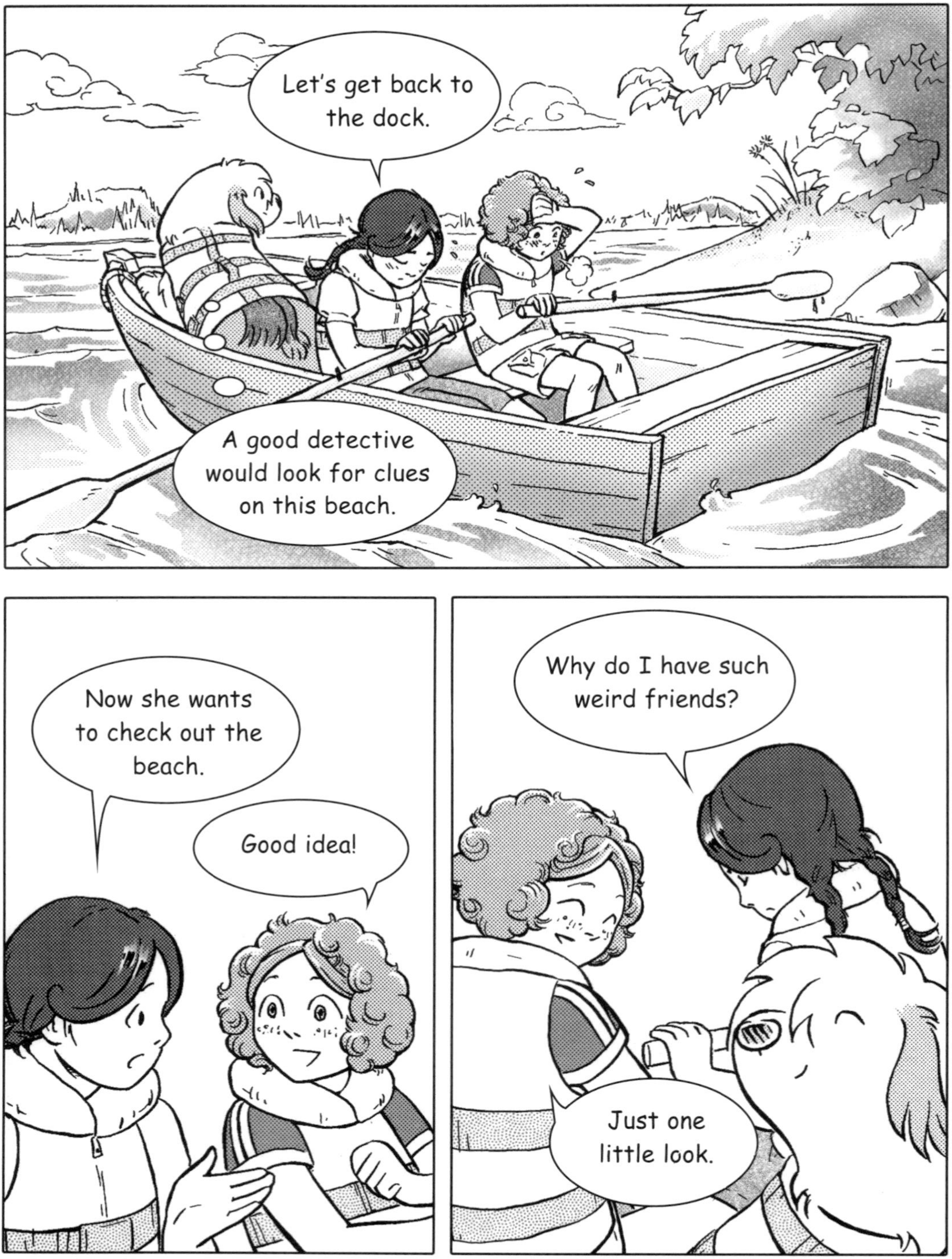
Let's get back to the dock.
A good detective would look for clues on this beach.
Now she wants to check out the beach.
Good idea!
Why do I have such weird friends?
Just one little look.

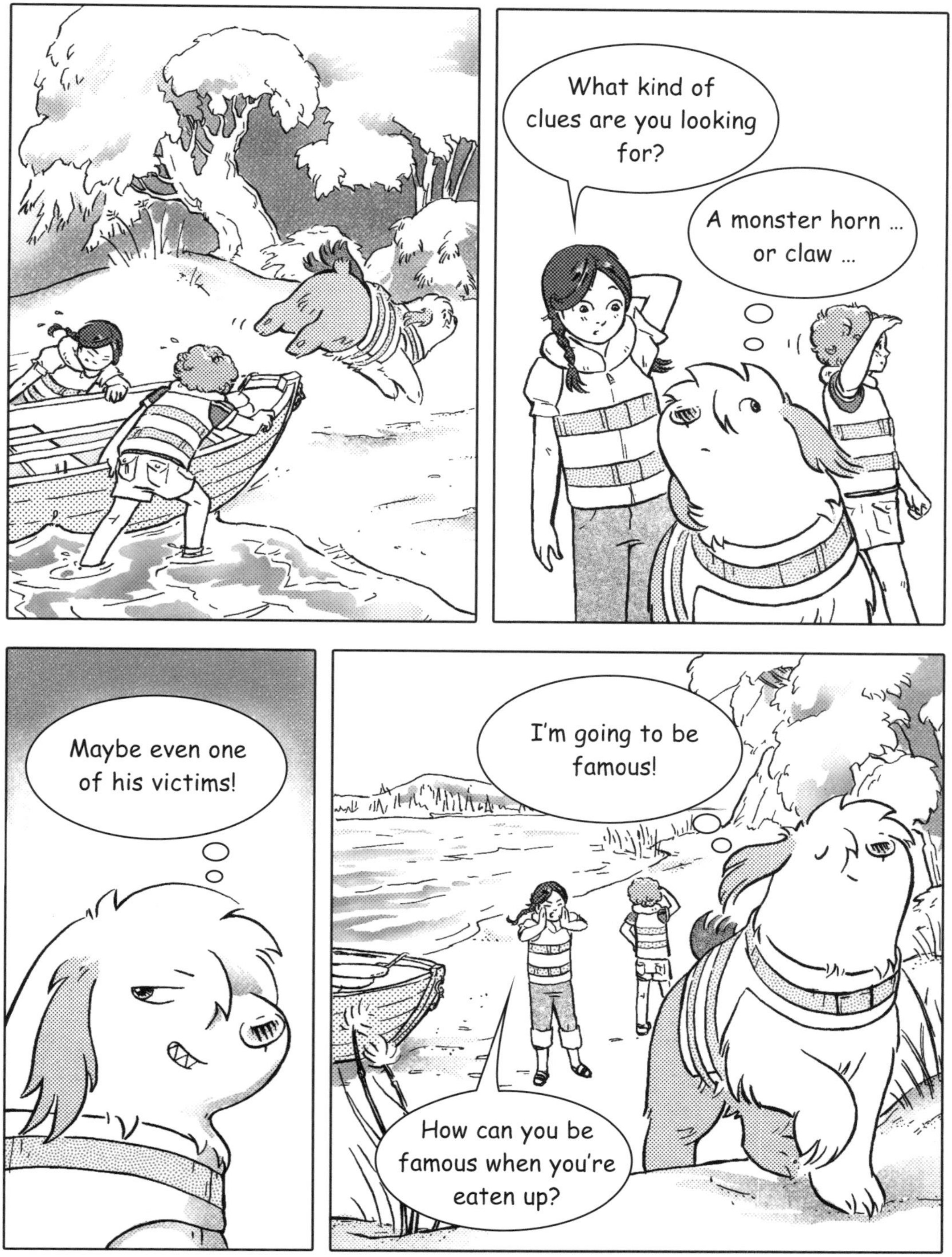
What kind of clues are you looking for?
A monster horn ... or claw ...
Maybe even one of his victims!
I'm going to be famous!
How can you be famous when you're eaten up?

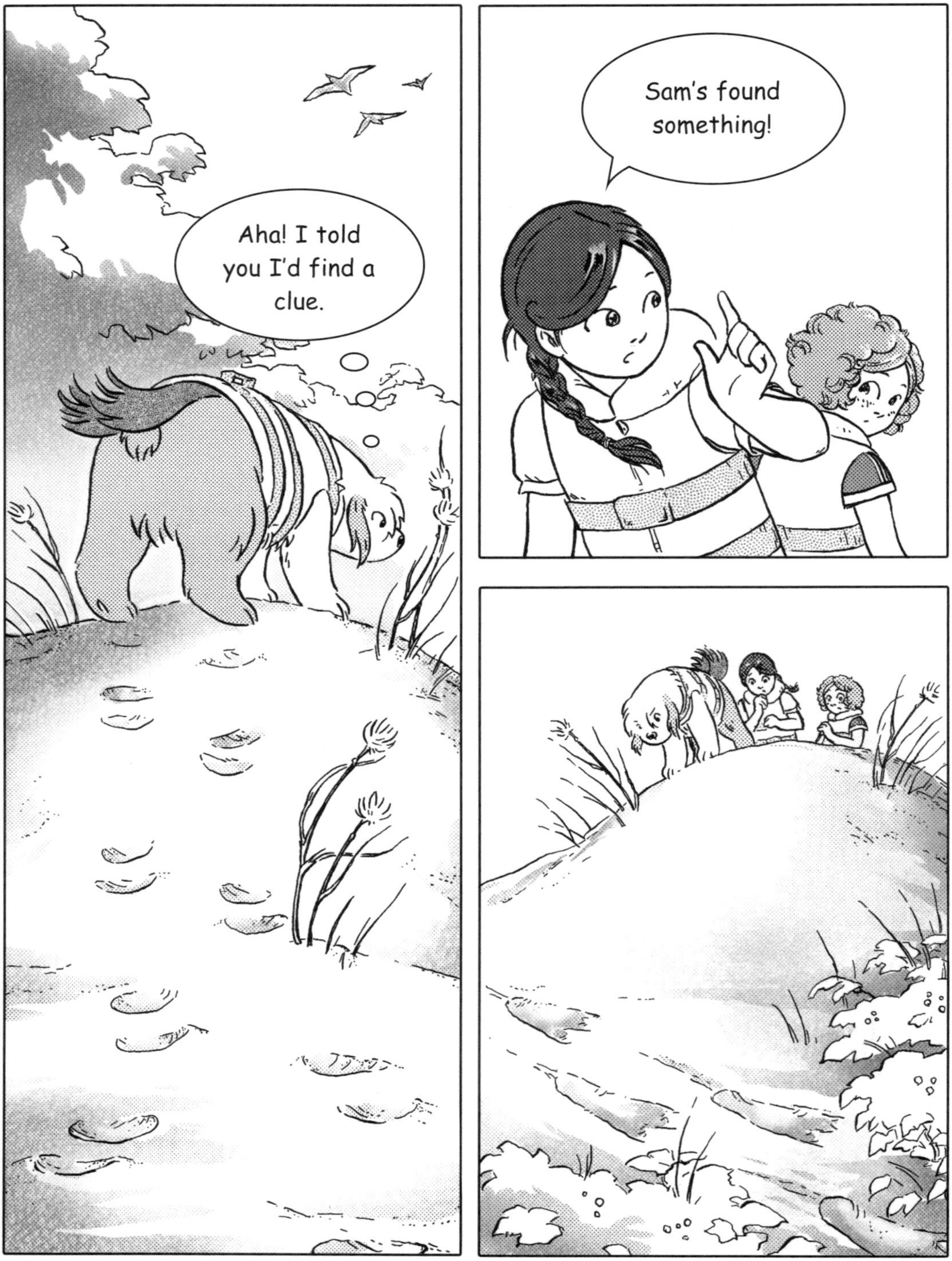
Aha! I told you I'd find a clue.
Sam's found something!

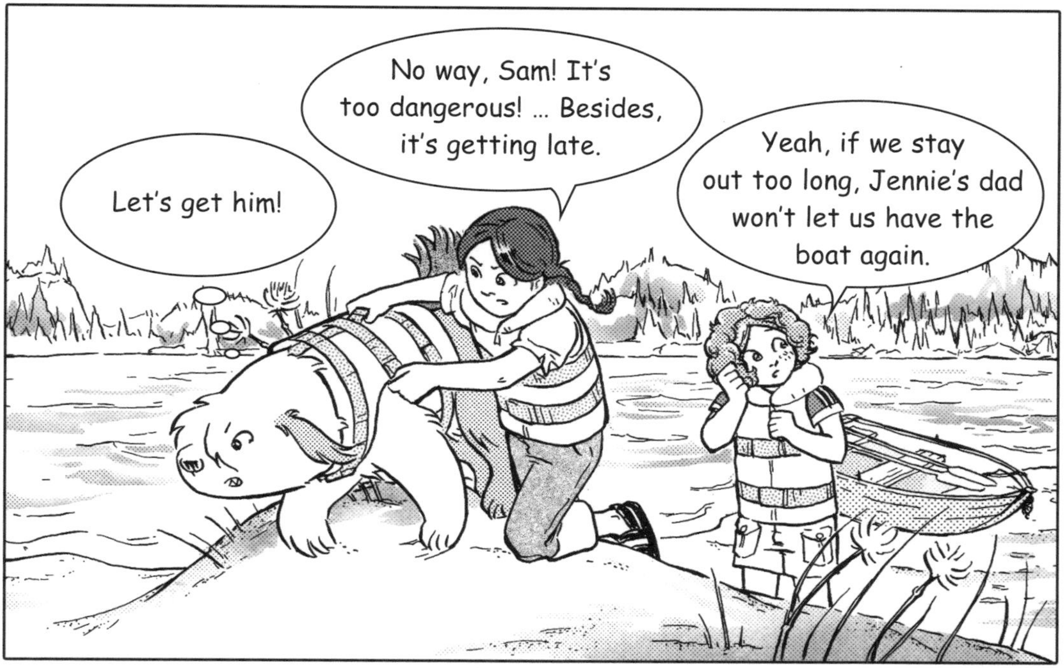
Let's get him!
No way, Sam! It's too dangerous! ... Besides, it's getting late.
Yeah, if we stay out too long, Jennie's dad won't let us have the boat again.

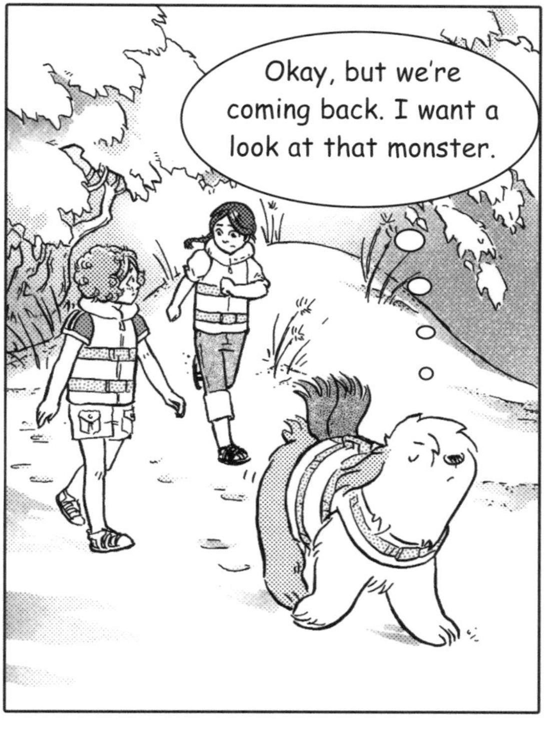
Okay, but we're coming back. I want a look at that monster.

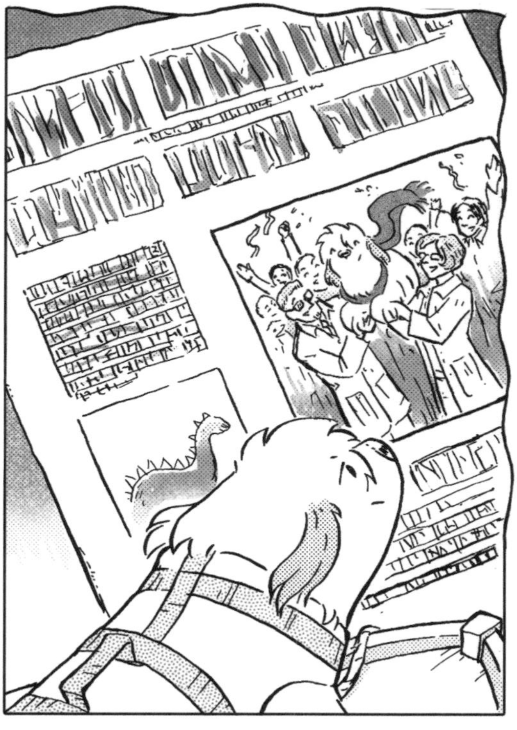

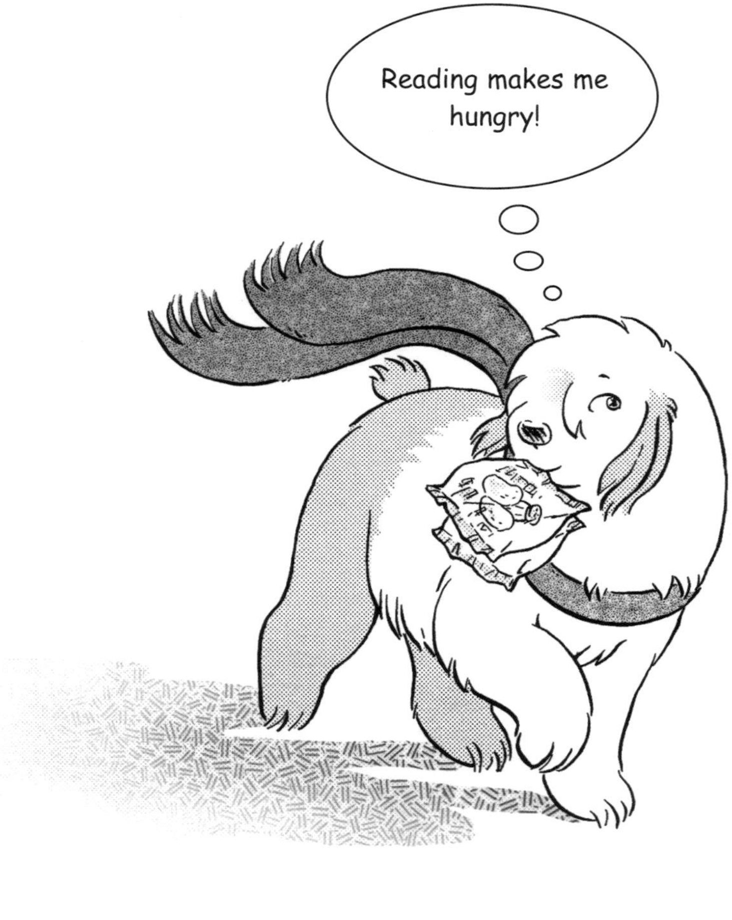
Reading makes me hungry!

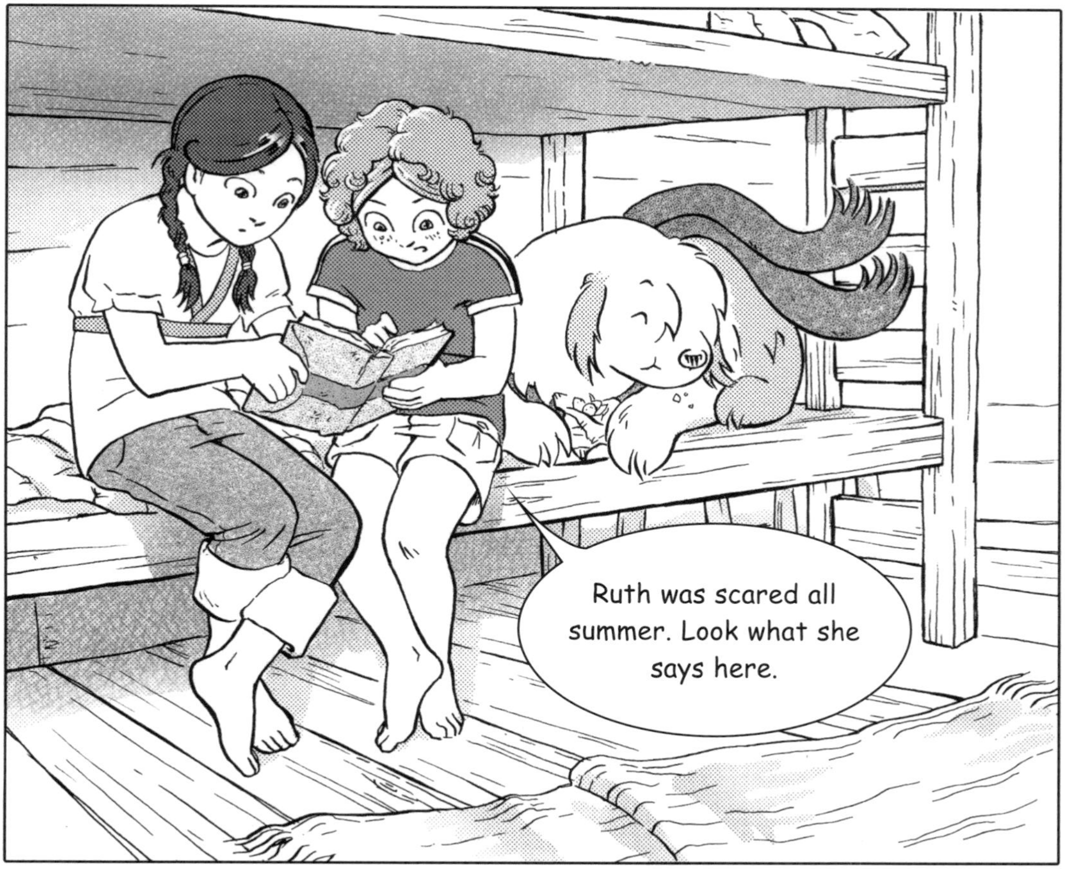
Ruth was scared all summer. Look what she says here.

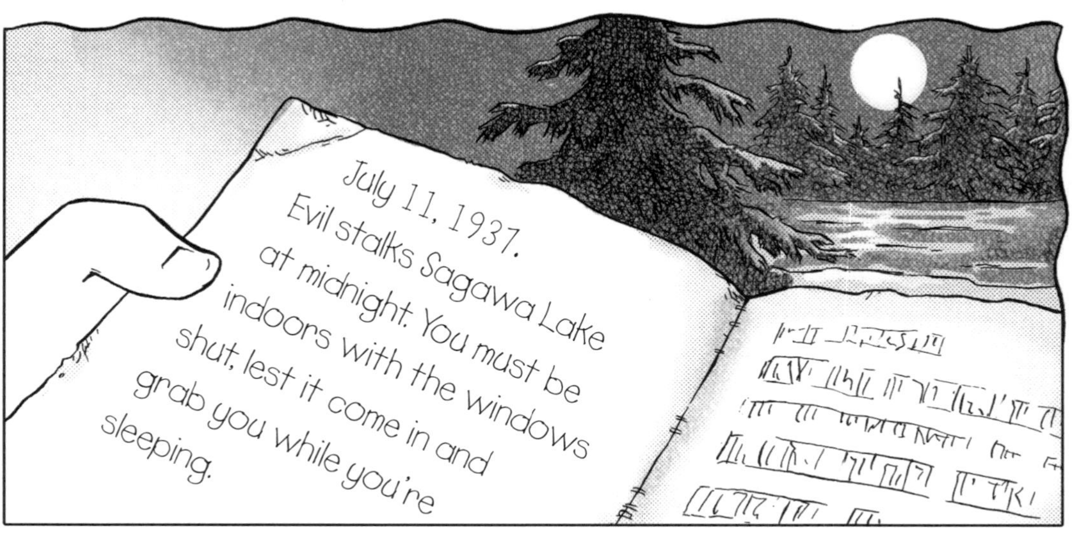
July 11, 1937.
Evil stalks Sagawa Lake at midnight. You must be indoors with the windows shut, lest it come in and grab you while you're sleeping.

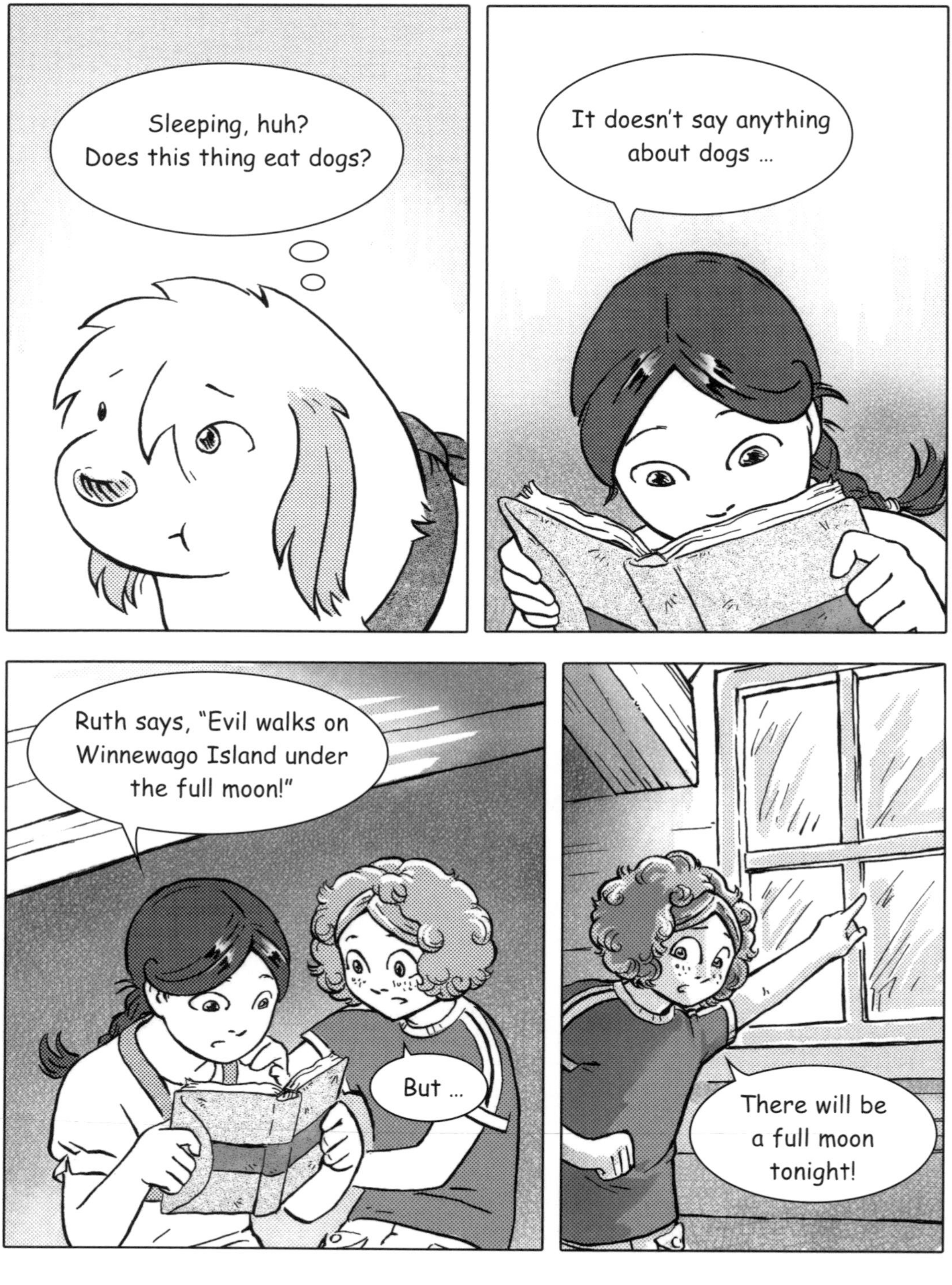
Sleeping, huh? Does this thing eat dogs?
It doesn't say anything about dogs ...
Ruth says, "Evil walks on Winnewago Island under the full moon!"
But ...
There will be a full moon tonight!

That evening ...

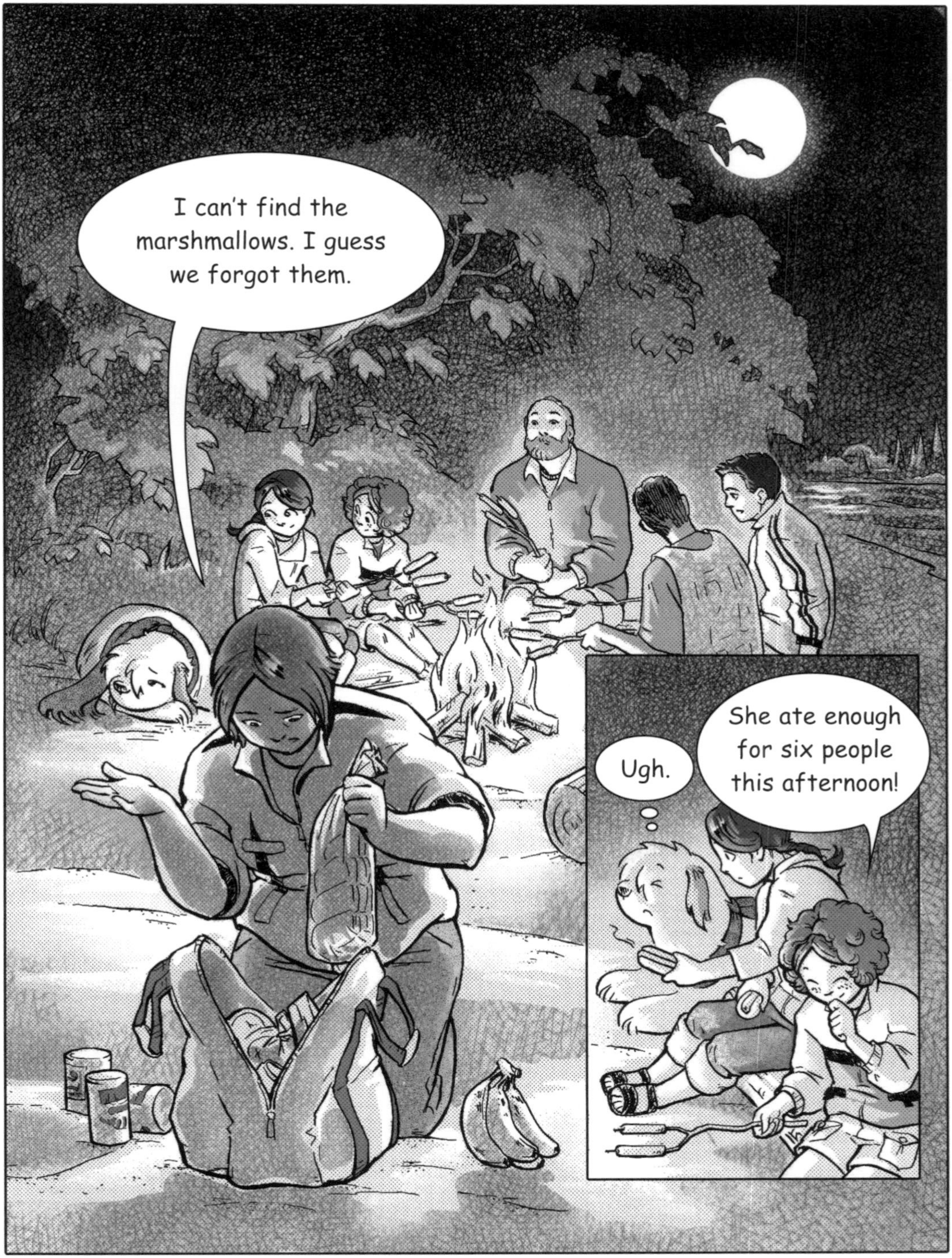
I can't find the marshmallows. I guess we forgot them.
Ugh.
She ate enough for six people this afternoon!

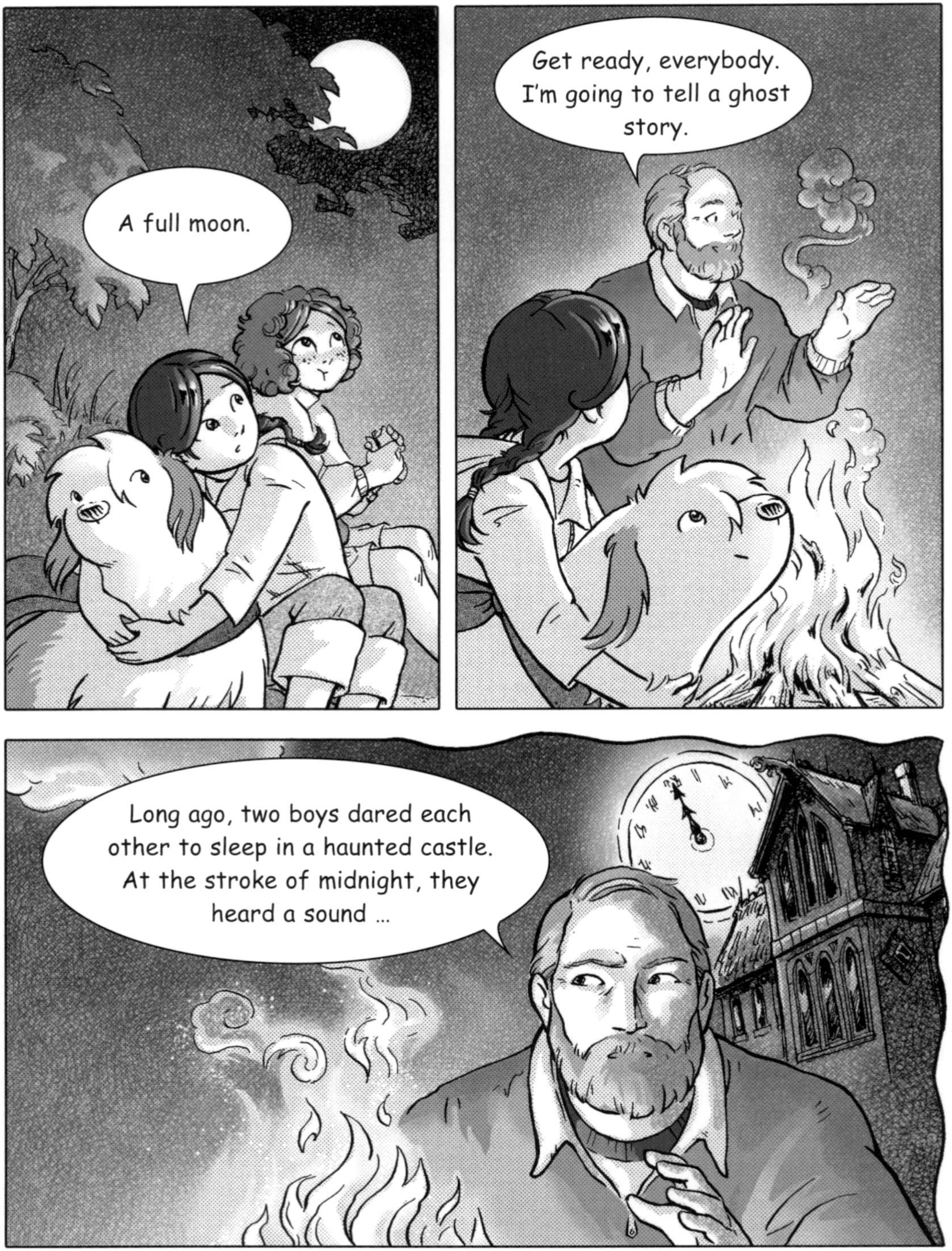
A full moon.
Get ready, everybody. I'm going to tell a ghost story.
Long ago, two boys dared each other to sleep in a haunted castle. At the stroke of midnight, they heard a sound ...

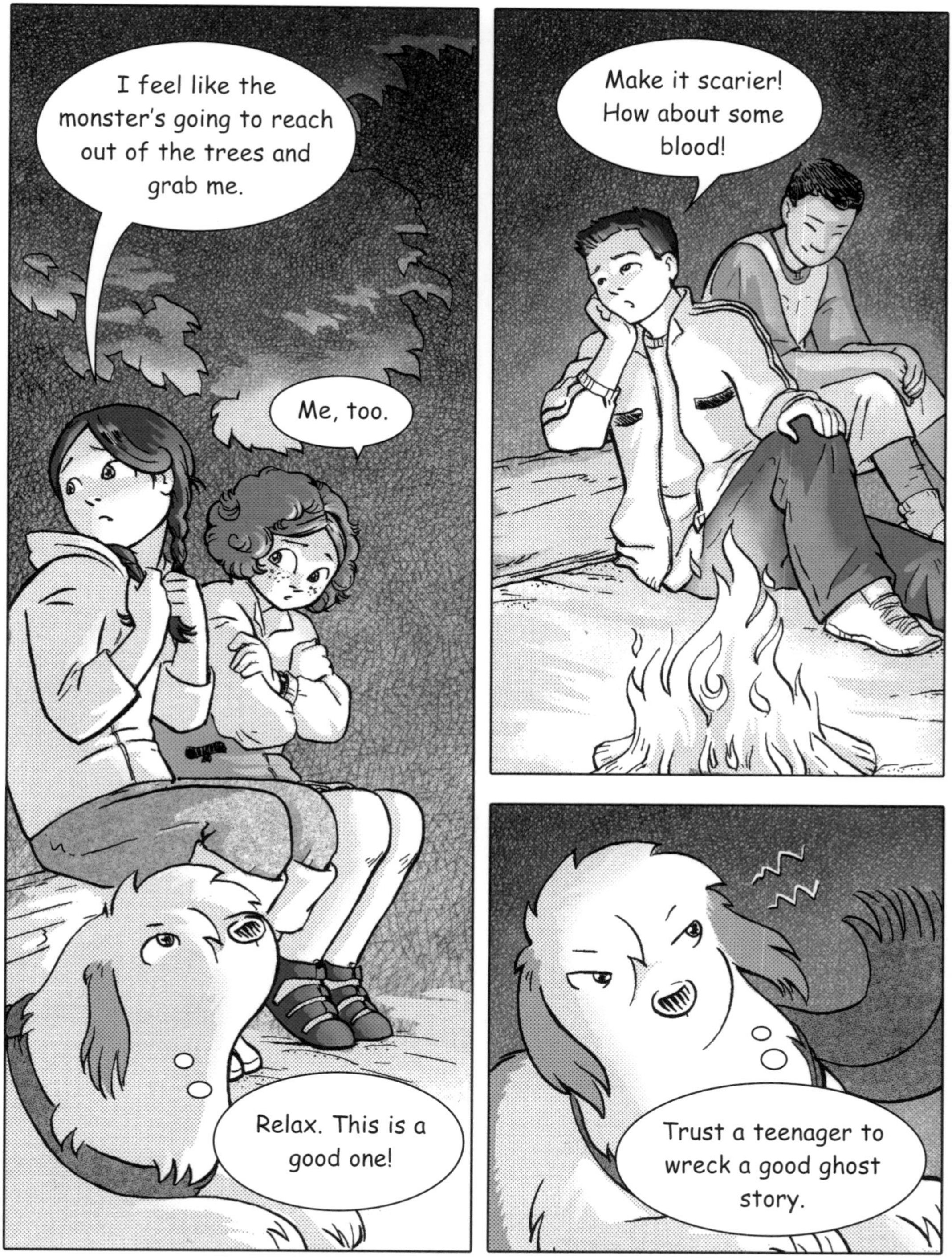
I feel like the monster's going to reach out of the trees and grab me.
Me, too.
Relax. This is a good one!
Make it scarier! How about some blood!
Trust a teenager to wreck a good ghost story.

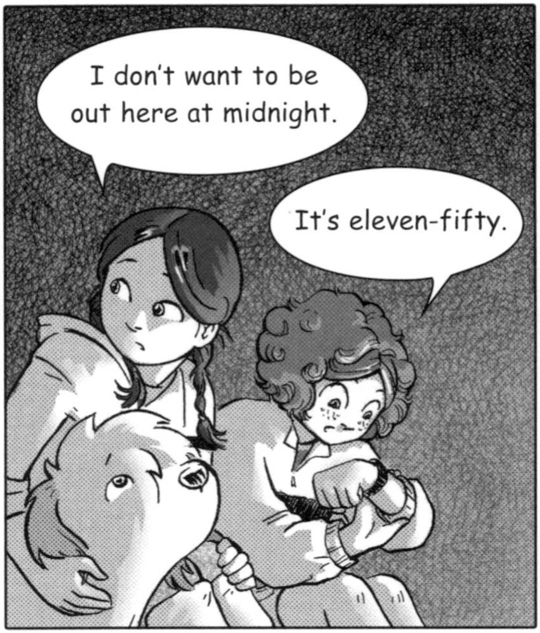
I don't want to be out here at midnight.
It's eleven-fifty.

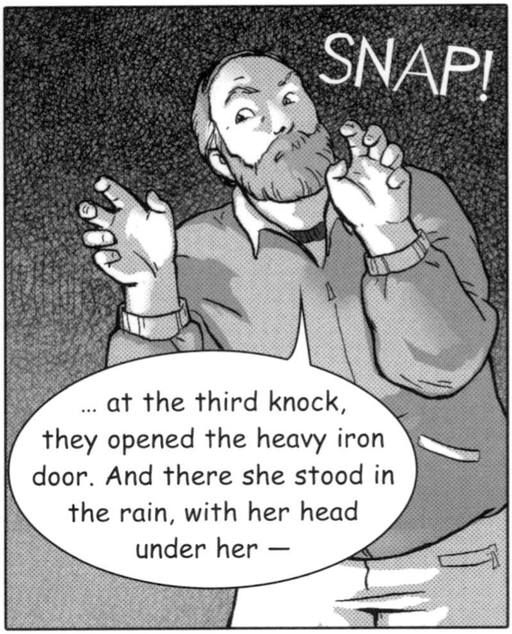
SNAP!
... at the third knock, they opened the heavy iron door. And there she stood in the rain, with her head under her —

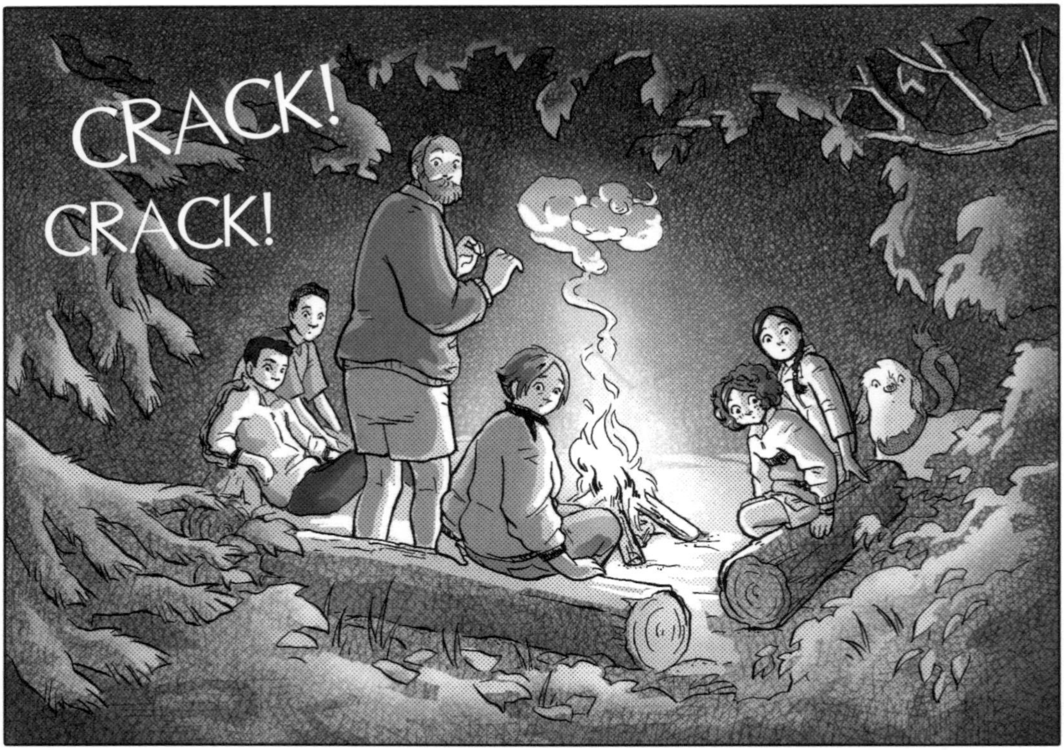
CRACK!
CRACK!

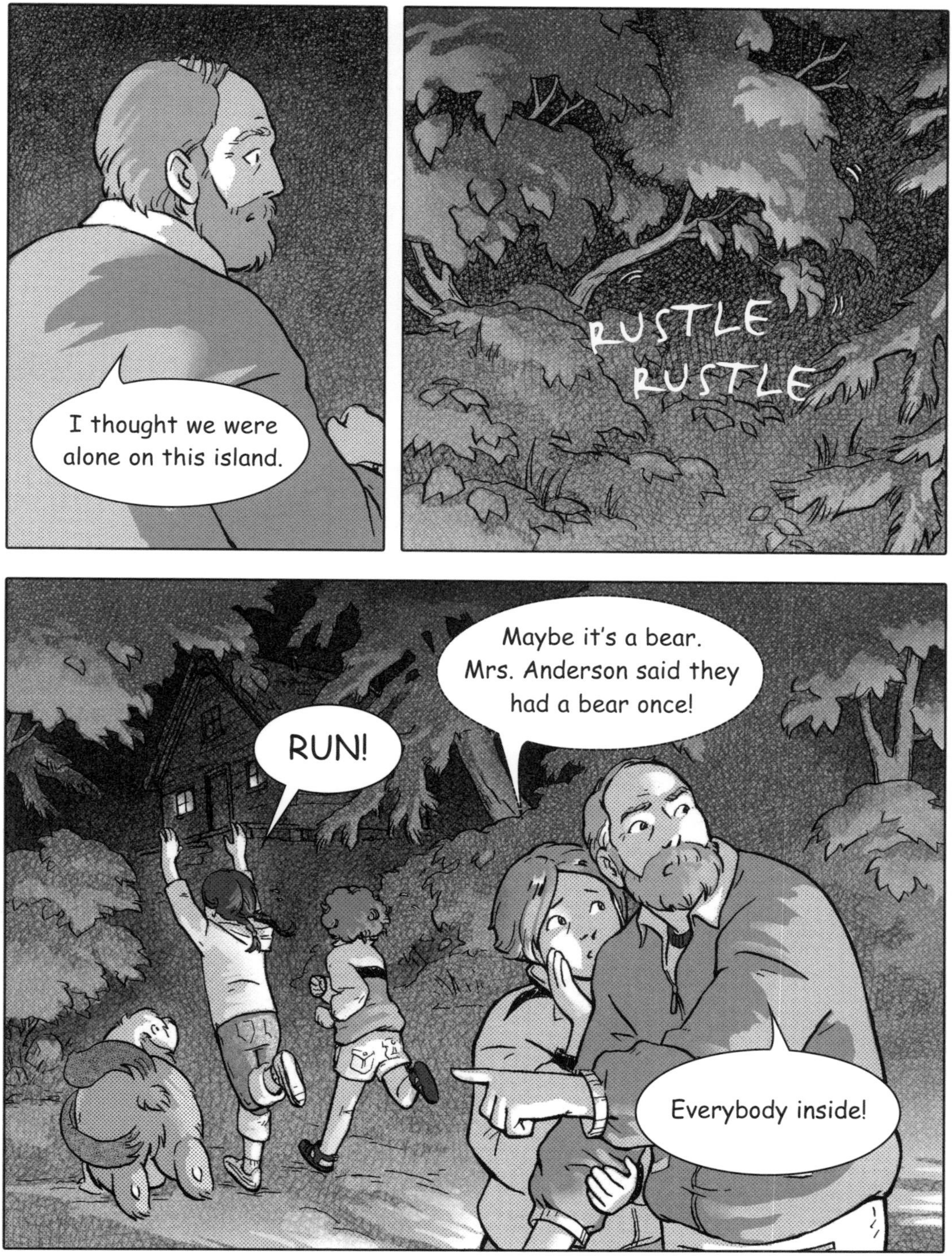
I thought we were alone on this island.
RUSTLE
RUSTLE
Maybe it's a bear. Mrs. Anderson said they had a bear once!
RUN!
Everybody inside!

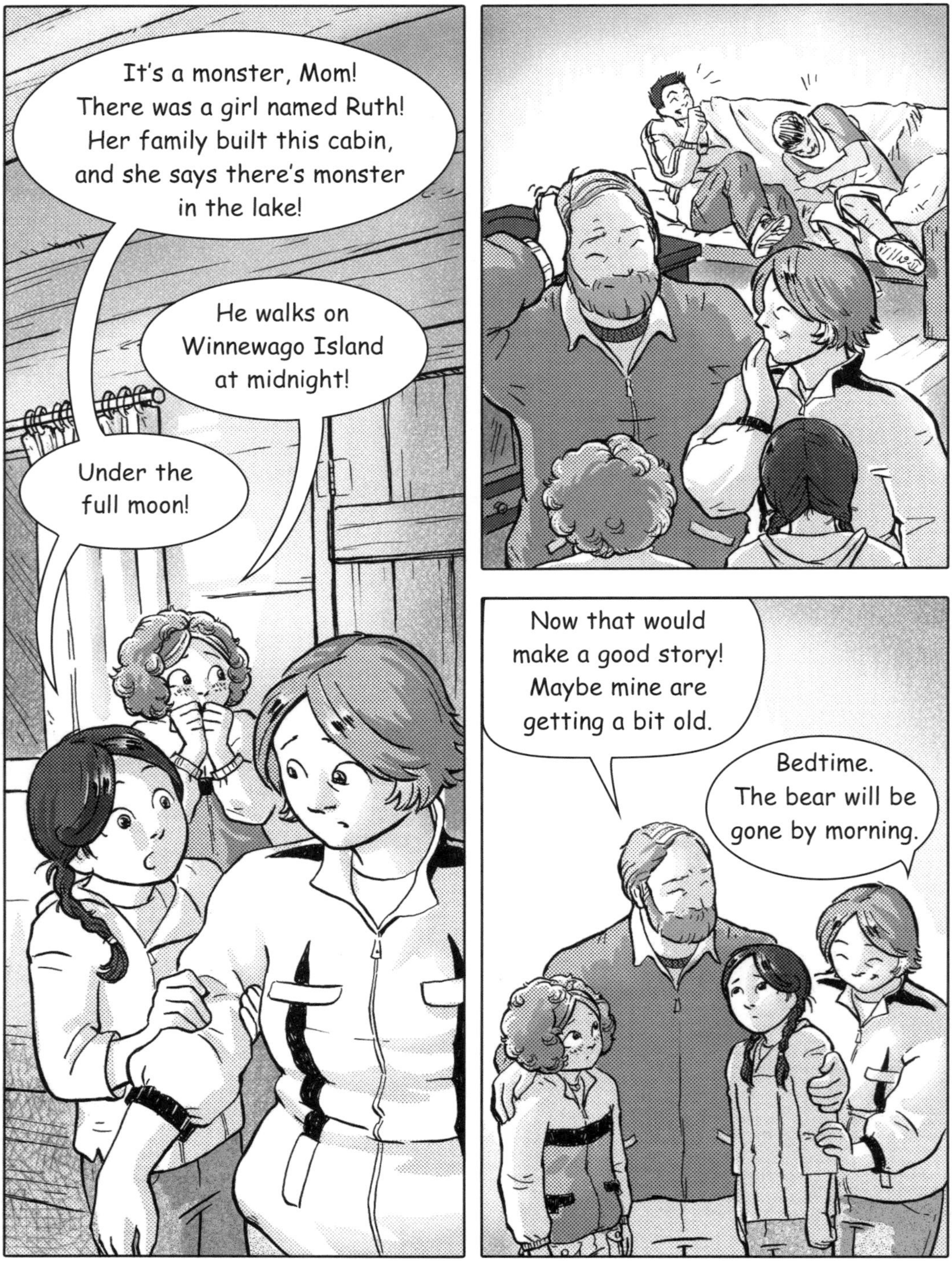
It's a monster, Mom! There was a girl named Ruth! Her family built this cabin, and she says there's monster in the lake!
He walks on Winnewago Island at midnight!
Under the full moon!
Now that would make a good story! Maybe mine are getting a bit old.
Bedtime. The bear will be gone by morning.

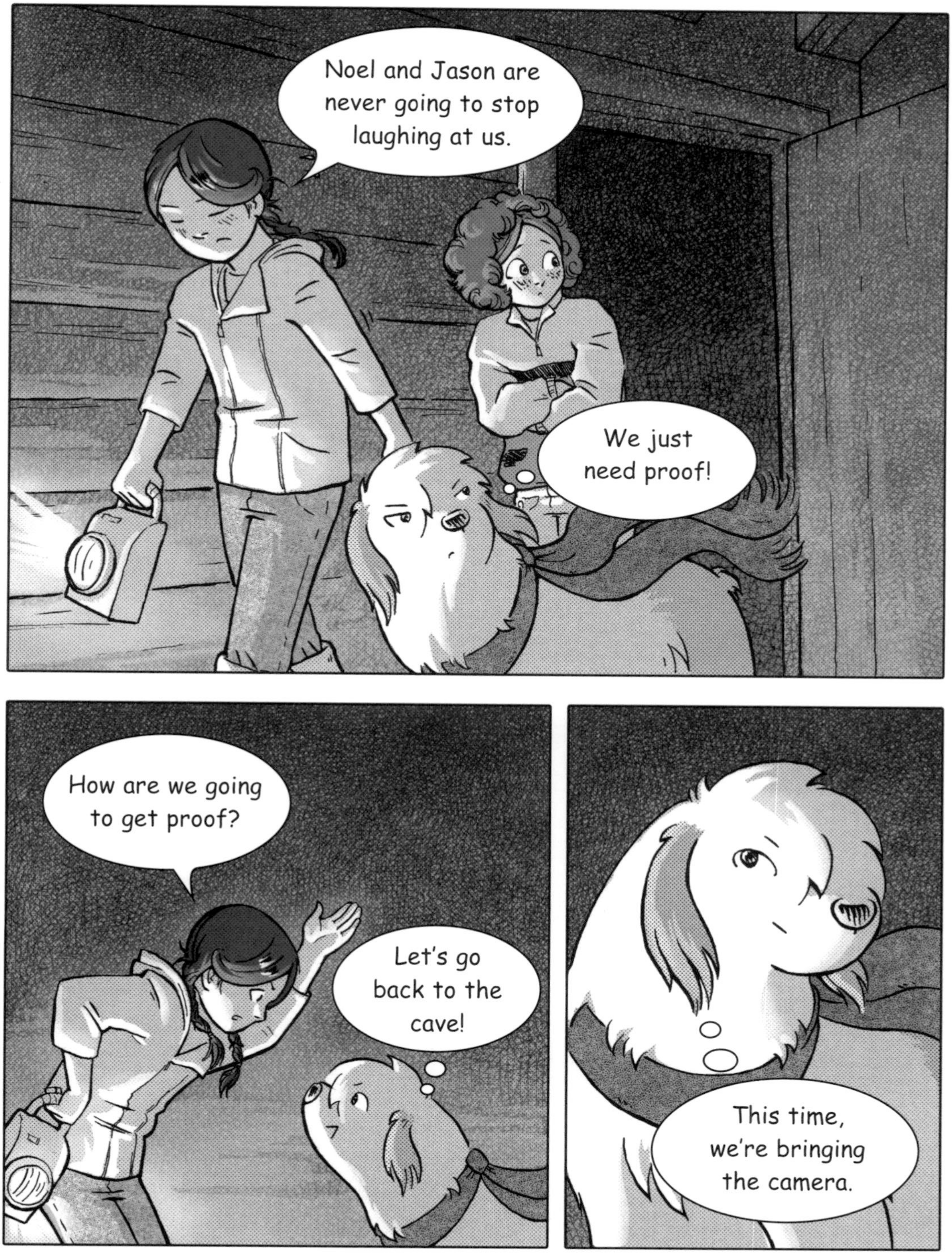
Noel and Jason are never going to stop laughing at us.
We just need proof!
How are we going to get proof?
Let's go back to the cave!
This time, we're bringing the camera.

Early the next morning ...

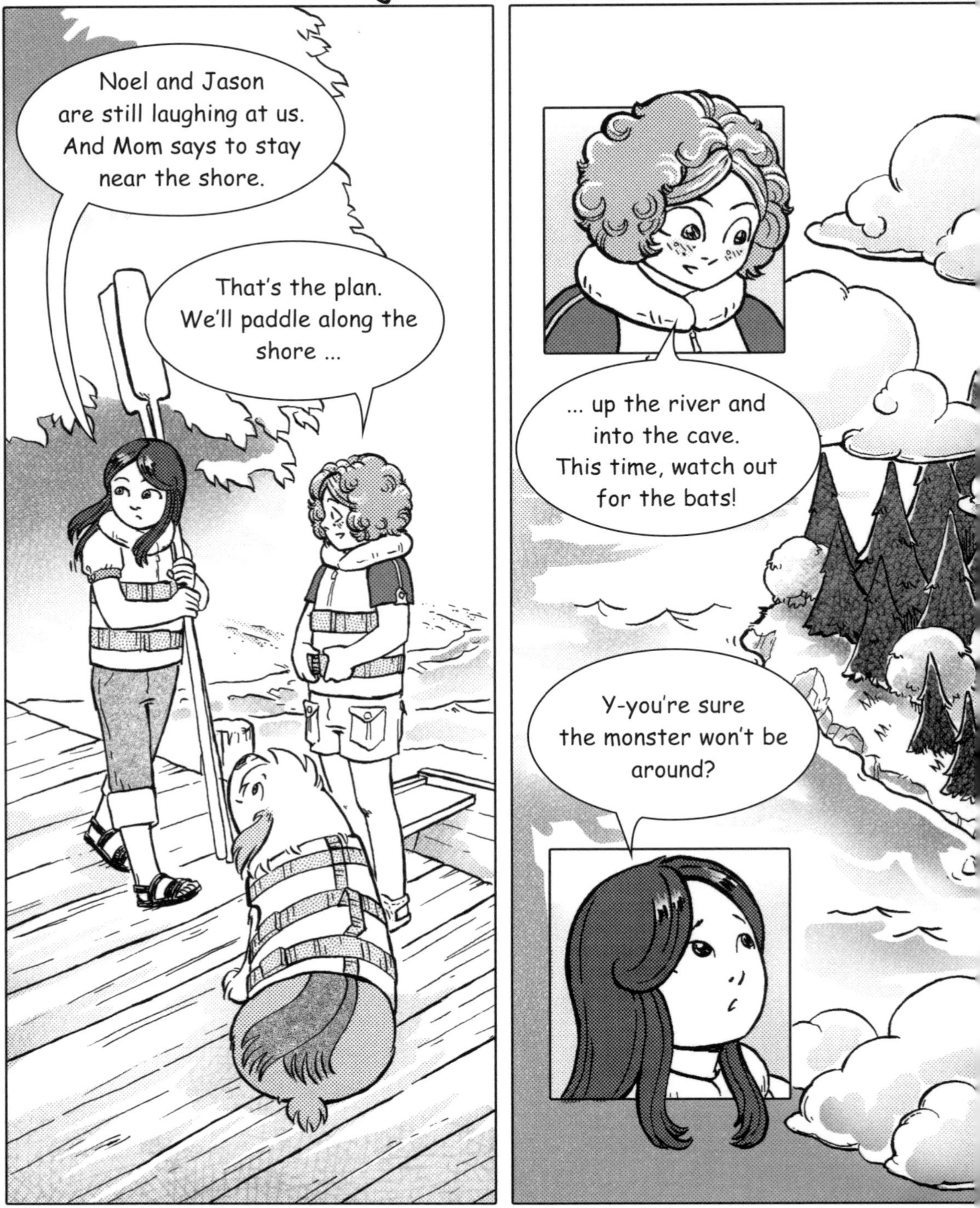
Noel and Jason are still laughing at us. And Mom says to stay near the shore.
That's the plan. We'll paddle along the shore ...
... up the river and into the cave. This time, watch out for the bats!
Y-you're sure the monster won't be around?

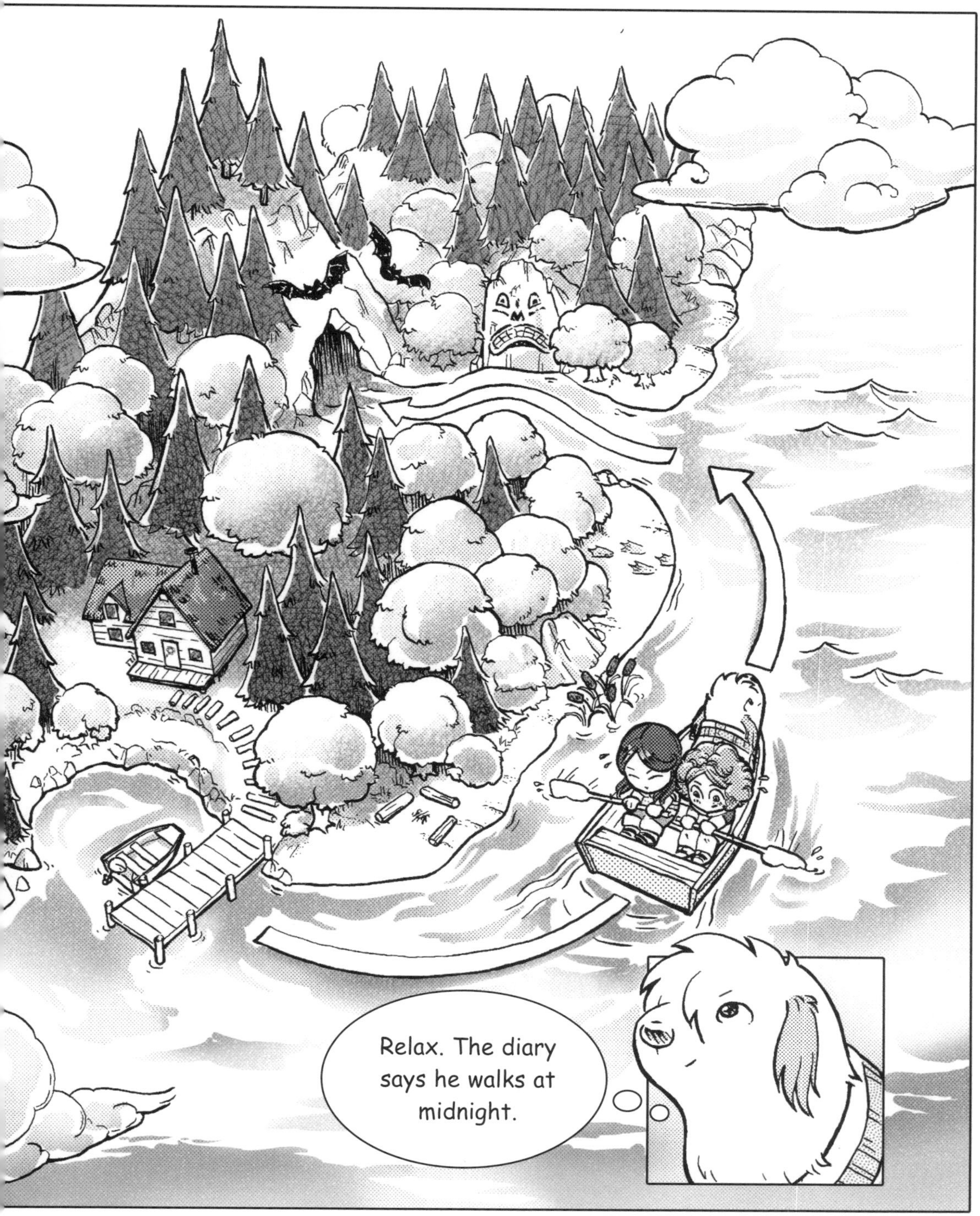
Relax. The diary says he walks at midnight.

Soon ...

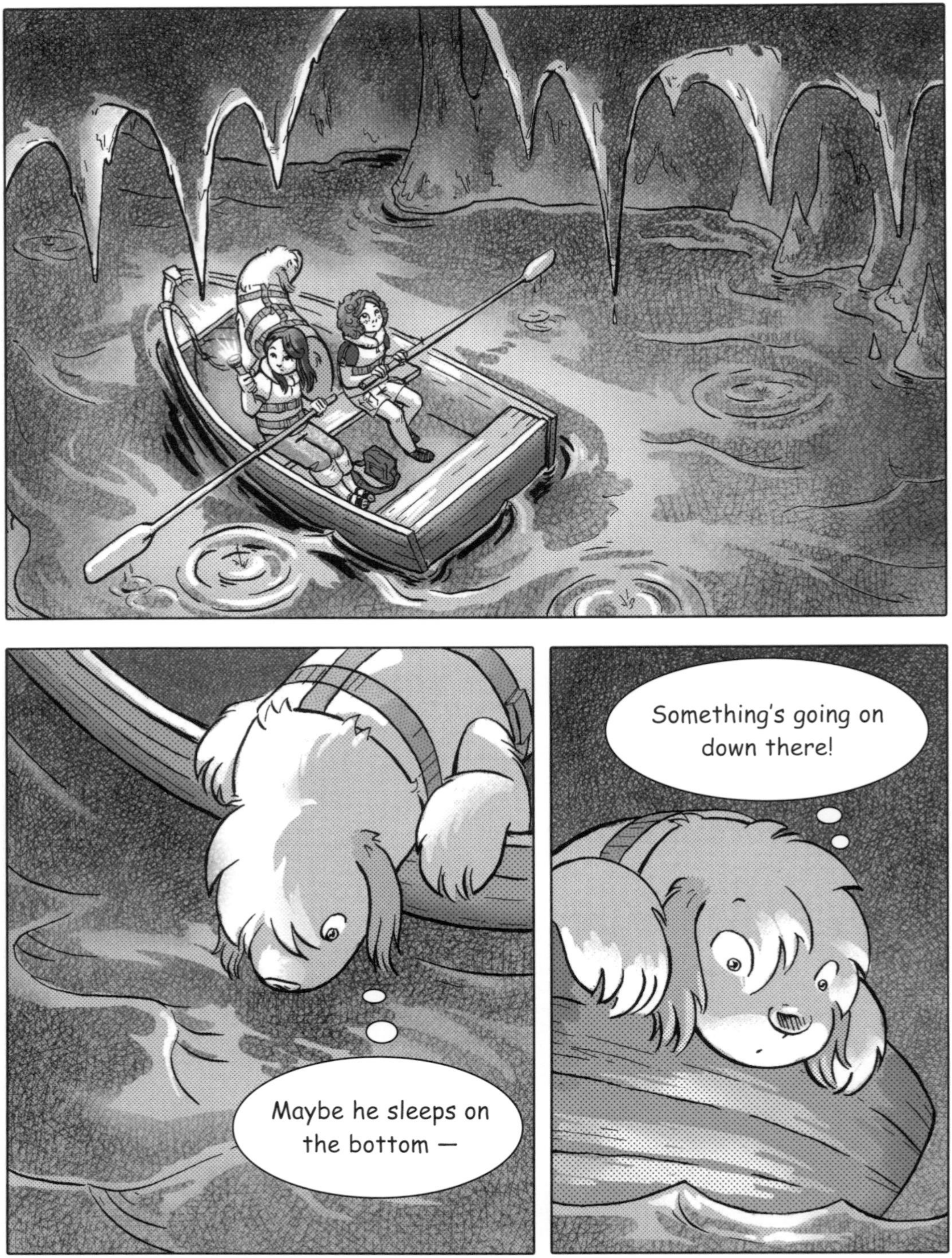
Maybe he sleeps on the bottom —
Something's going on down there!

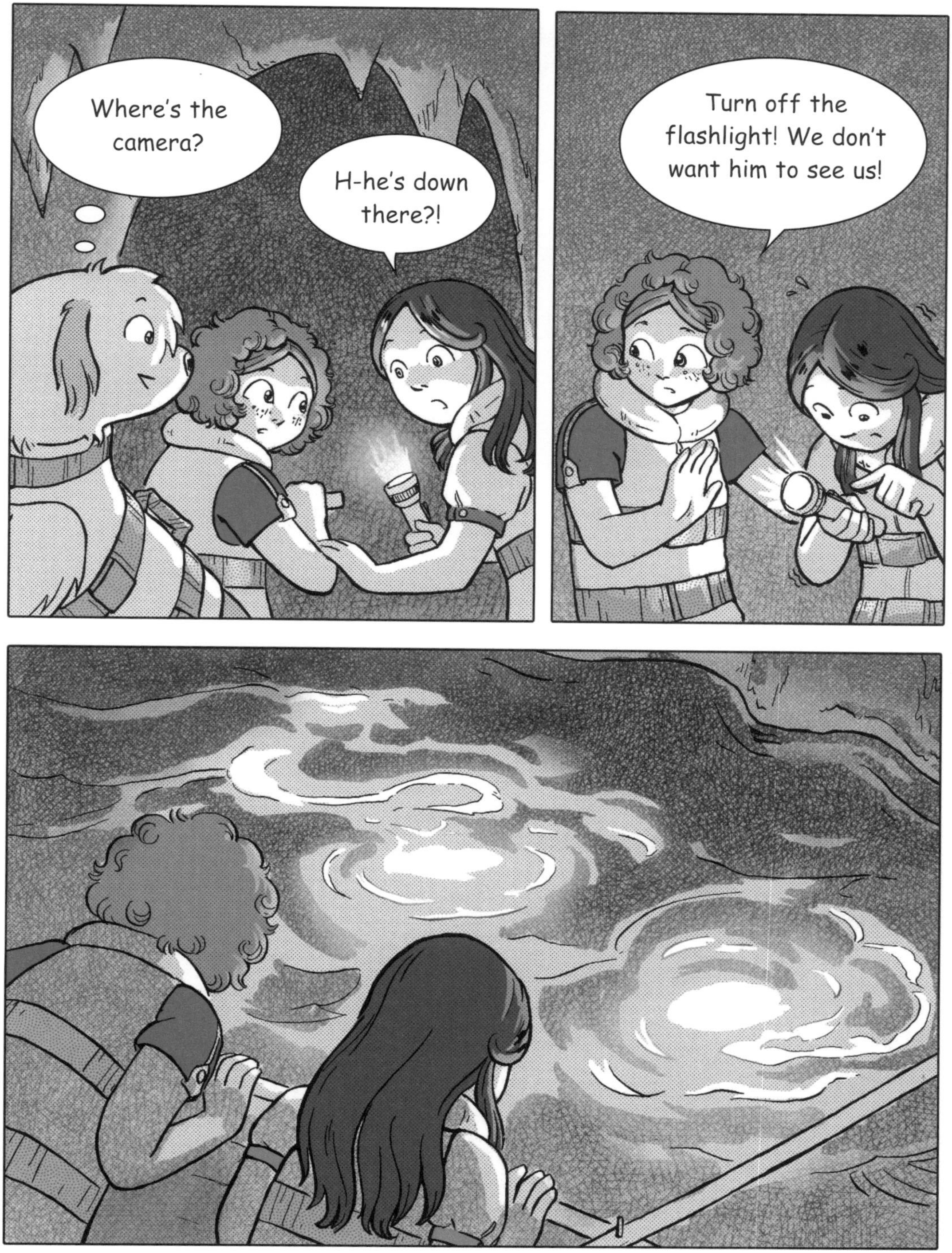
Where's the camera?
H-he's down there?!
Turn off the flashlight! We don't want him to see us!

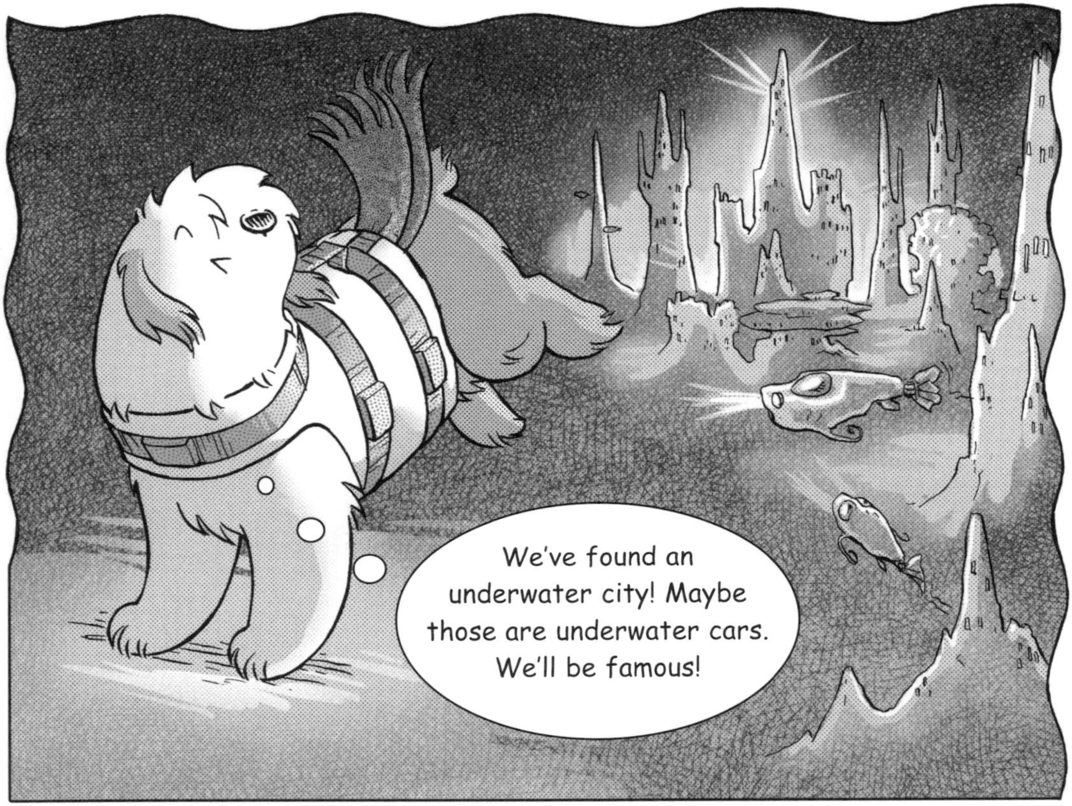
We've found an underwater city! Maybe those are underwater cars. We'll be famous!

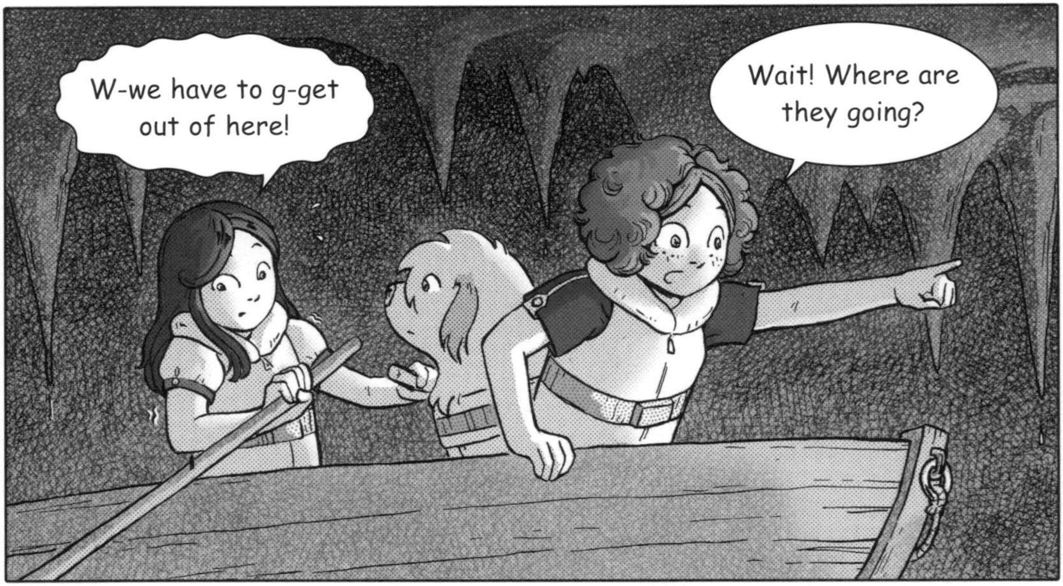
W-we have to g-get out of here!
Wait! Where are they going?

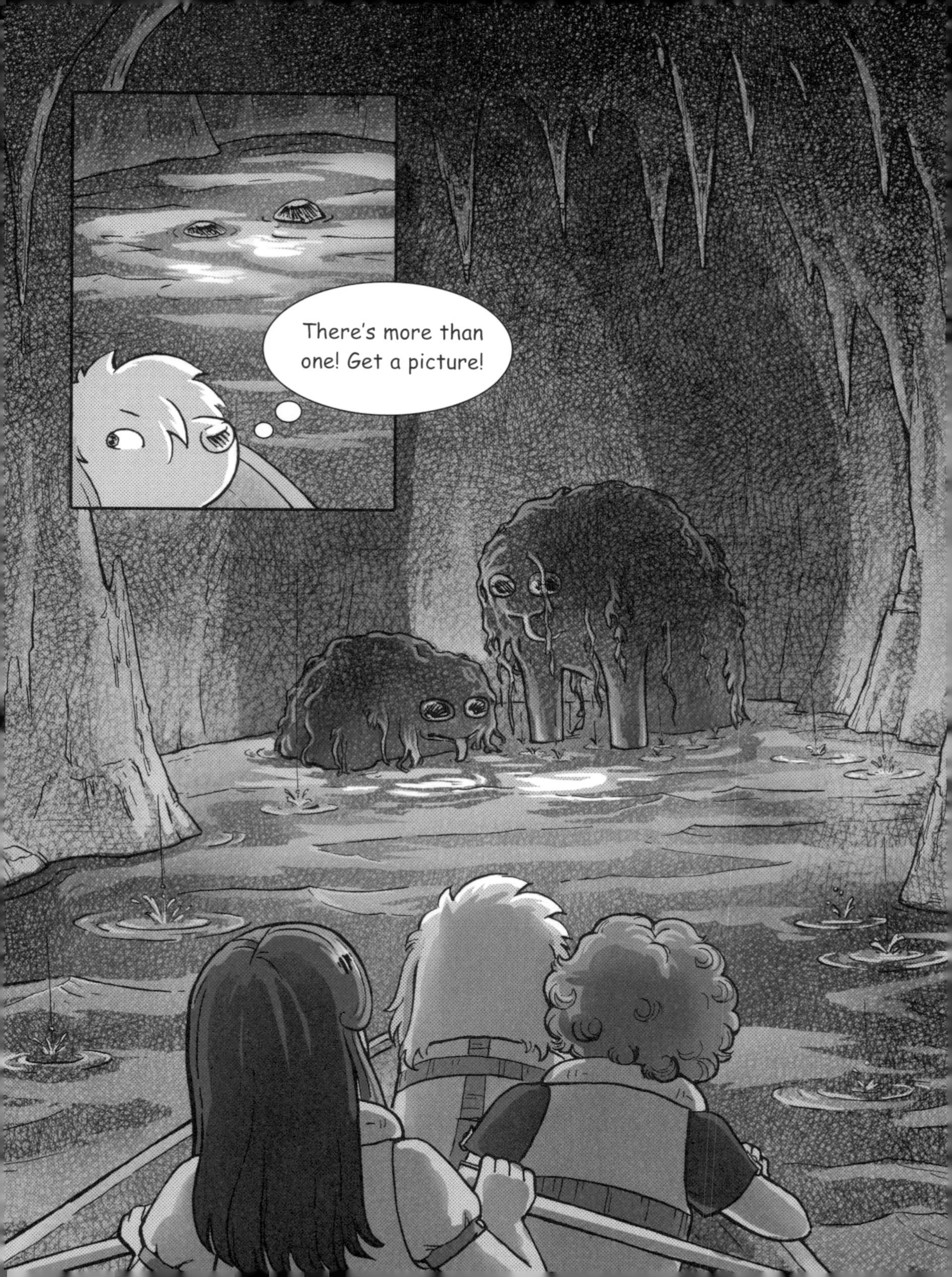
There's more than one! Get a picture!

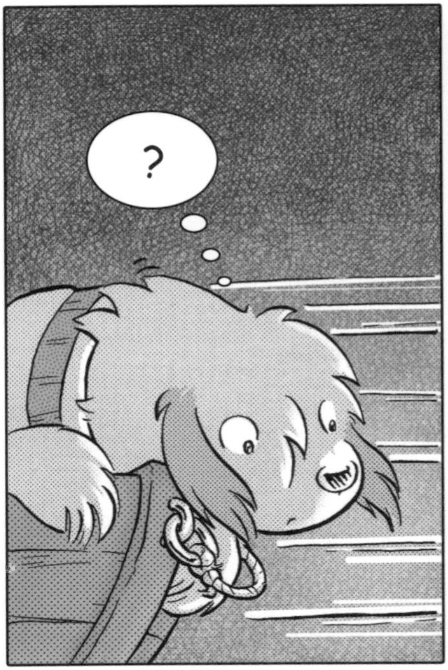
?

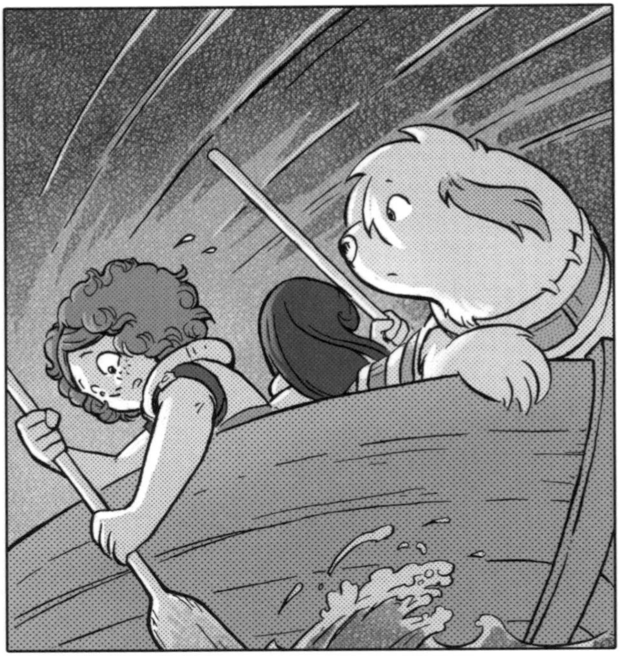

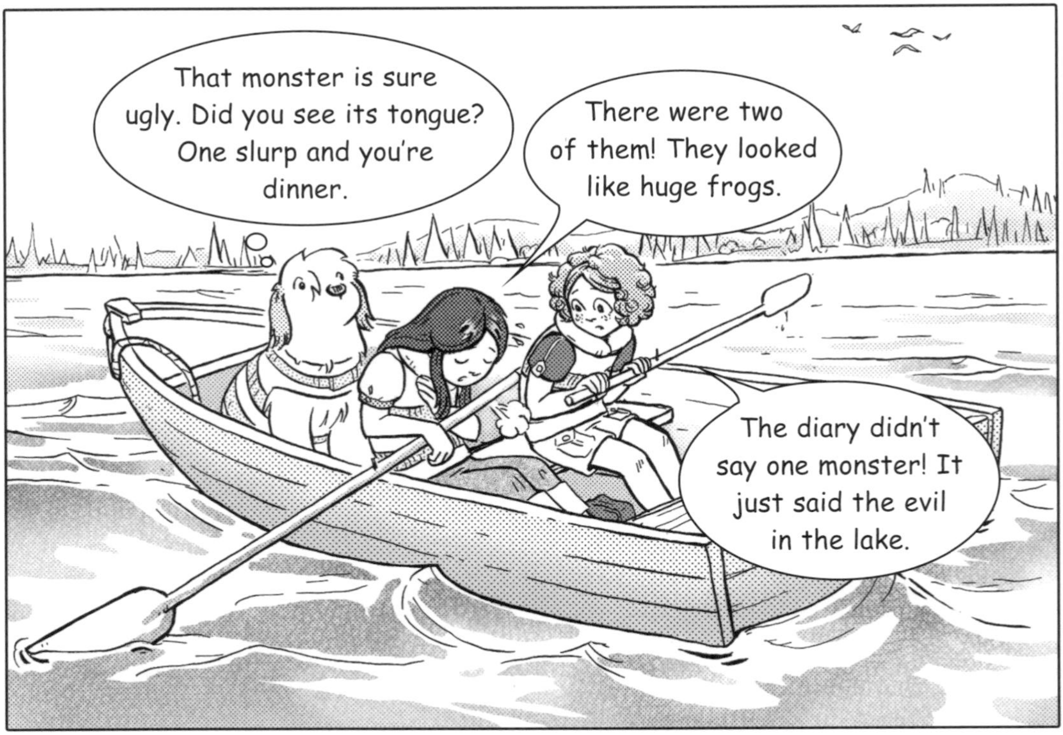
That monster is sure ugly. Did you see its tongue? One slurp and you're dinner.
There were two of them! They looked like huge frogs.
The diary didn't say one monster! It just said the evil in the lake.

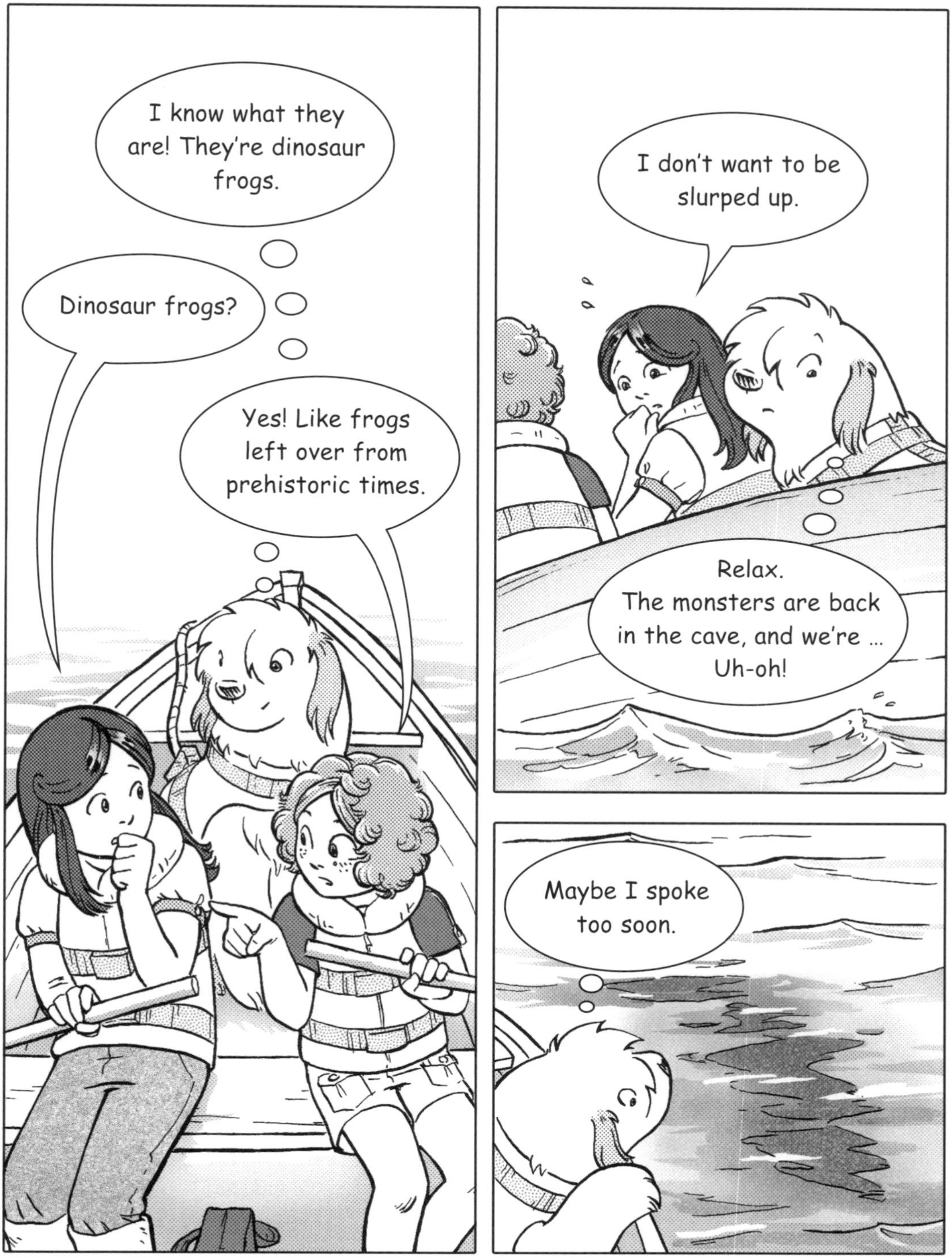
I know what they are! They're dinosaur frogs.
Dinosaur frogs?
Yes! Like frogs left over from prehistoric times.
I don't want to be slurped up.
Relax. The monsters are back in the cave, and we're ... Uh-oh!
Maybe I spoke too soon.

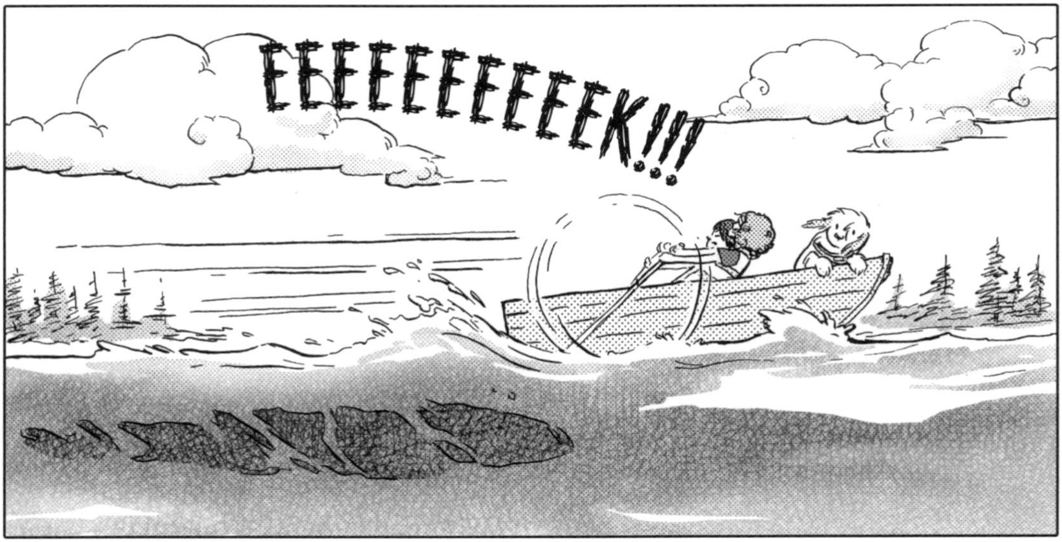
EEEEEEEEEEEEK!!!

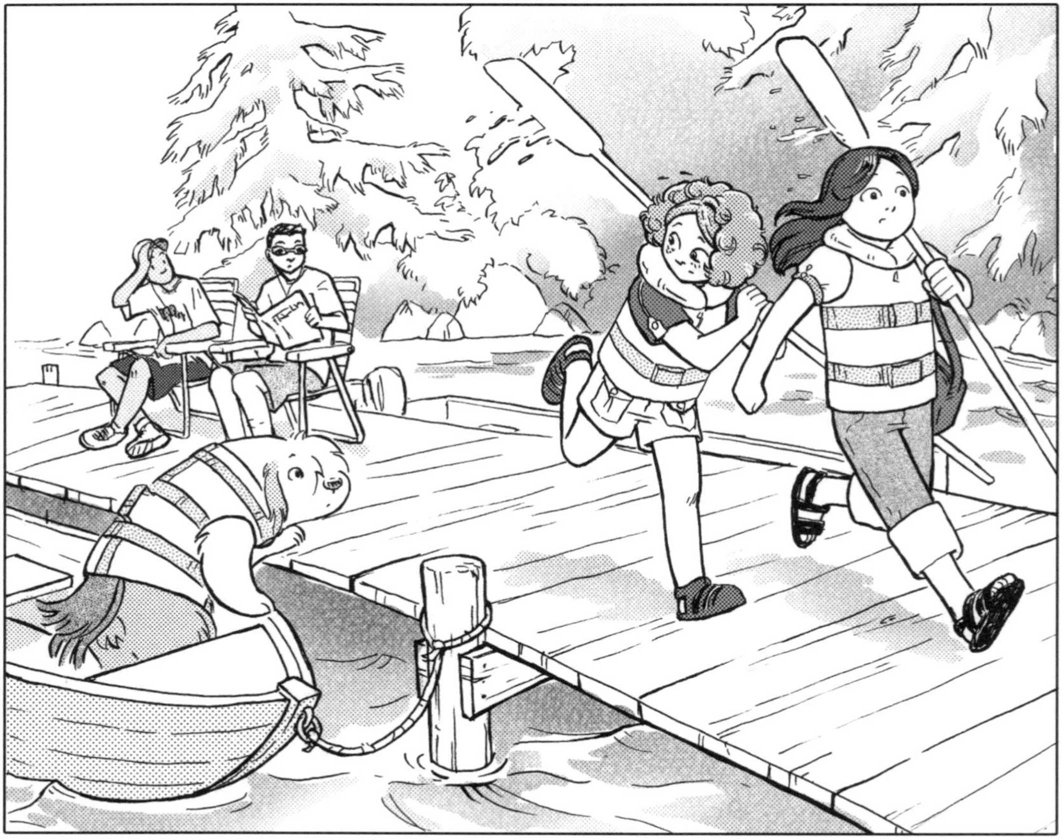

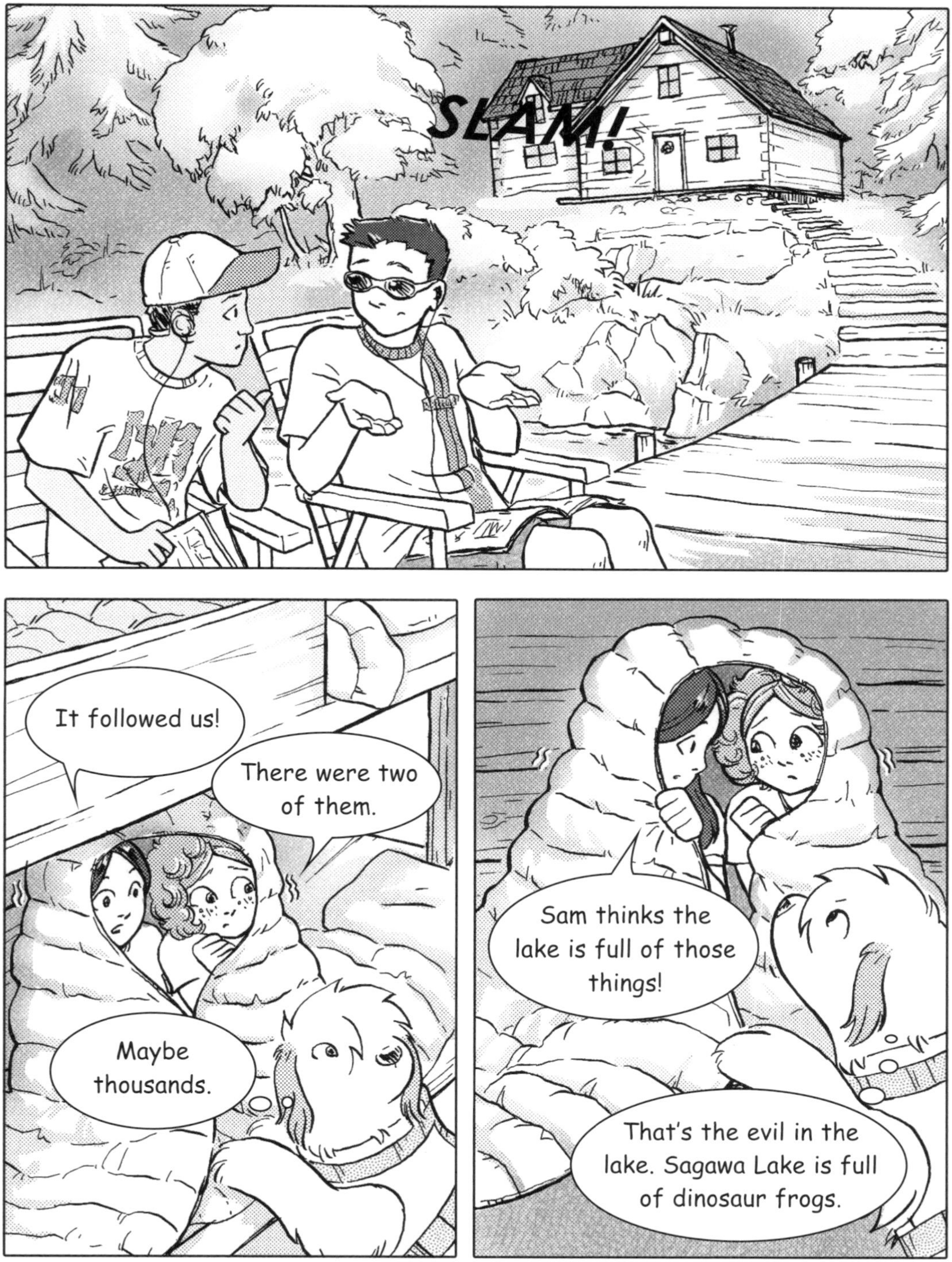
SLAM!
It followed us!
There were two of them.
Maybe thousands.
Sam thinks the lake is full of those things!
That's the evil in the lake. Sagawa Lake is full of dinosaur frogs.

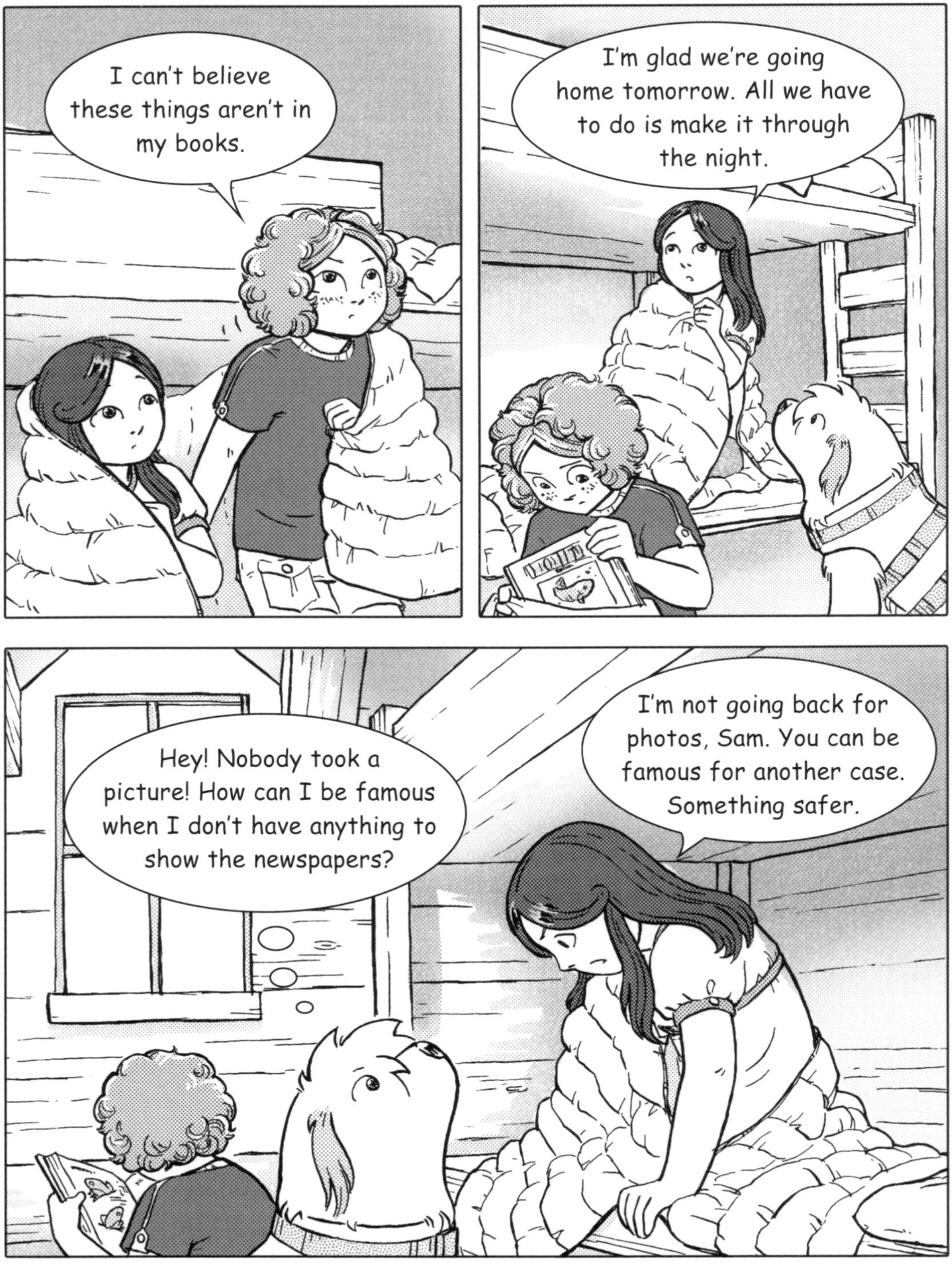
I can't believe these things aren't in my books.
I'm glad we're going home tomorrow. All we have to do is make it through the night.
Hey! Nobody took a picture! How can I be famous when I don't have anything to show the newspapers?
I'm not going back for photos, Sam. You can be famous for another case. Something safer.

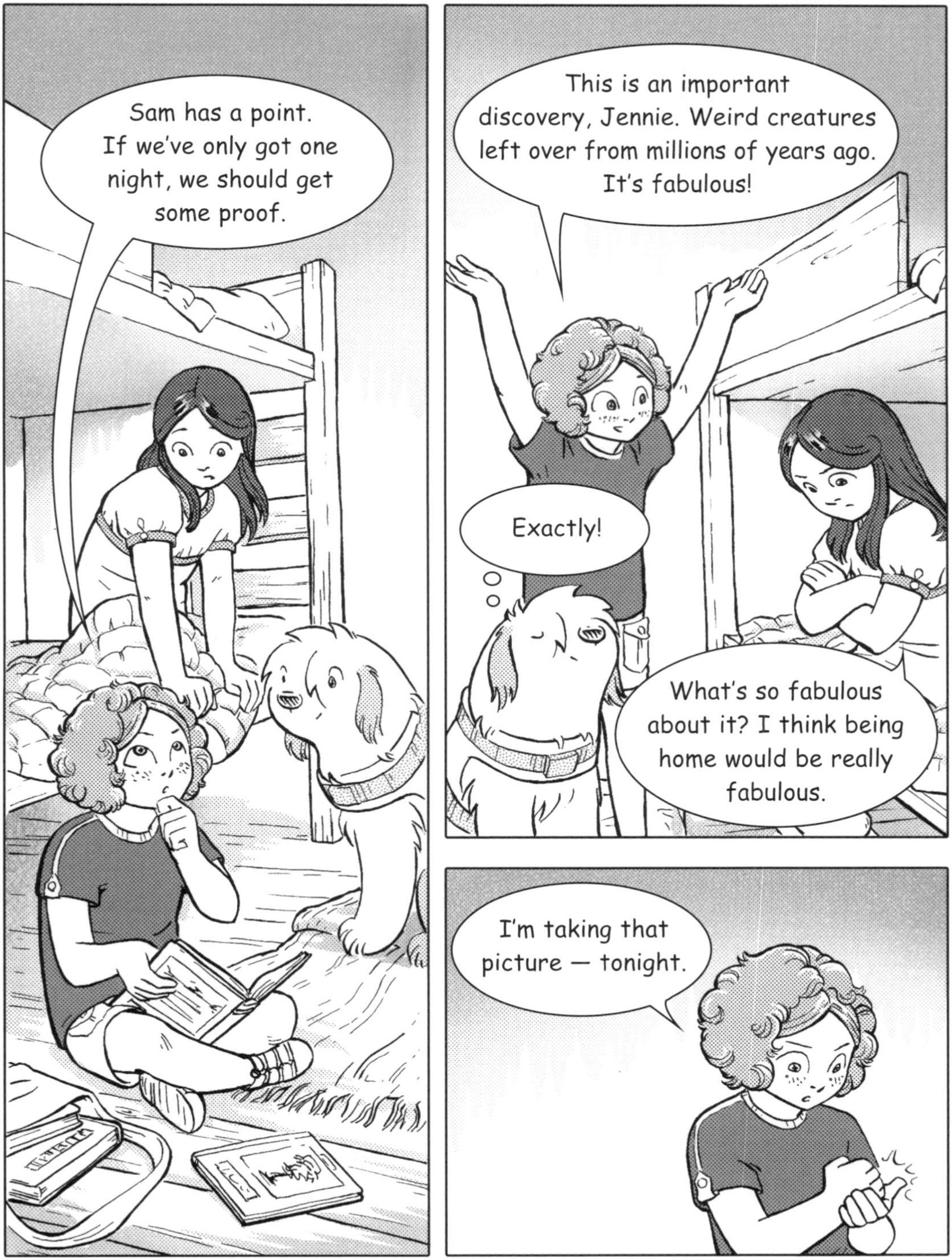
Sam has a point. If we've only got one night, we should get some proof.
This is an important discovery, Jennie. Weird creatures left over from millions of years ago. It's fabulous!
Exactly!
What's so fabulous about it? I think being home would be really fabulous.
I'm taking that picture — tonight.

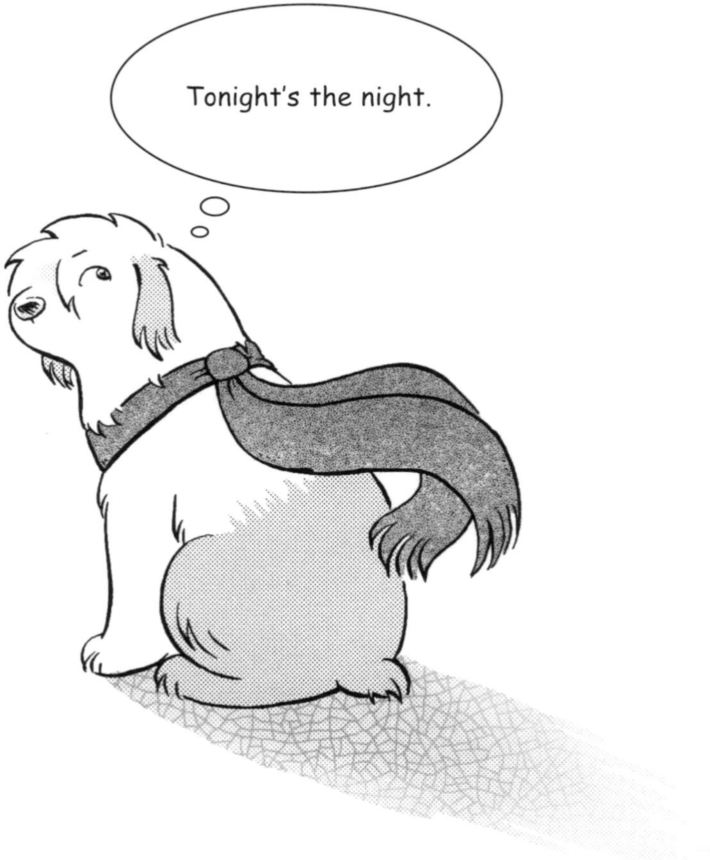
Tonight's the night.

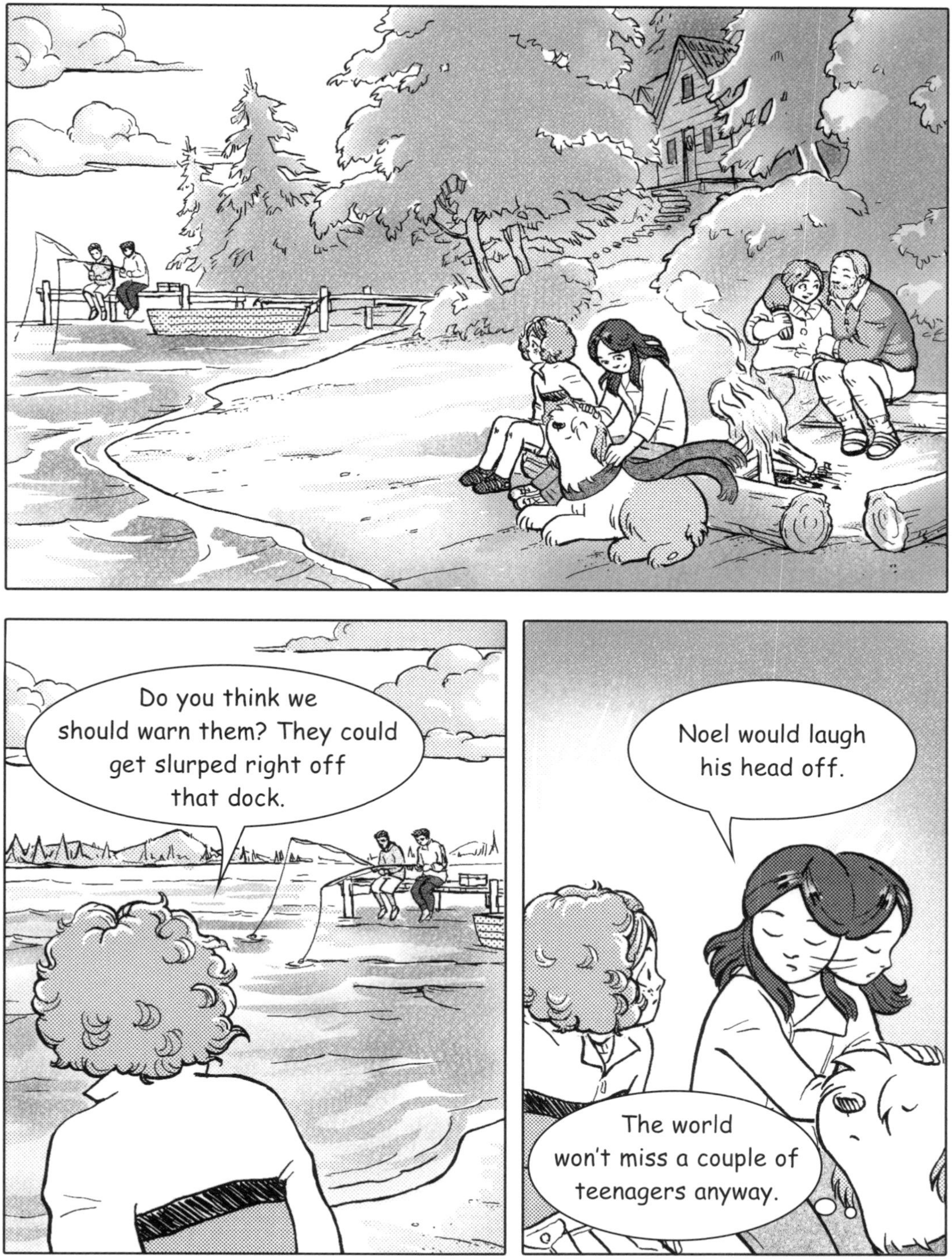
Do you think we should warn them? They could get slurped right off that dock.
Noel would laugh his head off.
The world won't miss a couple of teenagers anyway.

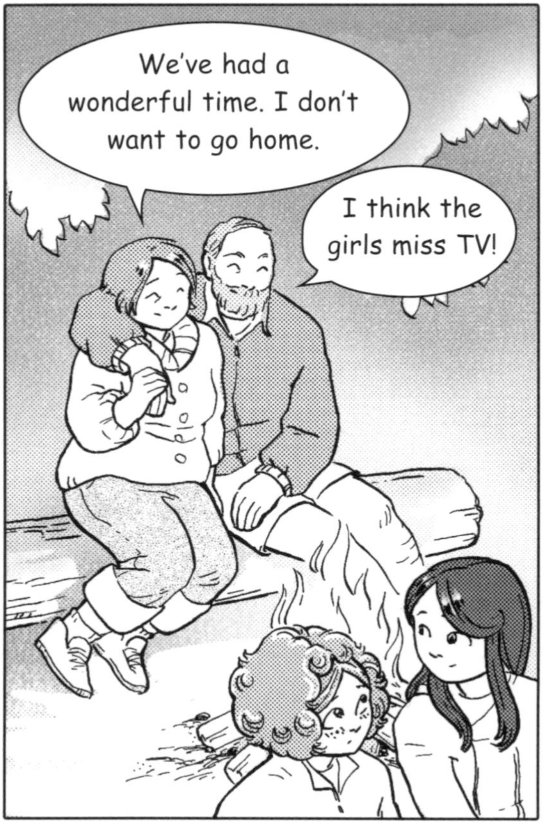
We've had a wonderful time. I don't want to go home.
I think the girls miss TV!

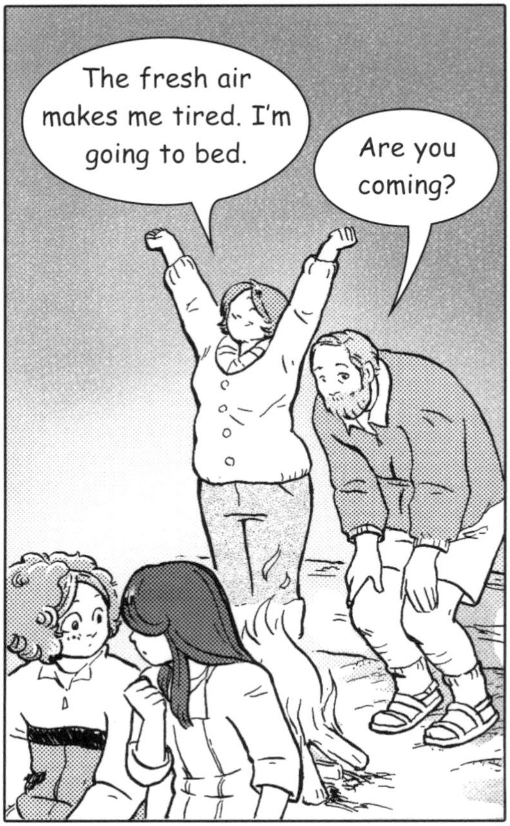
The fresh air makes me tired. I'm going to bed.
Are you coming?

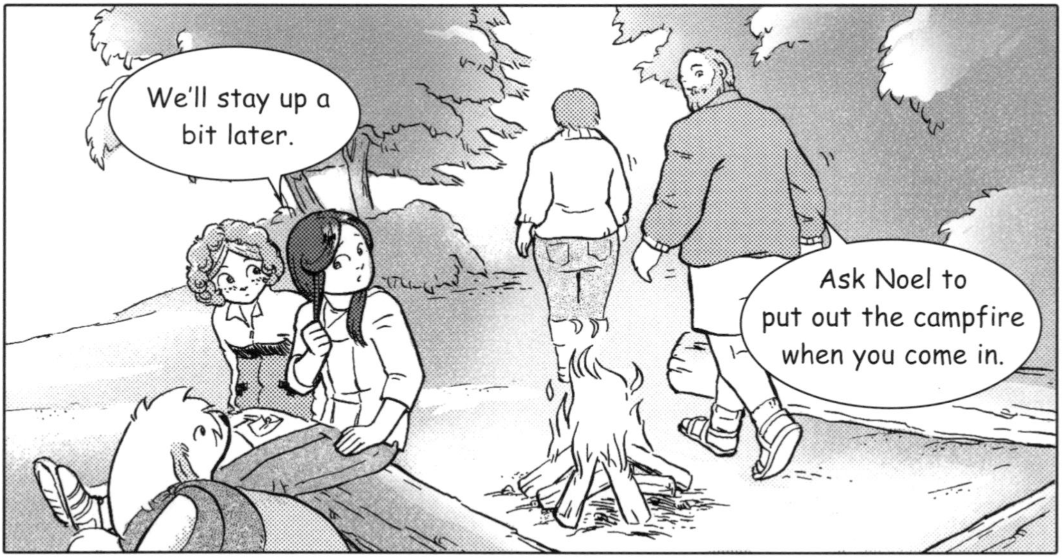
We'll stay up a bit later.
Ask Noel to put out the campfire when you come in.

Later ...

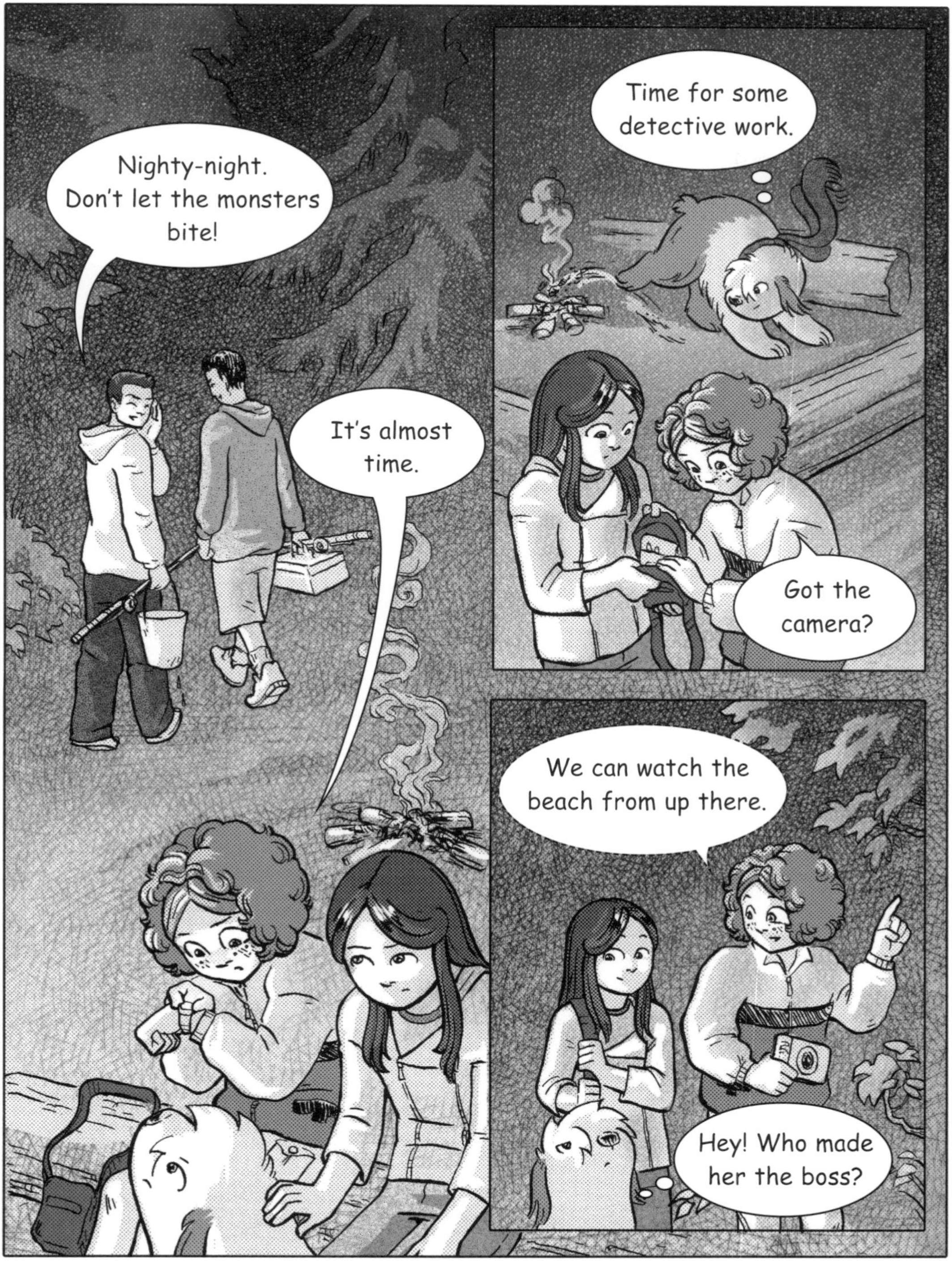
Nighty-night. Don't let the monsters bite!
It's almost time.
Time for some detective work.
Got the camera?
We can watch the beach from up there.
Hey! Who made her the boss?

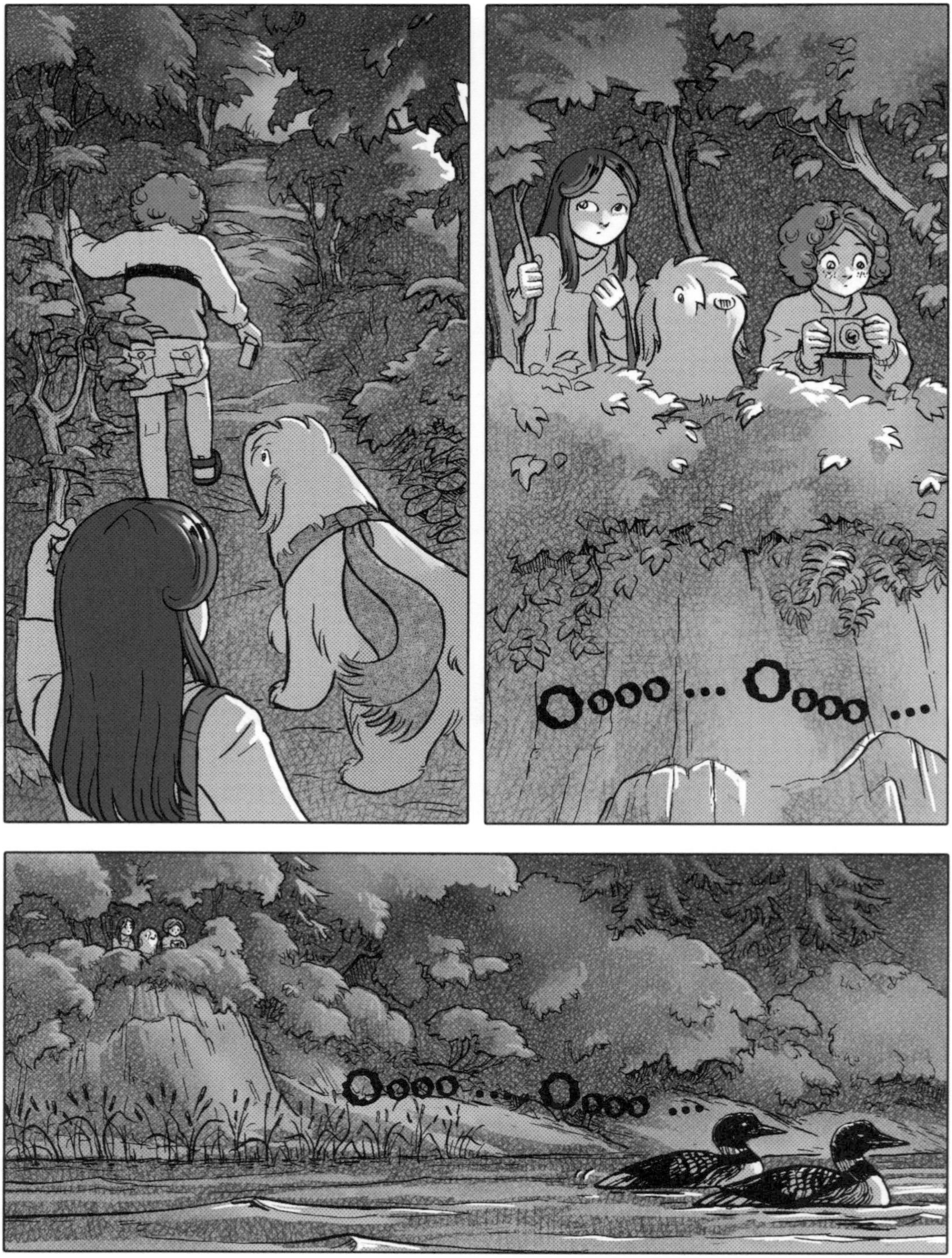
Oooo... Oooo...
Oooo... Oooo...

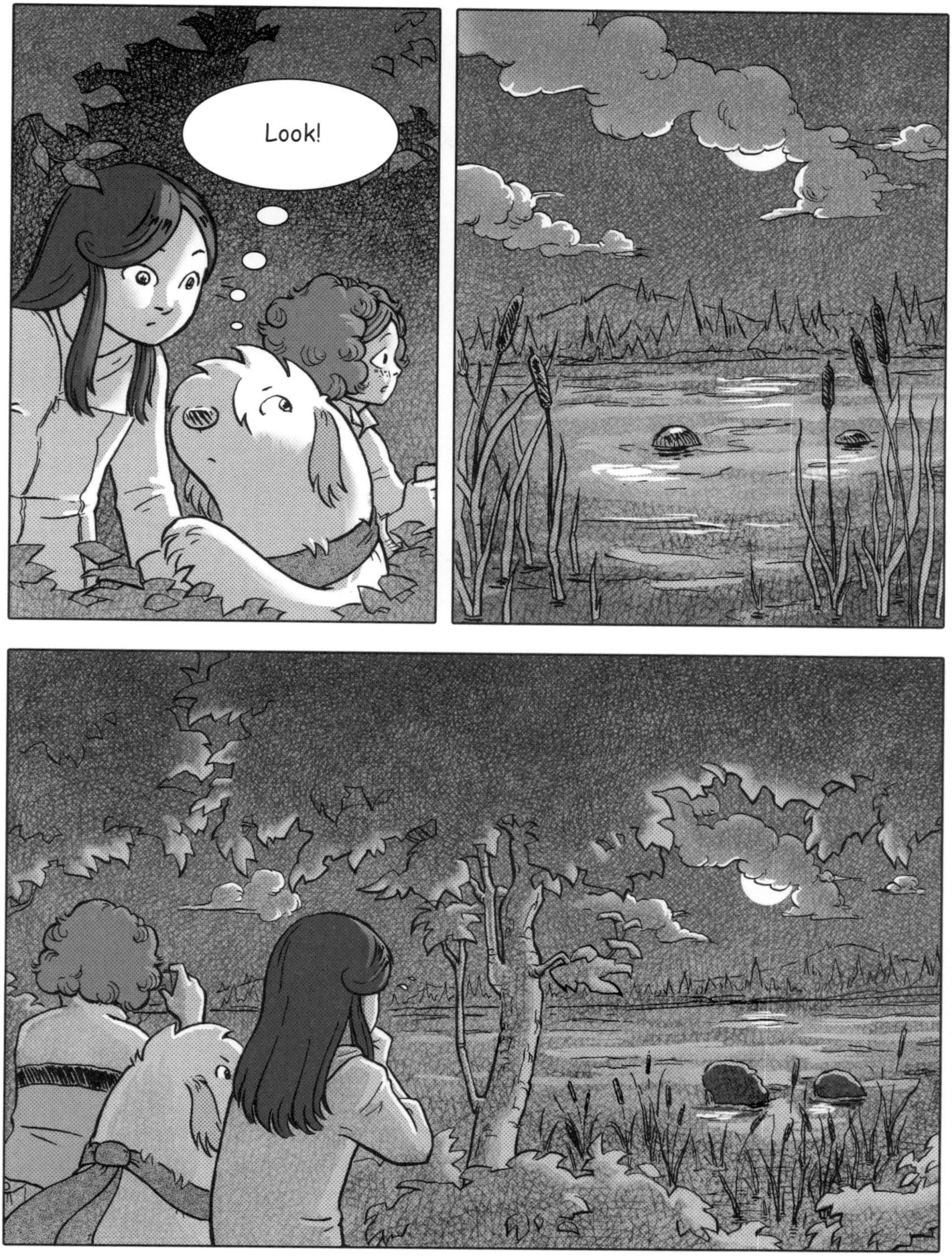
Look!

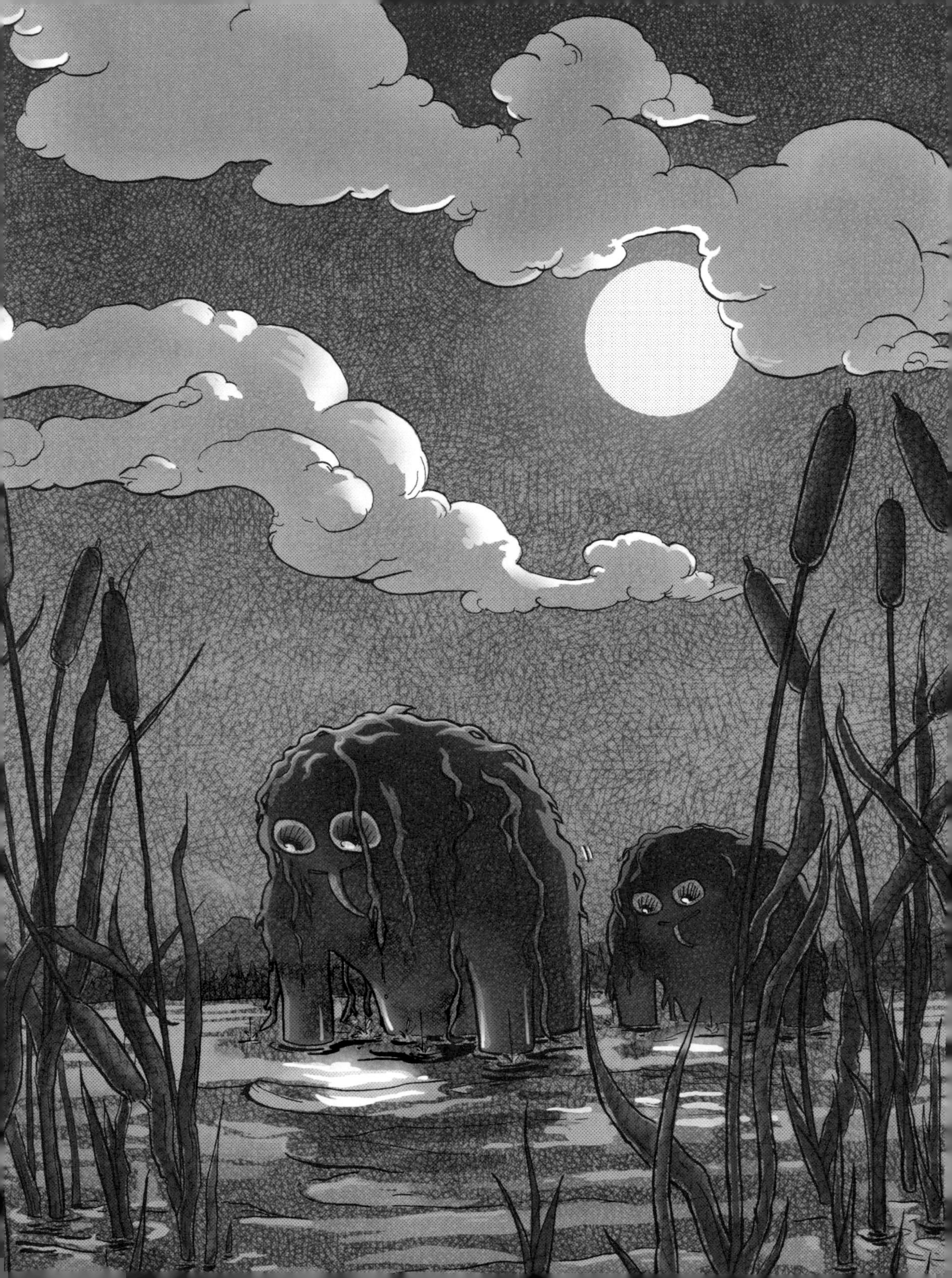

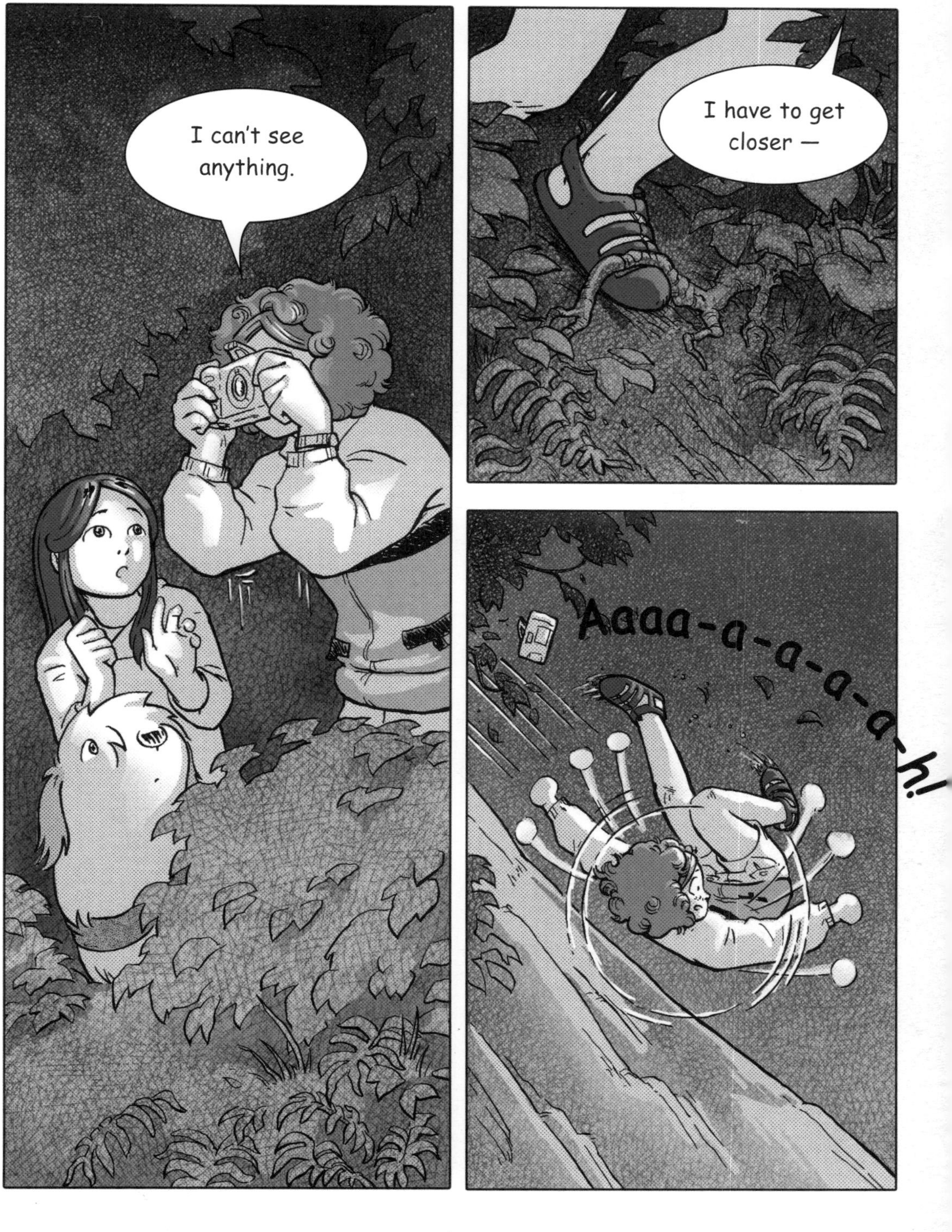
I can't see anything.
I have to get closer —
Aaaa-a-a-a-a-h!

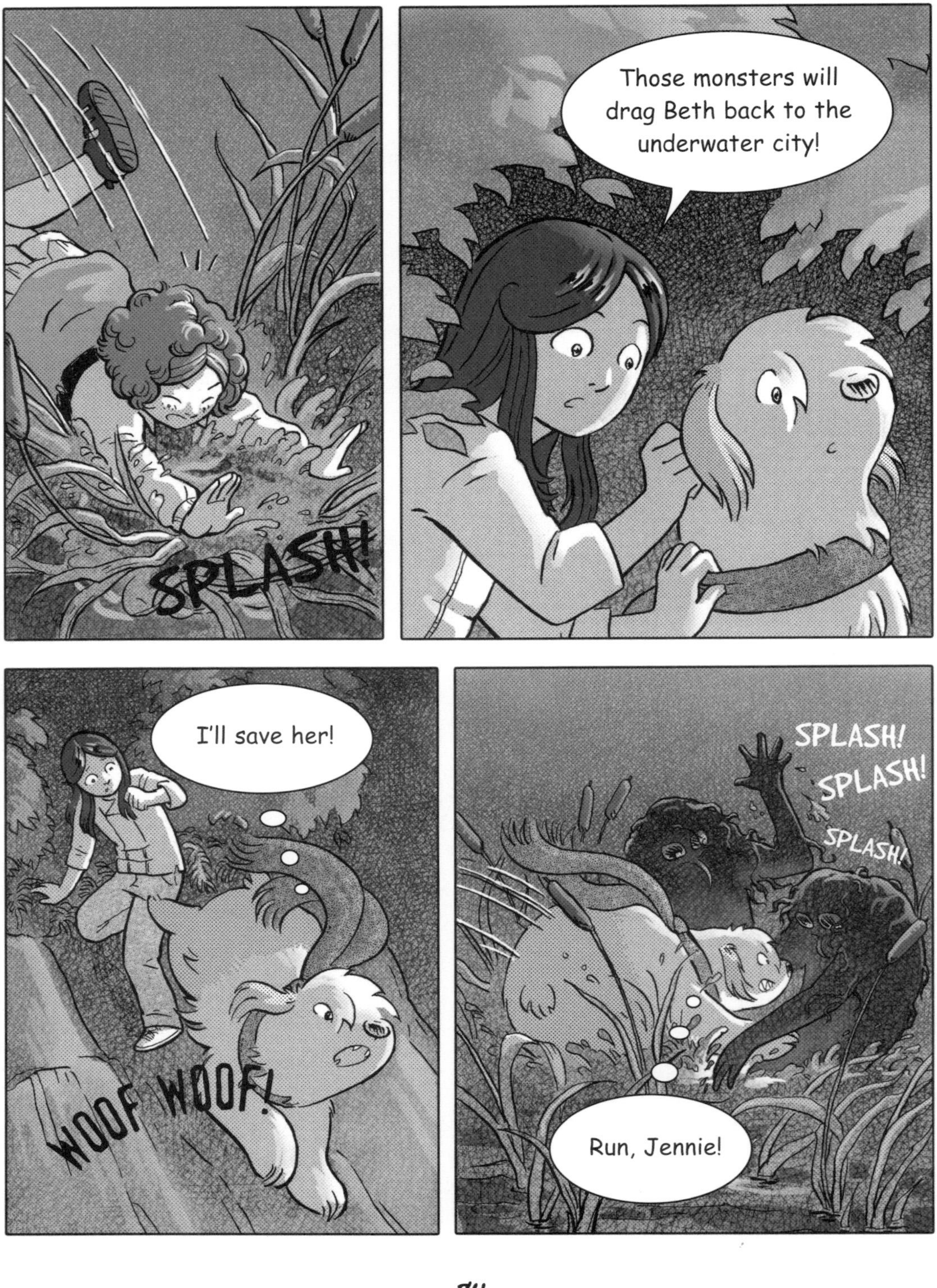
SPLASH!
Those monsters will drag Beth back to the underwater city!
I'll save her!
WOOF WOOF!
SPLASH!
SPLASH!
SPLASH!
Run, Jennie!

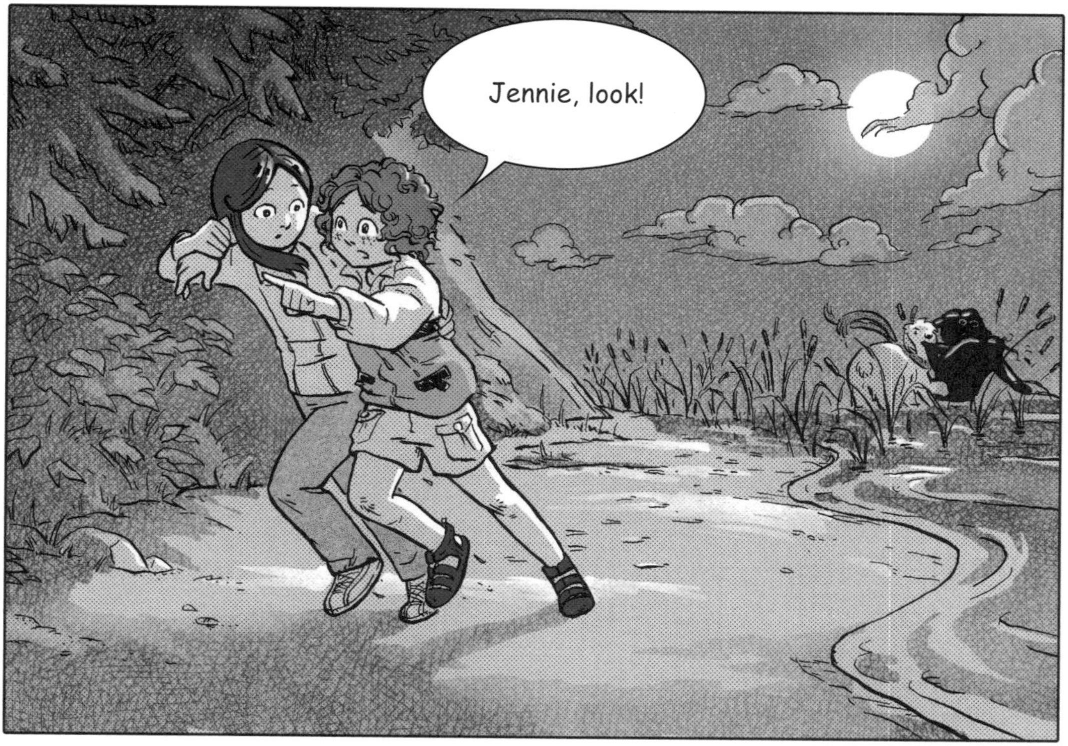
Jennie, look!

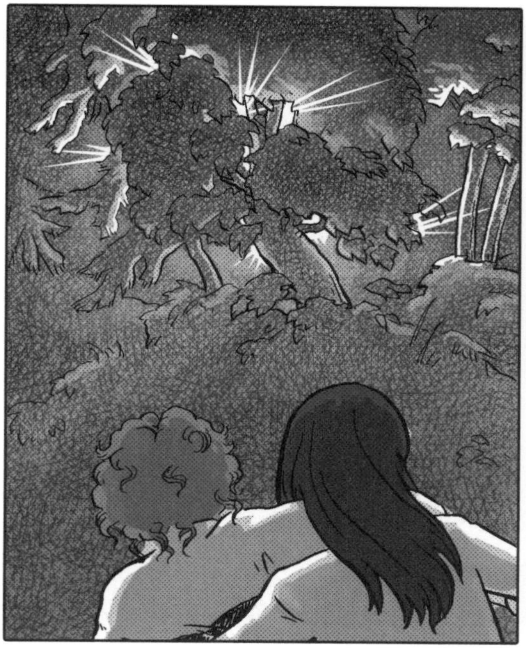

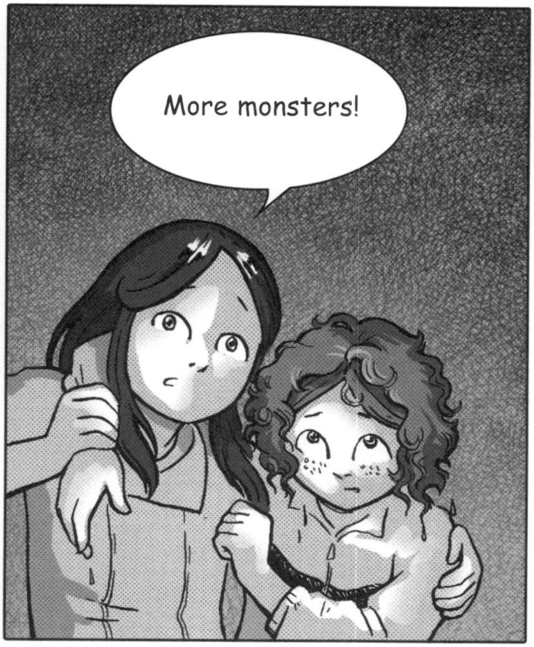
More monsters!

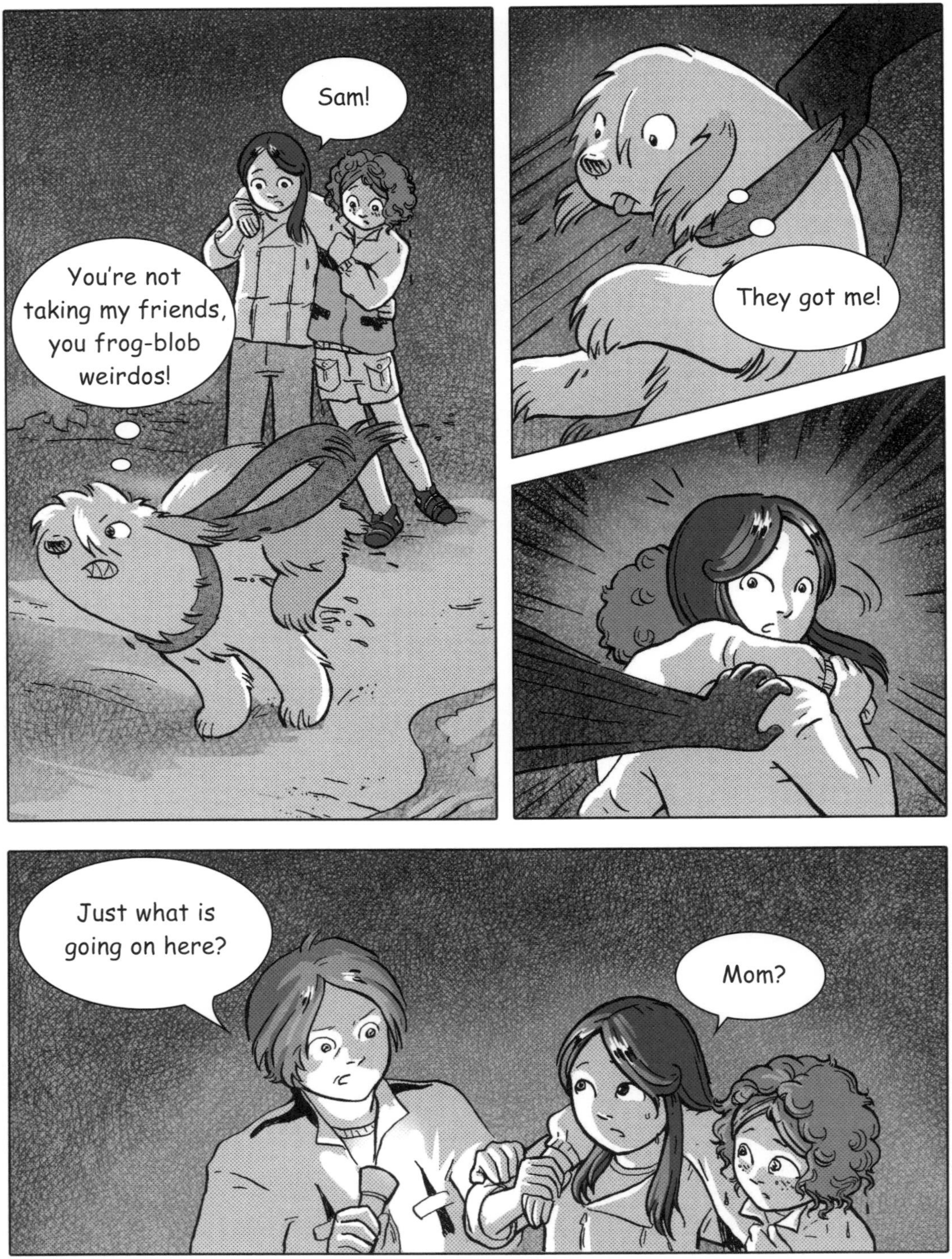
Sam!
You're not taking my friends, you frog-blob weirdos!
They got me!
Just what is going on here?
Mom?

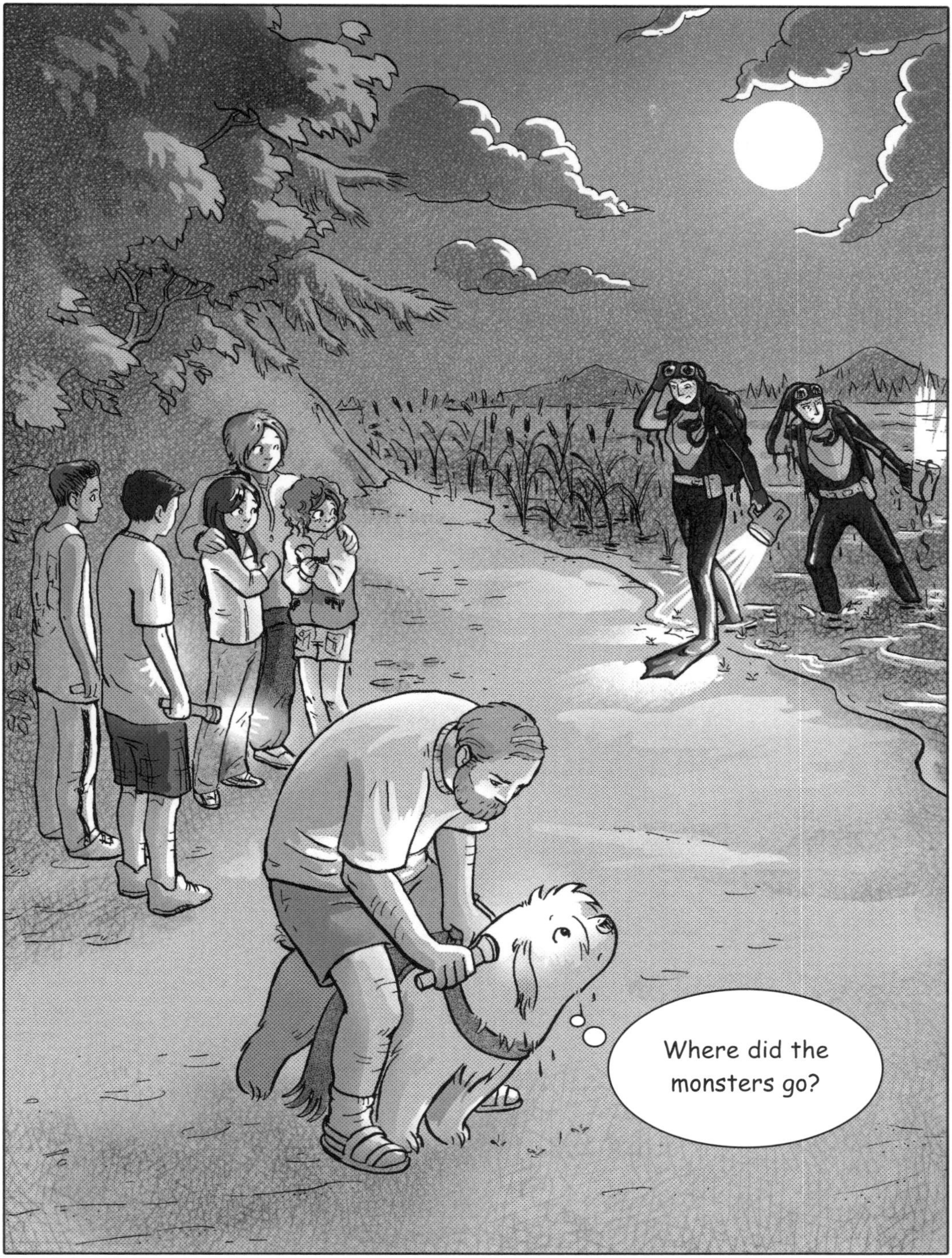
Where did the monsters go?

Back at the cabin ...

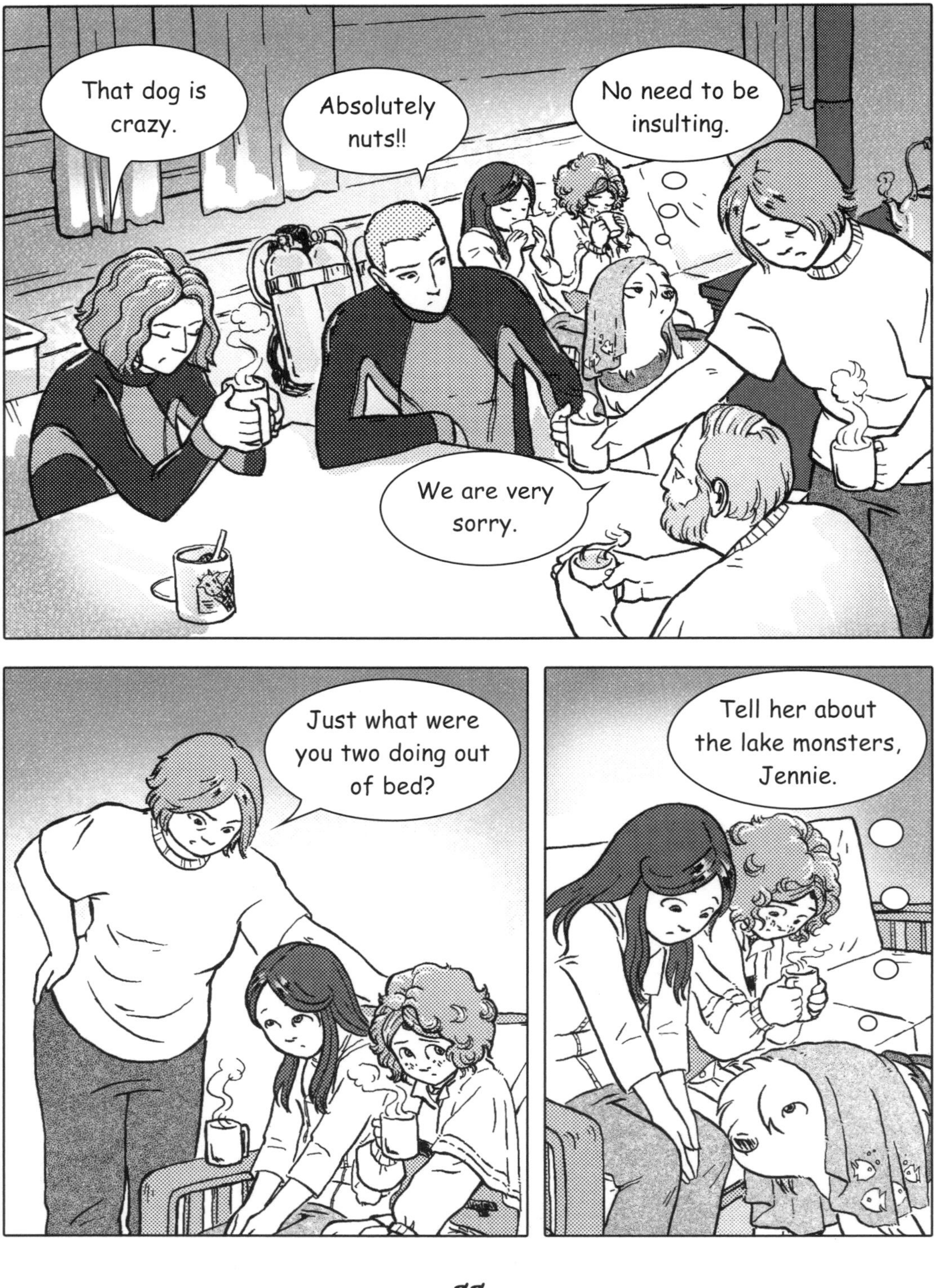
That dog is crazy.
Absolutely nuts!!
No need to be insulting.
We are very sorry.
Just what were you two doing out of bed?
Tell her about the lake monsters, Jennie.

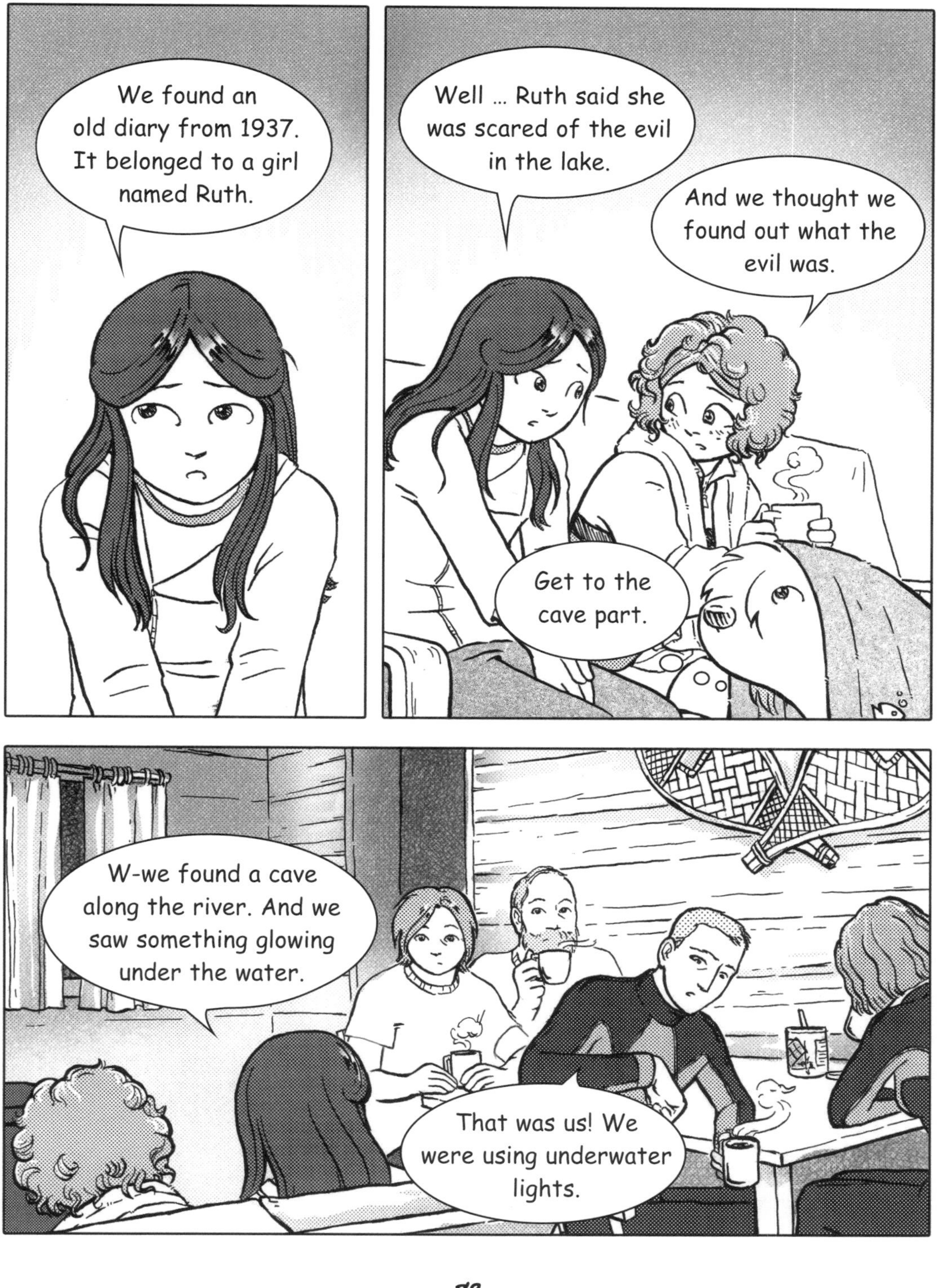
We found an old diary from 1937. It belonged to a girl named Ruth.
Well ... Ruth said she was scared of the evil in the lake.
And we thought we found out what the evil was.
Get to the cave part.
W-we found a cave along the river. And we saw something glowing under the water.
That was us! We were using underwater lights.

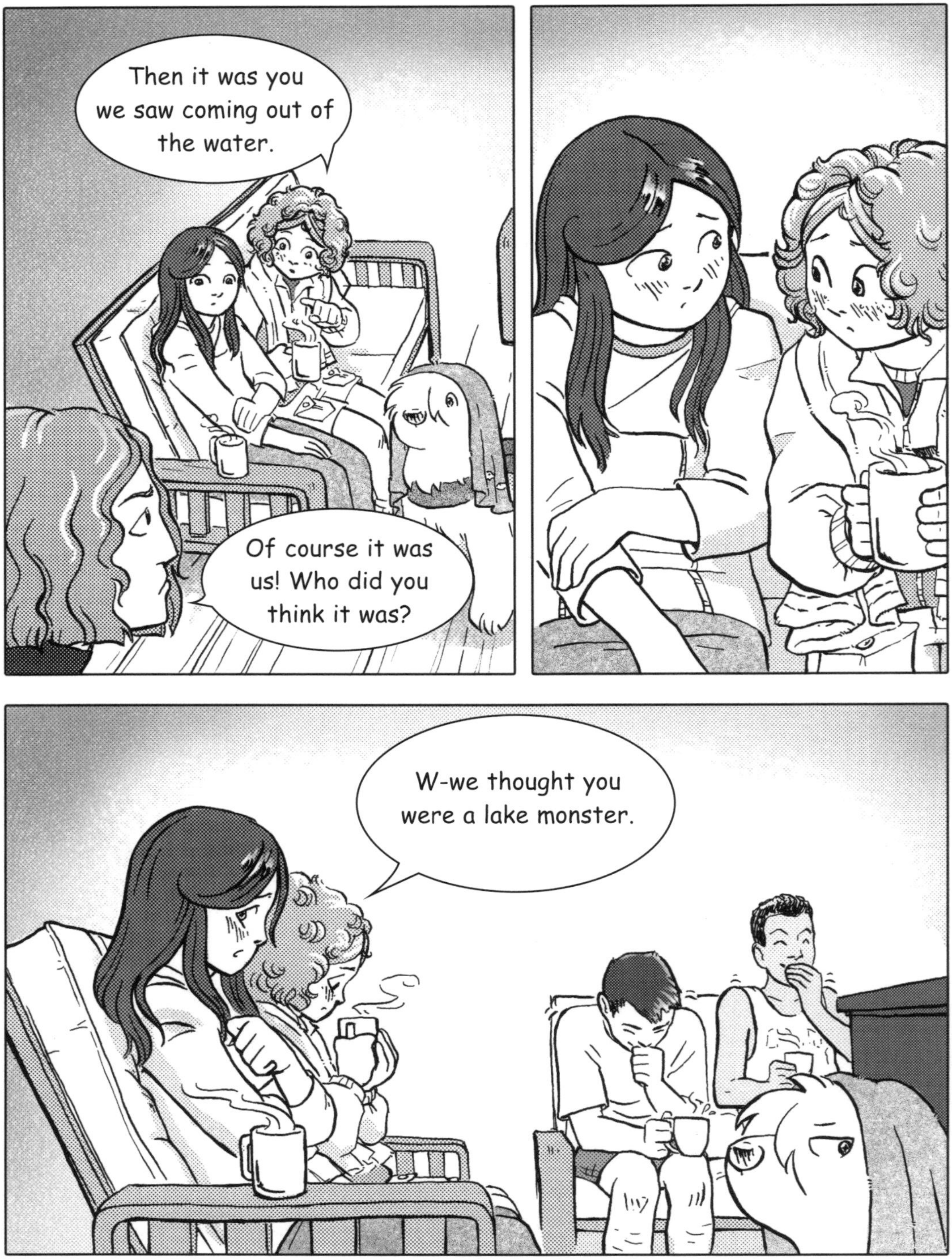
Then it was you we saw coming out of the water.
Of course it was us! Who did you think it was?
W-we thought you were a lake monster.

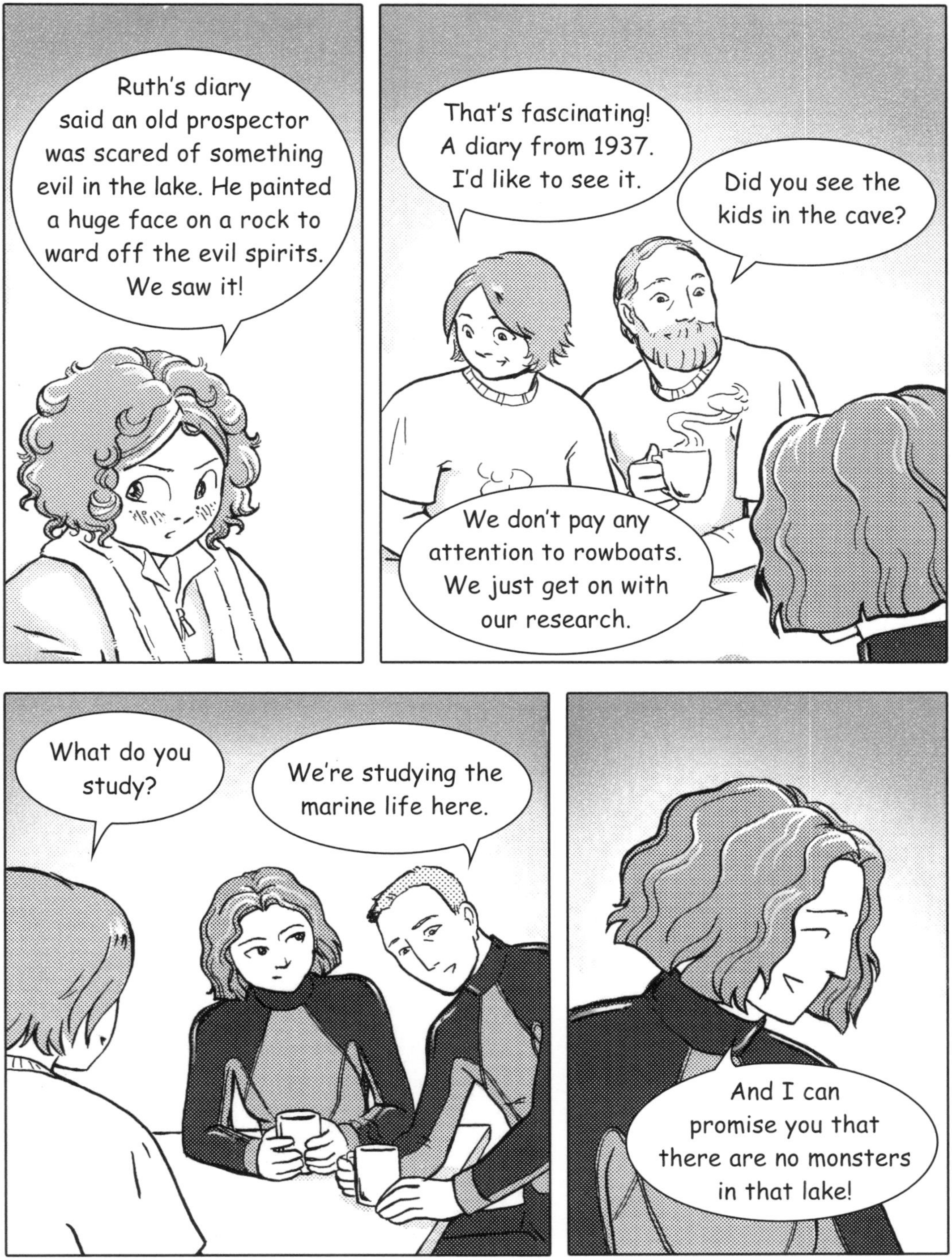
Ruth's diary said an old prospector was scared of something evil in the lake. He painted a huge face on a rock to ward off the evil spirits. We saw it!
That's fascinating! A diary from 1937. I'd like to see it.
Did you see the kids in the cave?
We don't pay any attention to rowboats. We just get on with our research.
What do you study?
We're studying the marine life here.
And I can promise you that there are no monsters in that lake!

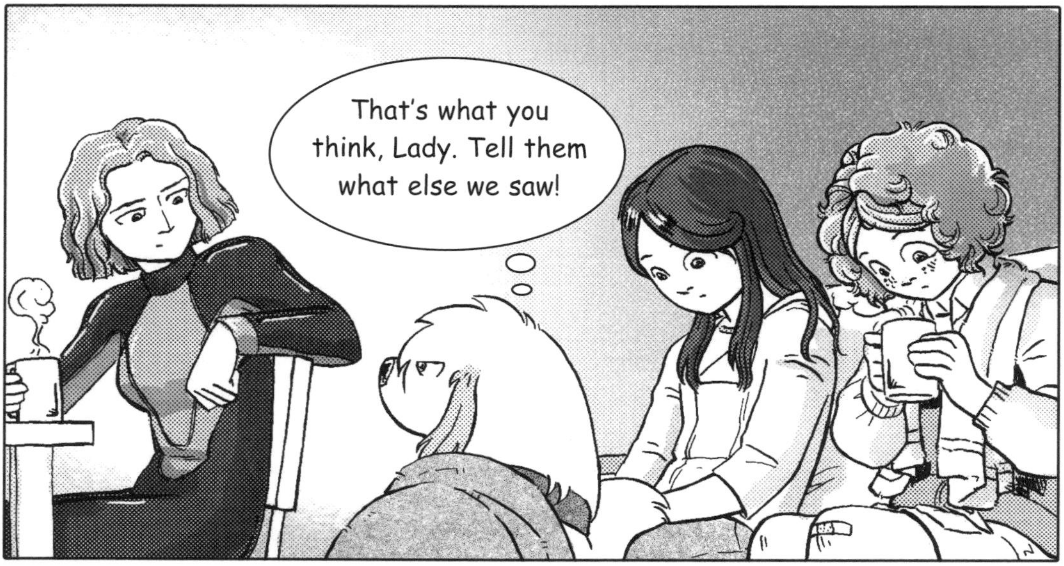
That's what you think, Lady. Tell them what else we saw!
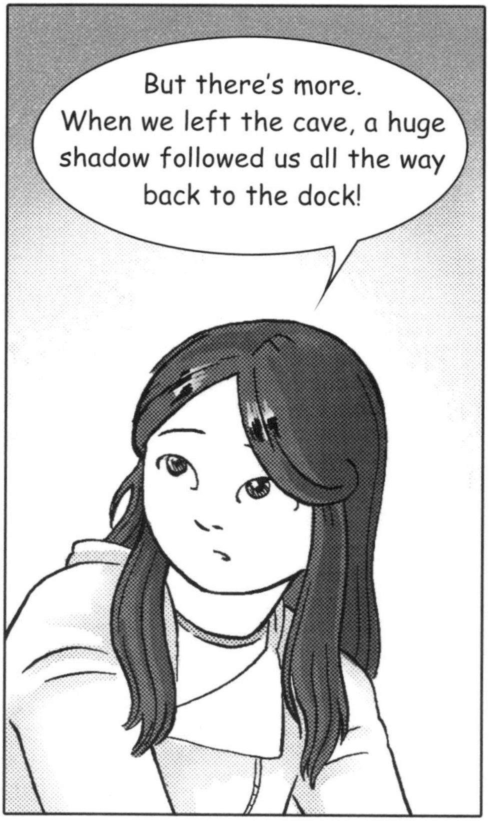
But there's more. When we left the cave, a huge shadow followed us all the way back to the dock!
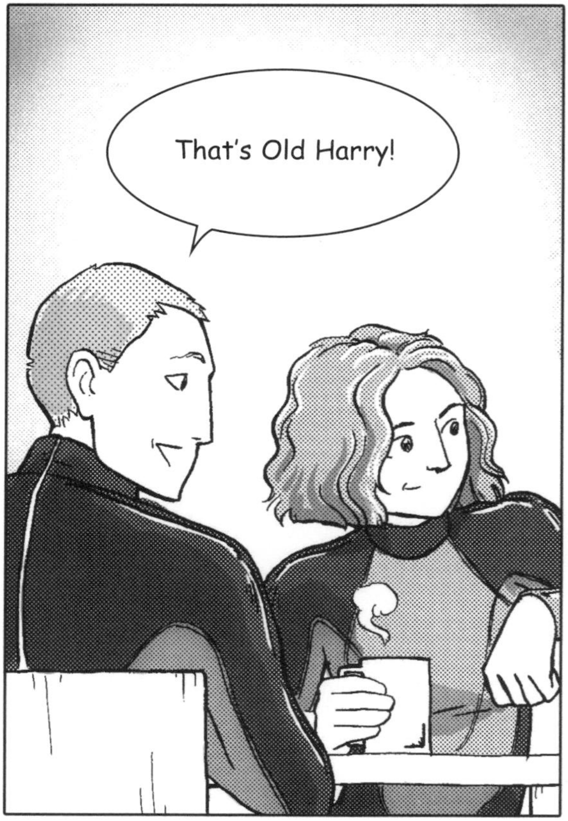
That's Old Harry!

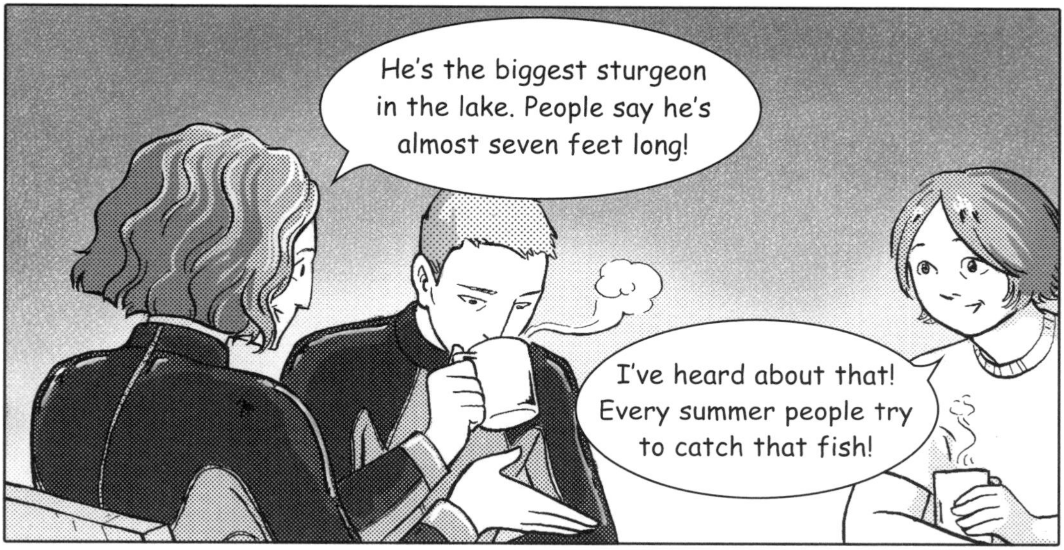
He's the biggest sturgeon in the lake. People say he's almost seven feet long!
I've heard about that! Every summer people try to catch that fish!

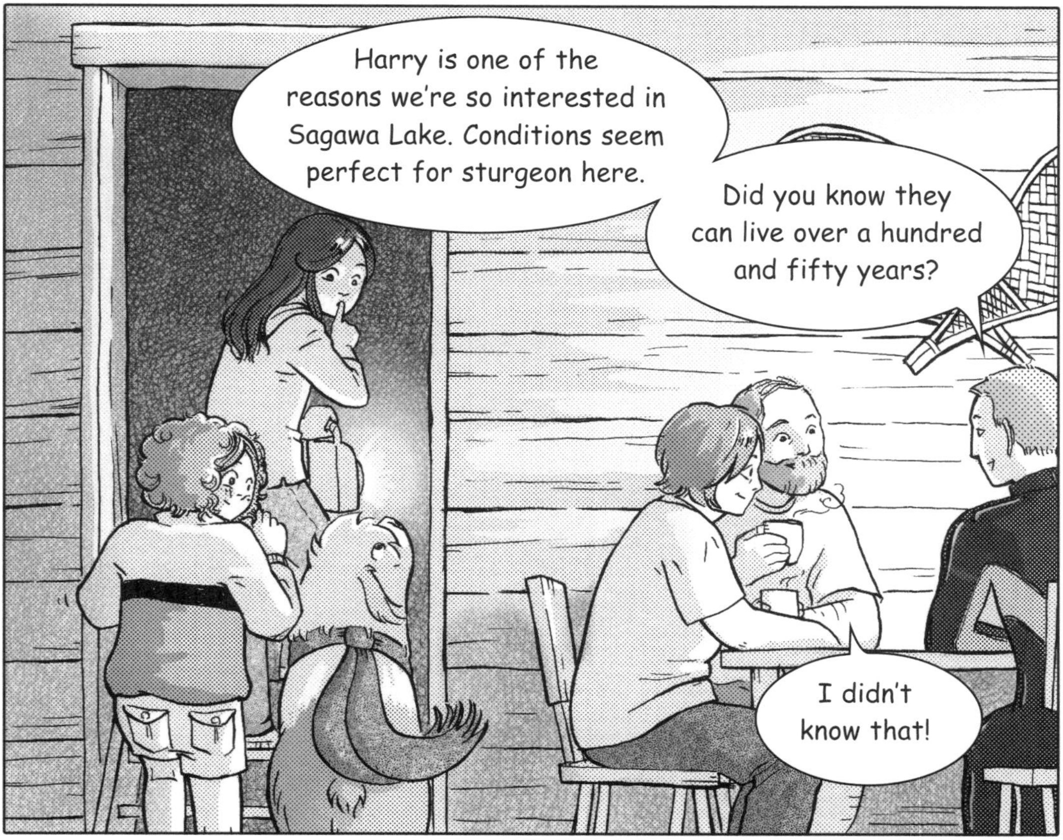
Harry is one of the reasons we're so interested in Sagawa Lake. Conditions seem perfect for sturgeon here.
Did you know they can live over a hundred and fifty years?
I didn't know that!

The next day ...

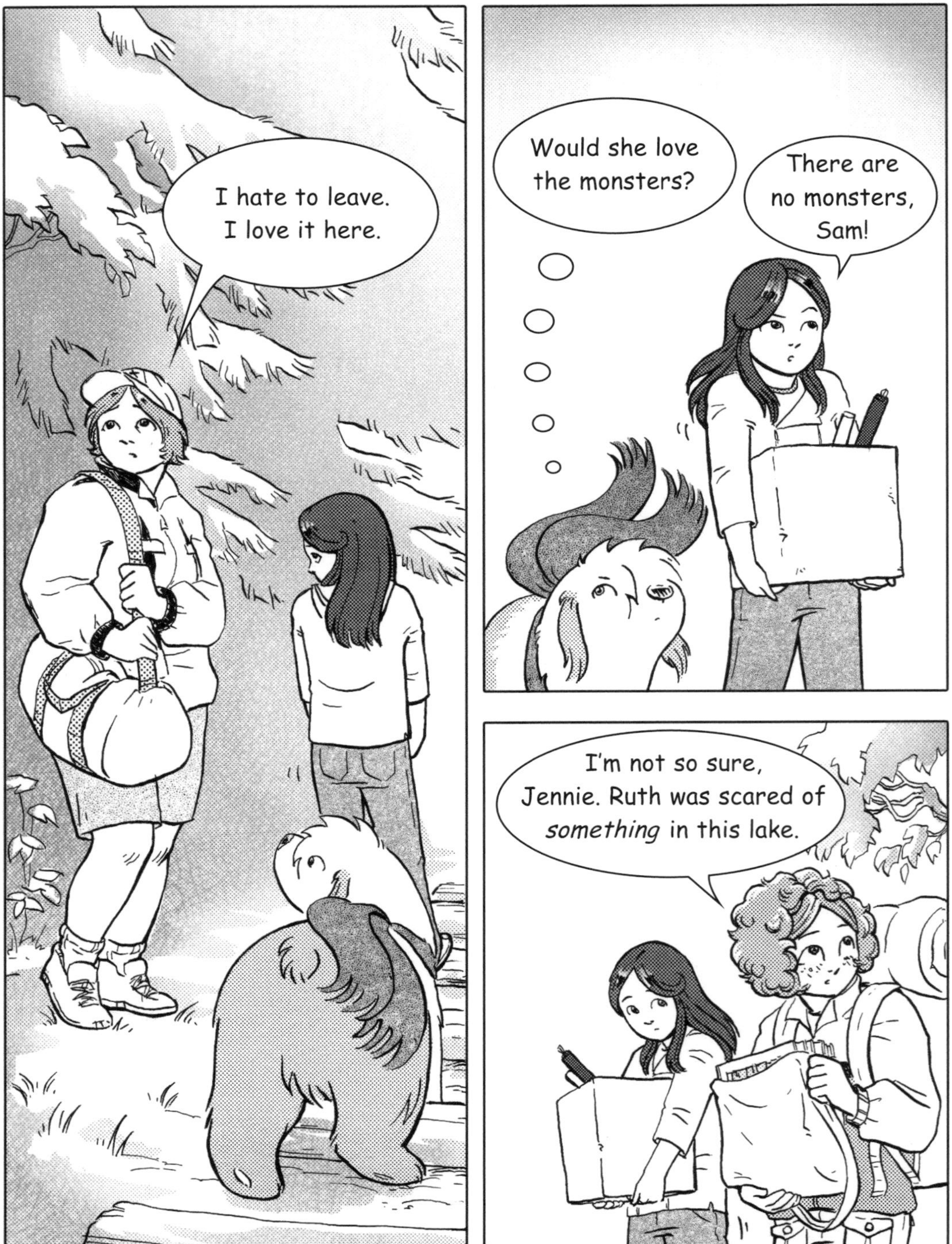
I hate to leave. I love it here.
Would she love the monsters?
There are no monsters, Sam!
I'm not so sure, Jennie. Ruth was scared of *something* in this lake.

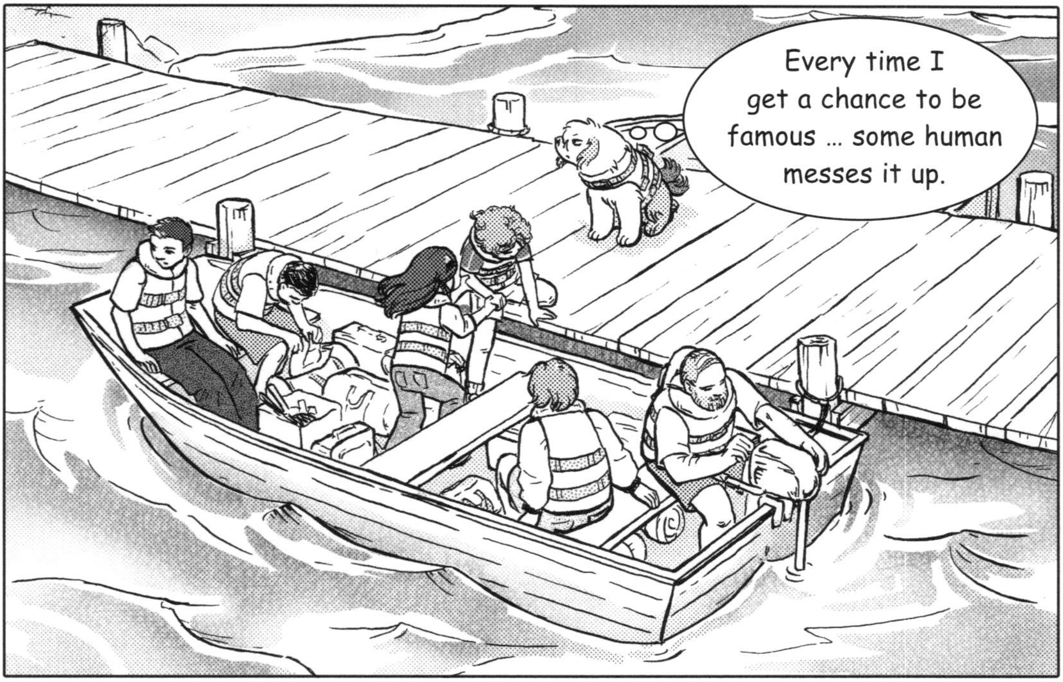
Every time I get a chance to be famous ... some human messes it up.

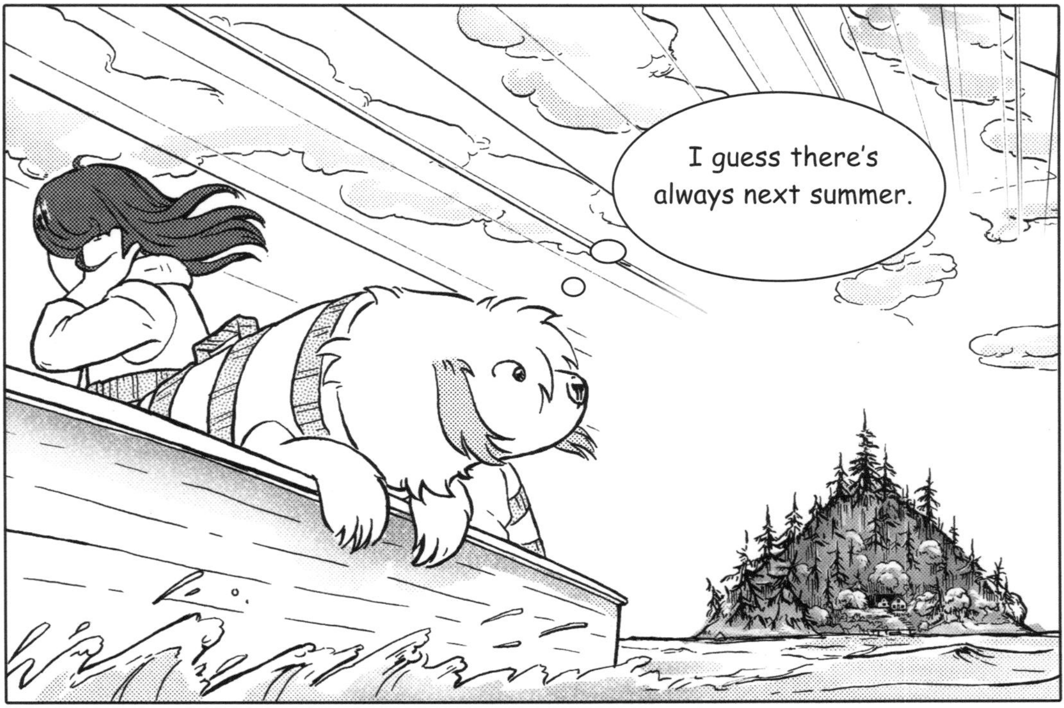
I guess there's always next summer.